Ashes

Sergios Gakas

ASHES

Translated from the Greek by
Anne-Marie Stanton-Ife

MACLEHOSE PRESS
QUERCUS · LONDON

First published in Great Britain in 2011 by

MacLehose Press
an imprint of Quercus
21 Bloomsbury Square
London WC1A 2NS

First published as Στάχτες by Kastaniotis Editions S.A., Athens

A CIP catalogue record for this book is available
from the British Library

ISBN (HB) 978 0 85705 016 8
ISBN (TPB) 978 0 85705 017 5

2 4 6 8 10 9 7 5 3 1

Typeset in 11¼/17½pt Minion by Patty Rennie
Printed and bound in Great Britain by Clays Ltd, St Ives plc

In Memory of Katerina Daniilidou

The rain was so hard that it cleaned the pigs and covered the humans in filth.

Georg Christoph Lichtenberg (1742–99)

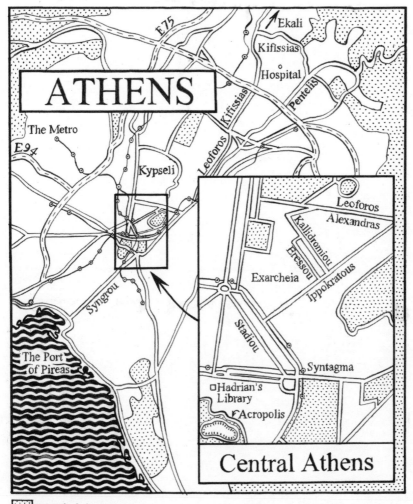

ATHENS

The Metro
E94
Kypseli
Syngrou
The Port
of Pireas

E75
Ekali
Kifissias
Hospital
Pentelis
Leoforos Kifissias

Leoforos Alexandras
Kallidromiou
Eressou
Exarcheia
Ippokratous
Stadiou
Syntagma
Hadrian's Library
Acropolis

Central Athens

Wooded Areas

CONTENTS

PROLOGUE

24.i.2004
Saturday, 11.15 p.m.

It's windy, really windy. They've smashed that streetlight again. Not kids this time; it was those people, the people who carry the darkness inside them. Better ring City Hall tomorrow. No, not tomorrow; tomorrow's Sunday – first thing Monday. They'll get on to it at once; they're always bending over backwards to make everything safe for the people who live in the nice parts of the city. I always hated those dark Saturday nights and always liked the matinées; they meant I could beat the dusk and the heavy sadness of the sky, and afterwards, at night, the city would light up and Leoforos Alexandras would smother both the darkness and the silence. God knows how many years I've been in love with Ippokratous – that street, it's like a knife slicing right through the heart of the city. What was his name again – the one who lived in the penthouse on the corner of Kallidromiou? The artist. No, he wasn't an artist – an architect, maybe. He used to like poking his tongue through the gap in my front teeth: the gaps between your teeth drive me crazy, my love, he would whisper. What was his name? Something Byzantine – not Konstantinos, of course. I was doing Anya in "The Cherry Orchard" at the time. So what was it?

I'll have some more wine and turn on the television, on mute so I don't wake them. It's probably very late. I'll have the wine first. Perhaps I should open the vodka that dear boy Noni brought me last week, completely ignoring that old tyrant's prohibition. Anyone would think he was Simeon the Stylite the way he carries on – still hopeful that I'll get off the drink one day, still believing that he can get off it himself. But when I started begging Noni, like a little girl, he took pity on me and turned up later with a bottle of Stoli. In return I gave him a photograph of me playing Medea – awful production in a basement theatre, genuine tragedy. I am still embarrassed just thinking about it, even more than I am about that "Yerma". Total fiasco – directors and their bloody special effects. Luckily I did "Betrayal" straight after – that shut most of them up, but even so, I don't like to think about it. Who does like thinking about betrayal, after all? No-one. I'm getting cold again. I'll get that vodka, fight ice with ice. Here I go, stumbling, talking to myself. Someone's left the window open. What was that play with the billowing curtain, remind me – a white curtain? I had to worry that someone might climb in, about being invaded, the end. I always cried on the last night, always, no matter how fed up I was by then after fifty, one hundred, two hundred performances. That's a lot, it ends up being too much, how can you escape the lie? That's why I prefer vodka. I'm going. I'm going to carry on, and the curtain can billow all it likes – who'd want to come in here anyway? Who'd want to get their hands dirty here in this wretched refuge of ours? No-one. No-one, my love. Now, when have I said that before?

Fight ice with ice. Let me break your seal, Stoli, my love. My red beauty, come here, give yourself to me, transparent like all my mistakes, dense as, oh damn you! Why are you doing this, you miserable fool? Why isn't anything coming out? Why isn't your liquid treasure pouring out? Come on, baby, drip, drip, drip – that's right – whoa! Not too fast. That's right, I'm holding you, not one tiny drop will escape me, my little darling. Who was it who called me that – "my little darling"?

There's light in the garden. That's good. That bloody wine has done me in. Spotlight falls on my almond tree. Another one, I don't feel good, damned wine, it's all your fault. Armchair – prepare yourself. My sweet throne, I'm coming, I'll get rid of all those shameless special effects in our peaceful garden. Who's that creeping around outside – who's after my vodka? It burns, the bitch. Shadows, I can see shadows, I can hear them walking, where's the door? It burns like hell: fight ice with ice, fire with fire, it's cold outside, shadows on the other side of the fence, I'll give up the drink, my love, you'll see, I'll stop drinking and I'll get well, and I'll come back to you, I'll be yours, I'm leaving now, but I'll be back so I can truly be yours. Who's doing the lighting? It's too soon, we haven't started yet, no, no, that's far too bright, why are you burning the almond tree? No! My face is burning, don't, why won't you listen to me? No, please, fire is never real for us.

CHAPTER 1

The Old House

Chronis Halkidis' son wants to switch to the channel with those deafening video clips; Halkidis begs him not to because the midday news is about to start. "Come on, father, it's Sunday. What are you so anxious to find out, anyway – the number of deaths on the National Road?" He snarls and stomps out of the sitting room in search of comfort from his second coke of the day. Two years tops, and he'll be as tall as I am, thinks the head of Internal Affairs of the Hellenic Police, suddenly noticing his son's broad shoulders. The boy stays over every other weekend, but he had only recently worked out what was really behind all the tension: having a policeman for a father is downright embarrassing. Halkidis lights up and settles into his armchair. Sod him. He'll understand soon enough. The boy will eventually get sick of his mother's brainwashing and at some point he'll no longer be forced to buy his son's affection by cultivating the ridiculous, fake camaraderie between a forty-five-year-old and a sixteen-year-old yob. At some point the promise of freedom masquerading as vulgar over-familiarity will become redundant, and they will not feel obliged to greet each other like N.B.A. players every other Friday when he picks him up, and he will not have to lay on endless supplies of coke, pizzas and beer, money and free tickets to basketball derbies, and he won't have to turn a blind eye every time the boy borrows porn under his name at the local video club. Surely, at some point love will take the upper hand?

Plastered in make-up, wearing a studied look of horror, the just-short-of-attractive woman who ensures his direct line to all the news stories recorded by her channel every Sunday afternoon had never quite learned to conceal her *schadenfreude* when describing the various disasters that befell other people: *The house burned to a cinder; there was nothing left after the fire – only ashes. Everybody inside the house burned to death. There is only one survivor. A woman, now fighting for her life in Intensive Care.*

A photograph of Sonia flashes across the screen, searing his face.

Sunday, 1.50 p.m.

Simeon Piertzovanis wakes up in completely unfamiliar surroundings, an incomprehensible wet dream etched onto his consciousness. The slats on the window slice up the icy grey winter light, the grey of silence and despair. It only takes a few seconds before he realizes he is at the Hilton and that the woman who had joined him in that most ancient of pastimes with such consummate skill was gone, and languishing in his inside pocket was a cheque for €3,000, a souvenir of one of those rare evenings when all the queens, kings and aces had collectively decided to reward him for his long-standing loyalty.

The sheets are suffused with a delicate scent, the time on his watch is 1.50 and the note on the bedside table reminds him with chilling clarity of the age of his nocturnal companion:

Nice one, granddad – didn't think u had it in u!!! Call u Monday! R.x

He crumples up the note in disgust and aims it at the champagne bottle which is still sitting on top of the room service trolley. *Missed.* He lights a cigarette and scans the room for the remote.

Sunday, 2.30 p.m.

Halkidis strides into the hospital flashing his I.D., barging his way through everyone from journalists, cameramen and nursing staff to the merely inquisitive. He finds the head of Intensive Care in a state of panic, hiding from the hordes of press in a tiny office. When confronted with the police I.D., his expression modulates to something approaching disgust.

"How is she?"

"Forty-six per cent third-degree burns."

"Will she make it?"

"Nothing's impossible."

"Her face? What about her face?"

Sunday, 2.30 p.m.

The photograph of Sonia flashing across the screen burns his eyes. The room starts to close in on him, the voice of the reporter disappears into a dark tunnel, the horror grabs him by the arm and drags him into the past, a past he had thought securely sealed, into a "then" he had secretly been proud of, to a painful but courageous elsewhere, to a landscape of shattered emotions and the sweetest kind of suffering.

The photograph on the screen gives way to another, and then another – each so similar and yet so different – two eyes which had been submerged in countless centuries, two lips which had contrived magical whispers, which had produced forgotten cries, which had given him . . .

Simeon screams her name.

He does not make a sound.

Sunday, 3.30 p.m.

He parks his ancient Golf behind a 4×4 belonging to the fire brigade. The young man at the wheel is busy texting. The sight of police I.D. startles him and he quickly takes Halkidis to the Fire Captain despatched by the investigating magistrate. He is a tall, thin, thirty-five-year-old with tired eyes and a warm voice. Halkidis at once realizes that the man is in shock.

"We've got one woman in a critical condition and two dead – an old man and a black woman, around thirty."

"Black?"

"Yes. The man was probably disabled; we found a wheelchair inside the house."

"How did it start?"

"We're still looking into it. Want to take a look?"

The captain takes him on a comprehensive tour of the scene of horror, and clears his throat loudly in an attempt to distract from his faltering voice. Outside there is an ancient burnt-out Hillman, two blackened fir trees, and a carbonized almond tree. The house was not big: a small living room overlooking the garden, three bedrooms, and a small laundry room round the back which was used as a storeroom. The black woman was found on the bed, burnt to a cinder; the man was outside her bedroom door, on the floor next to the wheelchair. The destruction was total.

"What about the other woman?" says Halkidis.

"Just say she was fortunate in her misfortune. She managed to get out . . . but not quickly enough, it seems, judging from her burns. She ran out onto the street and was seen by a passing driver."

"Was that who made the call?"

"As luck would have it, he turned out to be the only person in Greece who does not own a mobile phone. He rang the bells of a couple of houses a bit further down from here, but they're empty. He had to go all the way out onto the main road, Leoforos Pentelis, and stop another car. It was that driver who made the call. Valuable time was lost."

"Where did the fire start?"

"In the garden. You see that car, the almond tree, and the fir trees? In the small veranda at the front we found the remains of three canisters, which maybe contained petrol. There was an old stove inside the house."

Halkidis lights up. The captain rubs his eyes and continues:

"One of the fir trees was touching the outside wall. The window was open, so the curtain would have gone up just like that. It was a really old house, with dried reeds laid directly beneath the roof tiles. The beams in these old buildings stick out. Wooden floors, wooden ceilings, an open window to let the oxygen in. Wouldn't have taken more than a few minutes."

"How did it start?"

"Give us three hours to file our report and the house is all yours. Till then, I can't say anything."

"Any chance we're talking arson?"

The captain shakes his head. There's a strange sadness in his voice.

"Between you and me, in the majority of cases when a fire spreads from the outside in, it usually is. Especially in winter."

"Has anyone been talking to the press?"

"My job, Officer, is to save lives. That's what I do. That's what I know. I'm not good with words."

Halkidis gives him his mobile number, shakes his hand and hurries back to his car.

Sunday, 3.30 p.m.

A €50 note slipped to some miserable porter and a green surgical gown open the door to Intensive Care. Two security officers in the waiting room are sipping *frappés* and talking in low voices. The porter says something incomprehensible to them, opens a door, pulls a surgical mask over Halkidis' face and some protective plastic covers over his shoes and beckons him to follow. They negotiate a forest of tubes and machinery and stop next to a bed where the stark white of all the bandages floods his eyes, blinds and chills him. The porter has to steady him.

"What about her face?"

"Yannis – you have to let me have this case. I'm sure it was arson."

The Chief of Police is sceptical.

"Why is this so important to you?"

"It's personal."

"Absolutely not, Chronis, I need you here. Forget it."

"You owe me, Chief. Remember?"

Silence.

What the Chief of Police owed Halkidis was his job. Two years ago, it had been on the line when some of his so-called friends, officers who had very bright futures after the recent elections and the inevitable reshuffling of the public sector – and who also enjoyed cosy relationships with various celebrity journalists – found out about the Chief's affair with a beautiful young woman from Moldova he had met at a sleazy bar owned by a retired colleague. They grassed him up to Internal Affairs, letting it be understood that if the Chief could not see his way to doing them a few favours, they would feed the story to their scandal-hungry reporter friends. Halkidis investigated the case and closed it at once, after the girl in question told him that the Chief had rescued her from the traffickers who had brought her into Greece. She carried on the affair with the policeman, who for his part had set divorce proceedings in motion, intending to marry her as soon as he retired. The officers involved promptly withdrew their complaints when Halkidis warned them that Internal Affairs had a few queries of its own regarding their handling of funds allocated for the payment of informers.

"Come on, Chronis!"

"Yannis, I swear to God – this is a matter of life and death to me. She's a relative. A close relative."

"And how the fuck am I supposed to explain this to the top brass?"

"Since when did you feel obliged to explain yourself to them, when only last year they were —"

"O.K., O.K.," he cuts him short, feigning irritation.

"Thanks, Chief."

"As of tomorrow you're at H.Q. on Leoforos Alexandras. I expect daily bulletins."

"Of course, Chief."

"Just make sure for your own sake that you handle those journalists with care. If this actress really is as famous as you say she is, all hell's going to break loose."

"Don't worry, Chief."

"I'll make the call now."

"Who will you speak to?"

"To that old junta-socialist – the cabinet secretary's best man."

Relieved, he replaces the receiver. "Junta-socialist" was the least offensive nickname for Attica's Police Chief, a commander who, after gorging on half a suckling-pig washed down with ten litres of beer, would often argue that the only politicians who had genuinely cared about the country were Andreas Papandreou, the founder of the socialist P.A.S.O.K. party, and Giorgos Papadopoulos, one of the three colonels who engineered the '67 coup. His boss had often to keep him on a short leash because outbursts of this sort made the sweet pill of modernization he had been chewing for the last few years stick in his throat.

Halkidis lights up and sets to work. He bumps into one of his assistants out for a stroll with his in-laws round the Mikrolimano area of Piraeus, and tells him to get to the office in a hurry. The assistant is on his first coffee of the day and his hoarse voice betrays the excesses of the weekend. Halkidis instructs him to get hold of the preliminary fire report, orders himself a coffee and notices that the traffic down on Leoforos Syngrou is very light. He sits there trying to ward off the moment when memories and guilt will force him to open the engraved wooden box locked in the bottom drawer of his desk.

Sunday, 4.05 p.m.

The taxi is making its way up Leoforos Kifissias. The radio is tuned to Era Sport: violent clashes at a match in Thessaloniki.

"All that match fixing! Whichever way you look at it, it stinks."

"Why don't you turn it off, then?"

"Got to listen to something, mate, haven't you? Got to listen to something; silence does my head in."

Simeon decides instead to admire the new architectural marvels gracing the avenue.

"You get along with it alright, do you mate – silence?"

"What?"

"Silence – do you like it?"

"I'm on medication."

"What kind of medication?"

"Silencing drugs."

"What?"

He stood waiting for her outside the theatre, glancing at the magazines at the kiosk to kill time. She crept up behind him without a sound, and put her hands over his eyes. Her palms smelled of talcum powder.

"Guess who?"

"I don't know."

"Your evening dose, stupid."

The taxi driver will not let it go.

"I didn't know they had drugs for stuff like that?"

Simeon turns up the collar of his overcoat, leans his head against the window and closes his eyes.

Sunday, 4.20 p.m.

The coffee stain across the coroner's rushed draft forms a circle around the words "extensive third degree burns with".

Halkidis looks at his team, who are, quite reasonably, at a loss to understand his agitation. At the same time he thinks how lucky he is that the Assistant Director of Internal Affairs, an incompetent P.A.S.O.K. lackey, the minister's snitch, is on sick leave after a skiing accident on Parnassus.

"Kourkouvelas, take a team from Forensics down to the burnt-out house. Don't overlook anything you find. Dedes, you do the rounds of the neighbourhood. The house is isolated, but there are dozens of old houses within a 500-metre-radius of it. I want statements from all the neighbours and when I say all of them, I mean everyone from the five-year-olds to the deaf-mute grandfather. Ask at the nearby petrol stations if anyone has been in buying heating oil in jerry cans lately. But be very clear – not a word about this to anyone – that includes your bathroom mirrors. I'll take care of the woman."

The woman who survived, he was about to add, but something stopped him.

"Sir, may I ask what this fire's got to do with Internal Affairs?"

"You may not."

Sunday, 4.20 p.m.

The house is still smouldering. He steps over the orange plastic tape and walks across the fallen garden gate. A fireman calls out something to him. Simeon ignores him and slowly makes his way through the charred garden. The almond tree and the firs are no longer there. The sight of the burnt-out Hillman momentarily transports him to Thessaloniki, deep within two green eyes. There are fragments of pots holding geraniums scattered everywhere across the terrain of his childhood, smelling of death. The windows stand open like gaping wounds, and the roof with the swallows whose temporary flight used to grace the autumns back then with their magnificent cries, the wonderful red roof with that absurd chimney stack was gone. His knees start to cave in. He leans against the charred wall and his head is filled with images: Morenike laughing with the little one who is dipping her fingers into Noni's ice cream; Sonia with old Manthos, dizzy from all the wine and laughter, trying in vain to teach the little one a few words of Greek: *petalouda* – butterfly; *kryo* – cold; *zesti* – hot; *vrohi* – rain; *karamela* – sweetie. But the truth blazes in front of him, a truth which hurls him back into the past against his will.

That damned house was lost again, but this time for good. The first time was in the spring of '67, when his father left for a "holiday" on the prison isle of Gioura, indefinitely, and his mother rented it out, moving herself and her eleven-year-old mummy's boy in with her sister. The boy failed to understand why he suddenly found himself cooped up in a flat in downtown Plateia Amerikis, losing all his friends, the empty building lots where they would graze their knees, and leaving behind Klaras, the three-legged mongrel he had rescued from the dried-up riverbed next to the house.

His father returned from the island in 1970 to find his son much taller, much thinner and much angrier. His wife, instead of waiting patiently for him, had opted for the embrace of a well-to-do Citroën dealer somewhere in the Peloponnese. As she packed, she told her son she had a few things to see to and that she would be back soon. She told him to be sure to do his homework and never to take up smoking. Not one of those three things ever came to pass. His father did not even bother to go and look for her. "That's love for you, my boy. At some point, it passes." That was all he ever said on the subject. He retreated into the gloom of the accounts office at some paper mill and sank into depression. He lasted a surprisingly long time, until 1990, when he hanged himself in the Pedion tou Areos municipal park. His only friends, Loukas Marselos, a lawyer, and Lilis, a notary, fell out over which of them should assume the guardianship of the prodigal son. Piertzovanis was thirty-four years old by then, with a law degree he had never found any use for and a brain half-eroded by alcohol. Loukas won the argument and made him a partner in his firm. He muddled through, making slow progress until 1995 when a third heart attack finished off Loukas and the disappearance of a green-eyed, raven-haired beauty finished off Simeon. At least he had shown enough wit to make Achilleas, an ambitious young lawyer who did all the hard work at the office, his partner. That was how he could afford the luxury of an arrested adolescence, honing his skills at the card table, increasing his consumption of alcohol and attaching himself to unsuitable women. Then in '98 his mother turned up out of the blue, found Lilis and instructed him to transfer the deeds of the old house to her little boy. She held on to the usufruct, probably on the advice of the sage notary who feared that her little boy might simply hand the property over to a developer and lose all the money at the poker table, exactly as he had done with the small flat Loukas had left him. She did not ask to see him. He did not make any attempt to see her either.

A year later he met Sonia.

"That's quite a bit we lost today, Sir."

"Is there a quiet bar anywhere along Stadiou where they'd sell me a bottle? My treat."

"A bottle of what?"

"Paddy's."

"What's that?"

"Irish whiskey. Hard to come by these days."

"I'd rather have a yellow tequila."

"I've got credit too."

She looks at him and smiles.

"I'm sure you're aware that the old saying, 'unlucky at cards, lucky in love', isn't true."

"I haven't heard that one."

"Have you ever seen me in the theatre?"

"No."

"Then you don't know who I am?"

"I do recognize you, from photographs."

"No need to be so stiff with me. I'm only forty-five."

It was a lovely evening; first evenings always are. They got pleasantly drunk listening to the stories of the best barman in the universe, Aristides "the just", and popular old songs from Geramanis' radio show. After midnight he put her in a taxi, kissed her on the cheek, and promised to come and see her in her play. She said that she would have asked him back to her place but someone was expecting her. Simeon went back to the 16 bar for a nightcap and Aristides' verdict. Ever laconic, the barman restricted himself to an ominous "be careful".

It lasted a year and a half. In the autumn of 2000 she walked out on him and on the theatre. His pleas had fallen on deaf ears. "I'm cursed, my darling. I destroy everything I touch. Don't come looking for me. Promise?" He promised.

The lump in his throat is killing him. The hand on his shoulder is a friendly one. The fireman helps him up and he dusts himself down. He walks Piertzovanis out onto the pavement, and tells him "be careful".

Sunday, 5.05 p.m.

He is making some Turkish coffee on his little camping stove when his mobile rings. The Fire Captain on the other end sounds out of breath.

"We're definitely dealing with arson here, Officer. Someone threw some Molotov cocktails into the old banger abandoned in the garden. We've also found a —"

"A what?"

He listens to the heavy sigh of the captain.

"A child," he says through his tears.

Halkidis watches as his coffee boils over.

"A baby . . . three years old, maybe younger. It had shut itself in an iron trunk. Hid in there to escape the fire. Suffocated. She was probably the black woman's daughter."

His sobs are clearly audible still.

"Can you come round here?"

"Oh, I don't know."

"Please come."

"Where are you?"

Sunday, 5.05 p.m.

He's trying to get hold of Noni whose phone is switched off. After a while he remembers that Noni is at home on the other side of the world, and is due back in a couple of days. Images of Morenike and the little one keep coming back to him. It cannot be true; there must be some mistake. His mind cannot accommodate the horror. And then Sonia. Again and again. He does not know what to do, where to go or who to talk to. He refuses to accept the pain, the fear of having to face a tomorrow, which until this afternoon he had assumed to be sorted out; not a happy one, of course, not necessarily auspicious even, but predictable at least. He never imagined that anything could happen that would awaken such feelings, feelings that he considered non-existent, or rather killed off by all the generous pity he had shown her. "I'll just disappear in a cloud of smoke. I know how much damage I've done – I don't want to harm you too." Her last words. She was drunk on rose liqueur, and was slowly rubbing the soles of her feet, as though she was counting her wrinkles, so self-conscious that only her face and feet were allowed to stick out from under the sheet. 10 November, 2000.

Pity is synonymous with the end of an affair. Simeon had been counting on that old truism for the last few years, but why then was he stroking the photograph in his hand? Why was the video sitting there waiting to re-enact time at the simple push of a button – no, not re-enact – wrong word – to mock time? And even worse, why all the tears?

"Never again," he whispers at the photograph he had covertly taken one morning while she weighed herself on the bathroom scales, wearing an expression of indescribable despair. "Never again," he screams and instantly bites it back because that "never again" is sacrilege, it tempts fate. The weak heart is still beating, not like it used to when it clung to his back, but it's still beating, each beat feeding into the next, threatening to shatter his temples.

Sunday, 9.10 p.m.

On his own now. He is fiddling with the notes that the shattered Fire Captain had left him three hours ago. His assistants have turned up nothing significant. He is losing himself in the sketch of the house. He is besieged by questions: Why was Sonia living there? Who were the other tenants? What was the motive for the arson? He tries to think. He can't. Just as he cannot get the image of the little girl out of his head. He opens the window. It is quiet on Syngrou. He is cold. His brain aches. He goes back to his desk and unlocks the bottom drawer.

Sunday, 9.10 p.m.

The video is playing. "Lulu", winter '99. She never takes a bow at the end – she clasps her right hand to her heart and smiles at the audience instead. What is behind that smile? Joy? Gratitude? A farewell?

"*Relief. I smile because I've escaped them again tonight.*"

"*Escaped what?*"

"*The evil looks. Every evening, from the stalls.*"

"*No kind looks?*"

"*Only yours these days.*"

"*Don't exaggerate.*"

"*Most audiences hate actors.*"

"*How many people have you said this to?*"

"*You're the third.*"

"*Stop drinking. You've had enough.*"

Over the last few months, she had been filling plastic water bottles with vodka. Nobody got wise to her little trick; vodka leaves no trace on the breath.

He takes an old, dog-eared deck of cards out of the drawer: if he can crack the tableau, he will be alright.

Sunday, 9.25 p.m.

The contents of the drawer are spread out across Halkidis' desk:

A silver Zippo with his initials engraved on it; the first present she had given him.

A photograph of the two of them in the dressing rooms at the ancient theatre of Philippi.

The long black gloves she wore in "The Maids".

A flat flask of Dewar's, the one she had thrown at his head in Room 603 at the Galaxy Hotel in Patras.

Two cinema tickets from the Trianon cinema, "Identification of a Woman". Antonioni. It was snowing that day; they had had the place to themselves.

A packet of John Player's; all traces of the drunken red kiss vanished.

And those short notes she would always leave him at hotel receptions, summer '97. Nineteen notes; he had not looked at them since.

And a 9MM pistol shining through the semi-darkness.

Sunday, 9.25 p.m.

Simeon cannot take anymore. He changes the tape, turns the picture off and the volume up. He does not want to see her face, only to hear her voice. He had watched her countless times in that production, he almost knew her role by heart. He mimes along with her, whispering her lines, realizing he still remembers them.

"Do you think I'm crippled for life? Do you think that we'll be an endless army of emotional cripples who wander around speaking words to each other we don't understand and making us even more scared?"

Sunday, 11.30 a.m.

He greets the men from the Z-squad, the rapid reaction motorcycle unit, at the door, gets into his Golf and drives out onto Syngrou. He drives through empty streets, his mind in neutral. As though five years have not passed. He turns into Ippokratous and parks. Hotel Frida. He almost enjoys the look on the young receptionist's face.

"Are you going to, um, I mean, are you expecting someone?"

He does not answer. He goes up to the first floor, Room 12. There's a television opposite the circular bed, a low mirror next to it. The pink wallpaper with the purple geometrical pattern, the smell of air freshener and the sound of the leaking cistern.

Her smile as she waits for him.

"Are you tired, young Chronis? Oh – I keep meaning to ask you: does Chronis come from Chronos?"

She climbs on top of him. Her teeth gleam in the darkness.

He drops face down on the bed and breaks into furious sobs.

Sunday, 11.30 p.m.

I'm cold. What's she going to be like? Am I coming or going? I was always late for my dates. Fear. Terror. Terror is harder than fear, the word has a completely different ring to it; terror is when other people make you tremble, rubbing against your face with their looks of pity and the sense of the irreversible, hazy green figures whispering and plotting. Fear is sweet and calm, you are always afraid, you get used to it. I have always known fear. How clearly I remember his face when he told me he was leaving because he could not cope with my fear. Not the least trace of harshness on his face. Just love. A man in love, turning his back on love. The perfect melodrama. Curtains. Applause. The sound cannot conceal the enthusiasm of the audience. Then my final scene. Behind the curtain, this is where my play ends, above the secret trap-door which will swallow me up in an instant. Everyone will mourn such a convenient loss, but really, it will bring them pain, a lot of pain because they loved me a lot, and now they'll understand how much. Leave; I don't want you feeling sorry for me. I said the same thing to

23

the other one and can still remember how his face crumpled in grief. He was gentle, like a child. But you have to protect tenderness with harshness. Whose line was that? I would love to be able to say sorry to my most recent boyfriends. How I would love to do that.

26.i

Monday, 9.00 a.m.

He polishes off a second Turkish coffee, lights up, coughs, his eyes moistening, swears, spits into the rubbish bin, and makes a start on the newspapers. The word "mystery" seems to be a great favourite with editors: "Mystery blaze"; "Mystery fire"; "Sonia Varika – actress's last years shrouded in mystery". Not a word about arson. The Fire Captain had been as good as his word. He stubs out his cigarette and calls the woman who has been making his life much easier for the last five years.

Monday, 9.00 a.m.

He wakes up in a pool of sweat. In a matter of seconds, he has remembered everything. Despair penetrates his chest. It is an effort just to get out of bed and put on the coffee. He drinks it outside on the balcony defying the icy cold, the closed horizon, and devious thoughts crying out, "Leave; catch a plane to a different hemisphere, travel to some extended summer, go and melt under a foreign sun, get rid of the unbearable burden that is dragging you down."

His secretary is a thirty-five-year-old divorcee, short and always smiling, fluent in scores of foreign languages and as smart as they come. "I want you to find out who the house belongs to and anything else you can about the owner. Everything. Now. Drop whatever it is you are doing, and make sure we are up and running in Alexandras from tomorrow."

She takes the piece of paper he hands her and looks at him searchingly.

"Are we going to be working on this case?"

"Chief's orders."

Her questions multiply, but she manages to collapse them into a vague "of course".

"Fotini – we might have to —"

"Work overtime, even nights. Don't worry; I'm sure my 'darling husband' will be his usual understanding self."

"Well done, you angel, you genius. How does the old song go? 'What would I have amounted to on this earth without you . . . ?'"

"'A tramp – you'd have gone to ruin.'"

Smiling, she turns to leave. He picks up a blank piece of paper and, fully aware of the pointlessness of the exercise, starts making notes:

1. Arson. (Motive?)
2. 3 dead. (Relationships? Why didn't they wake up?)
   1 injured, S.V. – 50 years old. (Living there permanently?)
3. Nothing significant found in the house.
4. Owner – find today. (Whose name was the lease in? Fire insurance?)

He leaves his office, crosses the narrow corridor and opens the door to the meeting room. Dedes is talking to a well-dressed man in his thirties, his eyes red from crying. As soon as he sees Halkidis, he takes him to one side and explains to him in a whisper:

"Theophilopoulos. Son of the old man. He saw it on the news and went to the hospital, and after that to Alexandras. They brought him here a short while ago. Father was an actor, Varika's old mentor. They had been living together since Easter 2002. Apparently, he had never mentioned the black woman and the child."

Halkidis introduces himself and signals to Dedes to carry on.

"You were saying something about an old people's home, Mr Theophilopoulos?"

"Yes. He wouldn't hear of going. He wanted to be with Sonia. Said he enjoyed being with her. He wouldn't let us visit. Once a month he would come to the house; he never stayed long – played with his grandson and left. He seemed fine. He had stopped drinking, at least that's what he told us. He was still shaking, of course, but . . . I don't know – I suppose he might have been lying about the drink, but he was happy, so what were we supposed to do? We gave him an allowance; he had the pension as well. I can't take this in. I just can't."

The young man is weeping.

Halkidis sits down next to him and offers him a cigarette. He takes one. His hand is shaking.

"You mentioned that your father visited you occasionally. There was a wheelchair in the house. I suppose it was . . ."

"Wheelchair?"

"Yes."

"No, that wasn't his. He was in good shape for someone his age – apart from the drinking, that is."

Halkidis squeezes his arm and stands up.

Dedes looks up at his boss, inquiringly. No, Chronis has no further questions for the weeping man.

Sunday, 9.25 a.m.

He takes a small, old leather suitcase down from the loft and empties the contents onto the rug. The dust makes him cough. He sets to work, sorting through all these newly excavated traces of her: photographs, theatre programmes, cassettes, newspaper clippings, hand-written notes. He pulls a straw hat decorated with daisies out of a bag, the hat he had given her on May Day in 2000.

"Do you know how old I am, young man?" she had whispered, with a meanness prompted by a mixture of honesty and tequila, sloppily stuffing the hat back into the bag before literally throwing it back in his face.

He locks the suitcase, carefully dusts it off and goes out.

"Acropol Hotel, Halandri," he tells the taxi driver, who is wearing a Chicago Bulls baseball cap, the visor pointing down his neck, and listening to the very loud hip-hip on his radio.

"What are we listening to?"

The driver looks at him in the mirror, obviously surprised.

"Razastar – they're Greek. From Vyronas – the lead singer's my mate."

"Turn it up."

His mind was besieged by the rage in the young singer's voice:

"'Don't throw solitude a lifeline –/Stay. Don't leave/And go somewhere far away.'"

"Wicked, aren't they?" says the taxi driver, almost screaming to be heard.

Simeon nods in agreement, stroking his magical suitcase.

Monday, 10.35 a.m.

Fotini bursts in.

"I've found him! The owner."

"Tell me."

"Simeon Piertzovanis: Forty-eight. Lawyer. Unmarried. In 2003 declared earnings were €18,000. He rents in Exarcheia; office in Stadiou. No car; no bank loans; the house has belonged to him since 1998. His mother signed it over to him. Doesn't declare rent from it."

"Criminal record?"

"One arrest. Illegal gambling. Never went to court."

"Have we a phone number?"

"Just his home number at the moment."

"Get him. Put him through to me."

"Anything else?"

"Don't go near any journalists."

"Don't worry, I won't. You know . . ."

"What?"

"The actress who survived. I knew her. Well, what I mean is, I really admired her. I've got a signed photograph of her. I could never understand why she gave up acting."

"Perhaps we'll find out," Halkidis mumbled, lighting up.

"Go easy on the cigarettes."

Monday, 10.35 a.m.

Room 305 looks down on Leoforos Pentelis. Simeon is sitting on the double bed with the newspapers spread out around him, covered in filthy ink smears, absorbed in the photographs of her and the paeans to her talent and to her rarefied beauty, the insinuations about her addiction and her secret, possibly non-existent, love life.

He tosses the newspapers onto the floor and stretches out.

"This is our first time, Sir. Allow me to undress you."

"Be my guest."

"It might take some time."

"Even better."

"Don't be so sure; I'm a creature of talent – the tequila could keep me awake for hours."

"I'll do my best."

"What?"

"To last the course."

"What if you don't? If you fail to satisfy a woman who has got used to being captivating, a woman who has been making a living out of being captivating for so many years, a woman who lives and breathes creating false illusions?"

"I'll be made to pay for it."

"Will you? Ha! Tell me, what's the name of this depressing establishment you've dragged me to?"

"The Acropol."

"The room number. Do you remember it?"

"Two hundred and something."

"Two hundred and six. Right, so if you fail to satisfy me, you'll automatically give me the right to study your body, your mind, your

relationship with the world; I'll leave your soul out of it seeing that I'm an atheist. In short, you'll give up all your rights to me for the next twenty-six nights. Agreed?"

"But what if I do manage to satisfy you?"

"Then you win."

"Win what?"

"A chance to take part in the game of promises."

"Agreed."

He is holding a receipt from the Acropol dated 7 October, 1999. On the back it says: "You won the first night, young man. My first promise is that I will love you forever. What's yours? . . . Ha! . . . Now let's see what you're made of!"

Monday, 10.50 a.m.

"There's no answer, Mr Halkidis."

He bites his pencil. Fotini makes a face at the ashtray.

"Well, get a search warrant for his house, then."

"Yes, of course."

Fotini is about to leave, but then hesitates.

"Yes, I'm smoking. I know."

He pretends to stub it out and is rewarded with a big smile.

"Do you mind if I smoke?"

"Be my guest, Mr Halkidis. Is the coffee to your liking?"

"It's wonderful."

"I always stir in a little love with the sugar."

She gets up and brings an ashtray. She's wearing jeans and a T-shirt with the legend "Sacred Cows Make the Best Hamburgers" across the back.

He asks her what it means and she tells him she will explain the

story behind the T-shirt once they know each other better. Half an hour
later, they have agreed about the job. They shake hands.

"I have only three favours to ask of you, Mr Halkidis."

"Ask away."

"That you call me Sonia and I call you Chronis. That you'll never
feel sorry for me, even when I'm drunk. That each time you light up,
you'll remember how much it pains me."

Monday, 10.50 a.m.

The hotel bar is deserted, apart from one young man, who as soon
as he sees him neatly folds his copy of the *Athlitiko Echo* and turns
his attention to the espresso machine. Piertzovanis sits on a high
stool and peruses the menu.

He tries to remember what she used to drink in the afternoon
and how she tried to persuade him that her thirst was just her need
to prolong their outrageous celebration of the night before.

He has forgotten. Just as well. He will try to remember in his own
way. It does not matter anymore that for the thousandth time he
would be breaking the promise he made her three years ago, the day
they parted: "if I ever put one in my mouth again, it will mean that
I have forgotten you." He nods to the barman.

"A double vodka tonic, a gin fizz and a yellow tequila with two
slices of orange."

Monday, 3.30 p.m.

Halkidis is listening attentively to his assistants.

There is not much in the way of new evidence. The report from

Forensics does not help at all. The identities of the black woman and the child have not been established. An employee at the petrol station made a statement to the effect that four days earlier a young black man had bought three cans of heating fuel and had loaded them into a dark-coloured Toyota, or Mazda. He has not been back. Not one of the houses in a 500-metre radius of the burnt-out house is occupied. The nearest were on the other side of the dry stream bed and nobody there heard or saw anything, nor did they know any of the tenants. There was just one fifty-year-old man, highly strung, who would go out for a walk every evening, for about an hour and a half, and said he had sometimes noticed lights on in the house. At a mini-market, a kilometre away, the owner remembered the old actor – he would buy his *Radio-Teleorasi* guide from her every Friday, and a big bar of Ion chocolate with almonds. Neither of the two big supermarkets on the avenue had ever made a delivery to them and the employees did not recognize any of them.

"Right – they didn't eat and they didn't drink. So what the fuck did they live on?" Halkidis exploded.

"Someone must have been doing the shopping for them. Maybe that darkie who bought the heating fuel," said Kourkouvelas, one of the assistants.

"Perhaps. But where is the little shit now?"

"If he hasn't got a residence permit, he'll be scared," says Dedes. "And please, don't use the word 'darkie'. It's offensive."

Halkidis raises a hand to pre-empt another ideological struggle between *Synaspismos* left-alliance Dedes and the competent but ideologically unsound Kourkouvelas.

"Get the search warrant for Piertzovanis' house from Fotini. Go through the place with a fine-tooth comb. You're looking for anything, anything at all, that could be linked to the house or the victims. And from tomorrow, we'll be working out of Alexandras."

His team can't understand why their boss is looking so grim, but dare not say a word.

Monday, 3.30 p.m.

He collapses in a heap on the bed. There's a tune he cannot get out of his head: "All we ask is to be able to continue to alternate day with night – nothing else."

He cannot remember where he heard it, when, or who it was by. He falls asleep fearful that he will throw up on the bed, but he cannot get up, he cannot make it as far as the bathroom. He is incapable of caring about anything anymore because she has left him – again.

Monday, 4.45 p.m.

He is standing up, looking at her. He wants to stroke her hand, but the forest of plastic tubes makes him shudder. He wants to lift the sheet a little to check whether her toenails are varnished, but he is held back by the presence of the nurse beside him. He wants to whisper the tune, the one that always made her first smile and then cry, but is afraid that he will choke on his tears. Her breathing is normal; the green screens above her head form a perfect, silent nightmare that Halkidis is not sure he wants to end, but which he cannot endure for longer than two minutes, and which drives him out of deep contemplation into blank despair.

The doctor was very clear. "We'll know in seventy-two hours. The most severe burns are those from the waist down. Her face is in a relatively good state. There is always so much that can go wrong in these cases. Personally, I am not optimistic. Not pessimistic either."

He gets back into his Golf and lights up. Three missed calls flash in protest across his mobile, all from one or other of his assistants. He rings them back in turn. They each tell him that it would be a good idea if he had a look round Simeon Piertzovanis' house himself.

"Why?"

"There's an insurance policy, Sir."

Monday 4.45 p.m.

Sonia is holding him by the hand and leading him confidently down a narrow footpath. Rocks to the left, a grey sea to the right. Simeon is out of breath.

"We'll be late, young man, hurry up, we have to get to the end before it gets dark. The performance cannot start without me, so many people are waiting. What? You can't be out of breath so soon? O.K. Listen. This is what we'll do: I'll go on ahead and I'll drop the stuff that's in my handbag as I go, so you can see which way to go and that way you won't get lost. But get a move on, will you? I want you to see my entrance. It's my best scene. Don't be long, promise!"

In an instant she has disappeared from view and he starts picking up things she dropped from the ground, things he cannot believe could fit into such a small handbag: pink ballet shoes; green apples; a dressing gown; a wall clock; a bag crammed full of cotton wool; a sparrow which shudders and gives up the ghost.

Thank God, he wakes up. His mouth is dry. Darkness. The hum

of the traffic brings him momentary comfort. He turns on the light and buries his head under the pillow in an attempt to get rid of the terror, not the terror of the dream, but the terror that consumes him the minute he realizes that this is the first time he has ever dreamt about her.

Monday, 5.30 p.m.

He tells the team to go home and sinks into Mr Simeon Piertzovanis' threadbare sofa. In front of him on the glass-topped coffee table is the insurance policy. During all his long years in the force, the most valuable piece of advice he had ever heard was from an ancient prosecutor who said to him: "Young man, there's nothing that happens in this world that isn't motivated by money. Even those so-called *crimes passionnels* have the colour of money." He gives the policy a cursory glance and picks up his mobile. After a five-minute conversation with a cousin who works in insurance, he concludes that Mr Piertzovanis has something in the order of €150,000 coming to him as a result of the burnt house. He slides his pistol out of its shoulder holster and puts it on the sofa next to him.

Monday, 5.30 p.m.

The icy water is painful. He climbs out of the bath, gingerly, the dizziness dogging him. He rubs himself down with a coarse towel and catches a glimpse of his bony body in the mirror. With a head devoid of thought, devoid of memories, devoid of plans, he whistles without realizing that his eyes are dripping like a leaky tap. "This is the last time I sleep in a hotel," he vows and phones down to reception for his bill and a taxi. He does not dare go to the hospital. "Exarcheia," he tells the driver.

Monday, 6.30 p.m.

He remembers her imploring her sister Chrysothemis:

> *Nay, dear sister, let none of these things in thy hands touch*
> *the tomb; for neither custom nor piety allows thee to dedicate*
> *gifts or bring libations to our sire from a hateful wife.*

He recalls that stifling evening under the Acropolis most vividly: he remembers her exhilarated exhaustion, his lips on the perspiration of her throat in her locked dressing room. And now five years later he hears the lines again, the same words after every performance, *we got away with it again tonight, didn't we?* He hears her words and at the same time hears the key in the door, and for a moment thinks someone's coming into her dressing room and will catch them in the act. But it's not the same key. An exhausted man is turning it, and he's more puzzled than frightened at the sight of the Beretta pointing at him. His lips are moist. Silence. He's about 1.80, thin, between forty-five and fifty, casually dressed. Black overcoat, jeans, sweater, muddy suede boots. The frames of his glasses remind him of the style favoured by 1930s schoolteachers. Unwashed, dishevelled, grey hair. Bleary-eyed. Apart from the key, he is holding an old suitcase and a plastic bag with the logo *Cava Oinochoi* across it. Halkidis points to the sofa. But he just stands there, all at sea.

Monday, 6.30 p.m.

Simeon opens the door with a perfunctory movement. A faint light creeps from the living room. He goes inside and sees the pistol. The man holding it is tall and stocky, with short grey hair, unshaven. He is wearing a cheap, dark-coloured jacket, but it is the expression on his face more than the pistol motioning him to sit down that alarms him. He puts his suitcase and carrier bag down onto the floor, but he is still on his feet. Halkidis lowers the Beretta, puts it into his pocket and sits down in one of the armchairs. Simeon struggles out of his overcoat and tosses it onto the sofa. It slips slowly towards the rug. Halkidis observes him closely.

A wreck. Someone who has never let rip in his life. Someone who could so very easily kill a man, and just as easily regret it and confess everything.

"Who are you?" asks Simeon, collapsing onto the sofa, closing his eyes and deciding to drift off.

Halkidis realizes that it is going to be a long, hard night and decides to make a start.

"Police Colonel Chronis Halkidis. I'm investigating the fire at the house you own. I imagine you're aware of what happened there?"

Simeon shakes his head. He looks confused. He stands up, lifts the bag off the floor and, taking uncertain steps, heads for the kitchen. He fills a whisky tumbler to the halfway mark, adds some tap water, and comes back. He perches on the arm of the sofa. His hand is shaking.

"You look half dead," the tone was harsh.

"I frequently do."

"Exhaustion?"

"Gastro-oesophageal reflux, stomach ulcers, hypertension, alcoholic terror, sadness."

"Sadness?"

"That's what my doctor says."

"Your shrink?"

"My dentist."

Halkidis takes the sarcasm in his stride and continues, mildly.

"And the whisky helps, does it?"

"If I flush it through with enough water."

"I'll try to remember that," he says, offering a cigarette. *Cortina.* Low tar.

Simeon takes one, but is unable to light it. It falls out of his fingers.

"I'll be better in a minute."

He is barely audible.

"Take your time. I'm in no hurry."

"That's good."

CHAPTER 2

Simeon Piertzovanis
on the Verge of Collapse

26.i
Monday, 6.33 p.m.

I took the first sip and the burning sensation in my throat reminded me that I had to stock up on Nexium. The policeman looked terrible. It was not that he was unpleasant – if I had a child I might even trust him alone with him for a few hours – but I would never have him over for dinner. The only problem with policemen is the fact that they are policemen. In other words, the problem is generic.

"Why don't policemen use condoms?"

"I don't know. Why don't policemen use condoms?"

"Because they're cunts."

At least that was the theory of one of my friends, one he would elaborate on zealously, generally after his third drink, ever since he caught his wife in bed with a member of the Z-squad.

"Doesn't that warbling get on your nerves?" The question was almost friendly.

"Not unless I'm shaving."

He smiled, and stubbed out his cigarette.

"Don't be so prickly, Mr Piertzovanis. I don't know what your opinion of the police is, but whether you like it or not, we're going to have to work together. I need your help. This case means a lot to us. And I'm not saying that just because the victim is famous."

There she was again, standing in front of me, her eyes again, that tiny gap between her front teeth, the way she used to scoop the orange out of her tequila and bite into it.

"I'm so jealous of them – that's why I have to bite them; they're so lucky, swimming around in all that filthy alcohol and nothing ever happens to them."

The policeman's voice brought me to.

"Just a few questions and I'll leave you in peace, Mr Piertzovanis."

"Whatever you say, Mr . . . ?"

"Halkidis."

"That's it. You've already told me that."

Halkidis lit up. More than three packs a day. An even bigger idiot than me, I thought, as I noticed his overflowing ashtray.

"Shall I make you some coffee? I've only got Turkish."

"I'd prefer a whisky. Neat."

I gave him the bottle and told him to help himself.

"I've lost count of the number of coffees I've had today," he mumbled as though he was trying to justify himself.

"Not good. I've just about given it up. Stomach can't handle it."

"Fortunate in your misfortune then?"

"Something like that."

He moistened his lips and leant back into the sofa.

"Were you renting your house to Miss Sonia Varika?"

I finished my drink, refilled the glass and promised myself that the third one would be the last. The policeman's presence was compromising my grief. I had to get him out as quickly as possible.

"No; I just let her live in it."

"Why?"

"Old friend, calling in favours, returning favours maybe."

"So you knew her well?"

"No, not really. Hardly at all, in fact."

Halkidis looked puzzled. His eye fell onto the light blue plastic document wallet sitting on the table. I followed his gaze. The folder looked familiar.

"I forgot to mention that I obtained a warrant to search your flat," Halkidis said, looking me straight in the eye, possibly trying to work out whether the broken man sitting opposite him had anything to hide. "Can you remember the details of the insurance policy for that property?"

"Never even read it. A notary friend of mine arranged it for me. God rest his soul."

"When did you let Miss Varika move in?"

"Spring 2002."

"May I ask why?"

"No."

"Have it your way. As I said, I'm not in any great hurry and I can see that you are not at your best."

He pulled a notepad and pen out of his pocket, and just sat there.

"Alright, I'll talk," I said, hoping this would get rid of him.

He smiled as I switched into a more familiar tone. Perhaps he took it as a sign of surrender or a truce.

"Go ahead. Don't worry; these are just routine questions."

"A few years ago my mother signed the house over to me. Don't ask why; I haven't got a clue. I hadn't seen her since '69. I didn't get involved in any of the legal stuff. That was all taken care of by the notary I mentioned earlier. Sonia Varika was my friend. We used to play cards together; we'd talk; I'd go to her plays.'

"When did you first meet her?"

"21 July, 1999."

The policeman was visibly irritated. "Look – either you've got a very good memory or —"

"Or?"

"Or that date must be very important to you."

"It's my name day – St Simeon the Holy Fool. It was during the break in a game – she opened her diary to find a phone number and wished me a happy name day – the only person to do so all day."

"And you stayed friends after that?"

"Just good friends," I answered him with the decisiveness of a professional bearer of false witness.

"So why?"

"Look. We used to meet up very occasionally, but then out of the blue she gave up acting and shut herself away at home. I called a few times, but I realized she didn't want to see me. She was drinking pretty heavily. I bumped into her at a casino in the Christmas of 2001. She wasn't playing. She was standing next to a table in dark glasses, watching. And drinking. They don't charge for the booze at Loutraki. I took her back to her flat in Kypseli in the morning. When we got to the entrance to the block, she realized she'd lost her keys.

I offered to call the locksmith, but she didn't want me to. Do you know why?"

"I imagine that she preferred the idea of sleeping at your place?" he commented sarcastically.

"She was embarrassed. She wouldn't have been able to pay the locksmith if he had come. I made up the sofa for her here. She woke up late in the afternoon and told me she was €25,000 in debt to the banks and credit card companies and that she'd put her flat up for sale. I told her she was welcome to move into the house, and stay as long as she liked."

"Why?"

"It was Christmas. Didn't they teach you at school it makes the little Lord Jesus ever so happy when the faithful do good deeds on his birthday?"

Halkidis swallowed that along with the last sip of whisky. He refilled his glass and offered to pour me some more. I declined and went on with my story, careful not to leave the slightest crack through which he might suspect my real feelings for Sonia.

"She sold the flat in the January and moved into the house straight away. Three months later she phoned me and asked if I minded if she put up a retired actor there, her old mentor."

"Manthos Theophilopoulos."

"Yes."

"She needed a drinking companion," said the policeman peevishly.

"She loved him very much; he was the only teacher she had at drama school who didn't try to fuck her."

"Probably queer," he said, undeterred.

"Not wanting to and not trying it on are two different things."

43

He opened his cigarette packet and saw it was empty. I gestured towards mine.

"If I have just three of these, I'll wake up with no voice tomorrow," he said, lighting one of my Gitanes as though handling a stick of dynamite.

"She and the old man had a good time together. He took over the household chores and would break the silence whenever it was necessary. Sonia told me that it was he who had taught her the importance of pauses in the theatre."

"When did you see them?"

"Initially once a month. Then less often. The last time I went was back in the spring of last year, seven or eight months ago. I don't remember exactly. I knew that Sonia didn't want —"

"You to see the state she was in?"

"I've seen worse," I said, looking him straight in the eye.

"What do you mean?"

"You're the detective here. Work it out. But if you want a clue, there's a mirror in the bathroom."

He stubbed out the half-smoked cigarette, stifling a cough.

"What about the woman and child? Where do you know them from?"

"Morenike arrived in Greece about two-and-a-half years ago, escaped from Nigeria, pregnant. The little girl was called Rosa. She hadn't been baptized."

"What was she escaping from?"

"It's a long story, and not one that would be of any interest to your employers."

"What do you mean? My employers?"

"The state, Mr Halkidis."

"Why are you so hostile?"

What the fuck, I thought, the man's only doing his job. I muttered something resembling an apology and went on.

"Morenike entered the country illegally in 2001. Three months pregnant. Her brother Noni had already been living here for two years. He plays in goal for the national team."

"What's his surname?"

"Latouse."

"What about her husband?"

"There is no husband. There are men. She was raped. As you well know, if an unmarried woman gets pregnant in places like that, she can be stoned to death."

"Yes, I had heard something of the sort. Muslims, are they?"

"They're very poor. The money Noni's earning here is an awful lot by Nigerian standards. He got hold of a forged French passport for her and brought her over in September 2001."

"How did you meet her?"

Talk, so much talk. Why was I even bothering to talk to him? Because he seemed interested in the people I'd lost? Because I was dreading being alone now that night was falling? Because I was drunk and talking might stop me from crying? No, I wasn't drunk. Maybe I was talking to him like the relatives of patients do in hospitals, skulking in the corridors smoking, discussing the side-effects of chemotherapy on their loved ones while sucking hard on the tar and cursing those bloody fags that have been the death of the poor bugger, thinking that by speaking aloud its name they can break the spell of the tragedy.

"So how did you meet Morenike?" he said again. I pointed to the canary.

"You see her?"

He nodded.

"A few years ago I was living with a woman. She was a member of a support network for abused women. She would ask me to help out now and then with the legal side. After I managed to get an Albanian prostitute out of prison she gave me the canary. The prostitute was called Irina, which is why we named the bird Rina."

He was running out of patience but he didn't interrupt me.

"When she left me and went to Mexico with someone younger and better looking to work with the Zapatistas, she begged me to keep Rina. So I did, but only so as not to look like a complete arsehole. Anyway, I carried on helping out with her friends. That's how I met Morenike. I agreed to try to sort out her papers and get her a residence permit. Your bastard colleagues down at the Aliens' Bureau drove me insane, so in the end I married her. If you turn on your computer, you'll find out more than I can ever tell you."

"We're not that advanced," Halkidis said.

"Pity."

"Are you always so charitable, Mr Piertzovanis?"

"No, but Morenike had M.S. You know, wheelchair and all the rest of it. When the illness is at its worst, you need someone to help you eat, piss, wash and —"

The policeman was in shock. This did not please me particularly, but I certainly did not feel for him.

"A night full of surprises, eh?" I said, offering him another cigarette.

"You don't happen to have a different brand anywhere, do you?"

I fished a pouch of tobacco out of the fridge, a relic of the days when I was trying hard to kick the habit. Halkidis rolled himself a cigarette with the skill of professional dope head and waited for me to pick up where I had left off.

"Sonia was already living in the house. As soon as she heard the story, she suggested that Morenike and the child moved in. Noni was delighted because it was difficult for him to take care of them. Manthos was happy, everyone was happy, and they all lived happily together, I think."

"When was that?"

"Spring 2002. What difference does it make now?"

Halkidis picked up the file from the table.

"It says here that in the event of a fire, the policyholder will be entitled to a minimum of €50,000. The fire services insist it was arson. So you understand, I have to investigate."

"What did you say?"

"Somebody torched your house, Mr Piertzovanis."

I buried my face in my hands, trying to absorb what I'd just heard. Halkidis let me take my time by walking across to the window. His face vanished into the darkness of Eressou below. Rina made a half-hearted attempt to fill the silence.

"What were you doing on Saturday night, Mr Piertzovanis?"

"Are you out of your mind?"

"I'm a policeman."

His low voice did not succeed in concealing his anger. I poured myself another whisky. I did not water it down, but the explosion in my throat did not bother me at all.

"I was playing cards till nine. And then I went to the Hilton. And I spent the night there, with a friend. And I didn't wake up until the afternoon when I saw on the news what had happened. So stop fucking with me."

"Does this friend of yours have a name?"

I no longer had a clue what was going on. Halkidis decided to go easy on me.

"All I want is a name and I'm gone."

"I only know her first name. Rania. She said she'd call me on Monday."

"That's today," he said and started punching a number into his mobile. He spoke briefly, intensely and briskly.

I dragged myself to the kitchen, turned on the tap, diluted my drink and then leant against the fridge, trying to catch my breath. My visitor was saying something in the other room, but his voice flattened into an irritating buzz. I bent my legs, and sank to the floor. I had to turn this sense of panic into something, anger, hatred, if only to find the strength to scream and get rid of this intruder, or I would drown in the treacherous warmth of the alcohol.

"Are you alright?"

Halkidis was standing over me.

"I'll be fine."

His mobile rang. He listened for a moment and hung up.

"Is this where you plan to spend the night, Mr Piertzovanis?"

"I want you to leave."

"Fine. You went to the Hilton at 9.15, stayed in Room 808, paid €360 and left at 2.30 on Sunday afternoon. Of course, you could have slipped out for a couple of hours without anyone noticing. It's a big hotel, and Saturday nights . . ."

"Stop it. Please."

He helped me to my feet and into the armchair. The telephone was ringing. Rina protested about the noise.

"Aren't you going to answer that?" Halkidis said, gently.

The sound bored a hole though my brains and I closed my eyes. The policeman put the receiver close to his ear.

"Hello. Who shall I say is calling?"

He smiled.

"It's your alibi," he whispered, and continued the conversation cheerfully. "I'm a friend of his. He's having a bath and he told me to tell you if you rang that he's expecting you. Eressou. Number 16. Yes – third floor. The outside door is open. Don't mention it. Goodnight."

He replaced the receiver gently, looked at his watch and turned his attention to the canary.

"Don't worry. I'm not going to embarrass your girlfriend."

I lit a cigarette. "How did they set fire to the house?"

The policeman relayed the opinion of some Fire Captain, all the while keeping his gaze fixed on Rina.

"Who could have wanted to kill them?" I asked him flatly.

"I don't know, but I'll find them. And when I do, they'll curse the day they were born."

"I don't suppose you'd take so much interest in this case if a famous actress had not been living in the house."

"Why do you say that?"

"Because I live in the real world."

"Shall I tell you a story? It might help you see that you don't have a monopoly on sensitivity. It'll help pass the time too."

"One thing's for sure; you don't talk like a policeman. That's something."

"And you're not the only one with a law degree."

I could not think of anything to say, so I decided to concentrate on the progress of the burning cigarette paper on its ascent towards the filter. Halkidis sat down opposite me. He rubbed his eyes forcefully up towards his temples, as though he was trying to rid himself of the dirt of the day, and began talking in a calm, almost flat voice.

"I went to primary school in Kyparissi, in Evia. The school was an hour's walk from our village, Akres. After that it was high school in Psachna. We went by bus, stuffed in all together like sardines. The inspector couldn't even squeeze through among us to issue tickets. In '77 I got a place to read law. First attempt – no crammers, and managed to get my degree in five years. In the evenings I worked in a *souvlaki* place. Women never came near me. I thought it was because of my accent, or the smell of meat, or the fact that I didn't give a damn about politics. I had no idea then how complex-ridden I was, which is why I married the first woman who came along. In the army I had to do a month in prison after breaking the arm and smashing three teeth of some sergeant. Before that day, I had never hurt a fly."

"What did he do to you?"

"To me? Nothing. But he had made life hell for my closest friend."

"Why would he do that?"

"Because he was a gypsy."

"I see," I said, finding it very hard to follow him.

"That was twenty years ago and he's still the only friend I have. I was his best man, and godfather to his first child. I go down to Nafplion quite often to see him. He sells potatoes at the street markets – he's probably made more of his life than I have. My godson got into the Sports Academy last year."

"That's society for you, Officer. With a bit of hard work and God on your side, anyone can get ahead."

Halkidis responded to the sarcasm with a broad grin.

"Do I look like a religious man to you?"

"No. That's probably about all we have in common."

"Do you see why I'm telling you all this?"

"To pass the time and 'gain my trust'."

"Do you believe my story?"

The policeman's eyes were watering. He leant back in the sofa, his cigarette sticking straight out of his mouth as he snapped every single joint in his fingers, one by one. I shuddered, but this did not put him off.

"Do you know why I had to kick the shit out of that old pig?"

"Because you're a good person."

"Are you a good person, Mr Piertzovanis? Do you love your fellow men?"

"Not my strong suit."

"Have you ever harmed anyone?" he said, beginning to bear a frightening resemblance to James Ellroy's lunatic cop.

"What exactly do you want from me?"

"I want you to tell me everything you know about Sonia . . . and the fire."

His tone had become more aggressive which distracted my attention from the fact that he was referring to her by her first name. Something was eating at him, something was troubling him, but what?

His mobile rang. He looked at the number on the screen and tossed it to the other end of the sofa. Rina joined in with a tuneless chirp. I was desperate to get away, leave, disappear into the night, but instead I asked him:

"Why did you beat up that old pig?"

He drained his glass and began to look more relaxed. Rina stopped her cage gymnastics and fixed us with her gaze in turn.

"That little gypsy kid would cry himself to sleep every night under his blanket," he said a short while later.

The doorbell startled us. Halkidis ordered me not to say a word, and nodded to indicate that I should open the door. I did as I was told, slightly doubtful whether or not I would recognize my conquest of the night before. There, on the threshold stood a young woman who could not have been more than twenty-five, her black hair full of gel, and three earrings in each ear. Her eyes shone with intelligent rebellion. Her hands were dug deep inside the pockets of an expensive leather jacket and she was chewing gum. Her make-up was subtle. She hoisted herself up on tiptoe and kissed me on the cheek.

"I'm not late, am I?" she asked mischievously.

I helped her out of her jacket and showed her to the living room where I introduced her to Halkidis without explaining what line of work he was in, something he did not hesitate to do himself, without, it must be said, any hint of pride. The next few minutes were scenes straight out of Woody Allen as the irritable Halkidis tried to find a subtle way to test my claim that this young woman and myself really had spent the night in the Hilton shagging each other senseless while the old house was being torched. Rania really made him suffer; she was unable to decode his euphemisms or innuendos, and just stood there, chewing her gum provocatively, answering with brazen ease. At any other time, I would have enjoyed it, but decided instead to pretend that the focus of my pleasure was the canary, teasingly poking little pieces of paper through the bars in her cage for her to snatch in her beak. The canary was playing her favourite game of transforming these little pieces of paper into tiny pellets but Rania, on the other hand, the longer it went on, the less she could have cared about her interrogation. "I don't have to tell you what I did. I did whatever I pleased. What am I being charged with, anyway? In what way have I broken the law?" and Halkidis was flailingly trying to win a trick that was lost before it was even played.

"Come on, young lady. No need to be so annoyed. I'm just doing my job; a simple 'yes' or a 'no' will do. It doesn't cost you anything. Are you absolutely sure that Mr Piertzovanis was with you the whole time from 9.00 in the evening until the following morning?"

Rania pulled out a packet of filterless Camels, stuck her chewing gum onto it and lit a cigarette, her hands shaking with annoyance. Halkidis was desperate but did not dare ask her for one.

"Yes. I can confirm that between 10 p.m. and dawn I was on top of that gentleman over there."

He gave her a blank look. The young girl's audacity had completely wrong-footed him.

"Shagging, Sir, making love, having sex, fucking – or whatever it is you call it in the police force."

I had to stifle a laugh. Halkidis choked but somehow found the sheer nerve to ask her for a cigarette. She pointed to the pack in a gesture that implied that his time was up. But he was not giving up.

"When did you first meet Mr Piertzovanis?"

"The day before yesterday."

"Can you tell me where?"

"At a gambling club – Glyfada. I went there out of curiosity, with my brother and a friend of his. The gentleman, the one presently feeding his canary, won all their money, and on the way out offered to buy me dinner at a restaurant of my choice. I chose the Hilton so that we could avoid any unnecessary transfers. You know, you have dinner in one place, go for a drink somewhere else, and then somewhere else again for a ... Anyway – because he didn't have a car and I'd left the Porsche with the gardener, I borrowed my little brother's Saab without telling him. I don't suppose he went and reported it stolen, did he?"

Halkidis looked as if he would gladly have slapped her, but instead carried on playing poster boy for the human face of the Hellenic Police and restricted himself to a vague shake of the head.

"I hope I've satisfied your curiosity."

"Quite the opposite: you've piqued it."

"You find it odd that my taste in cars falls at the luxury end unlike my taste in men, is that it?"

She looked at me, the picture of innocence, and then said, as sweet as you like, "I hate to say this, darling, but you look like shit!"

"And what is it that you do for a living, if you don't mind me asking?" said Halkidis, refusing to concede that this brash young woman had stolen the show.

"Surely you're not suggesting that I practise the oldest profession in the world, are you, Officer? Not that I would take offence at such a suggestion, it's just that I don't have the qualifications. I've just started post-graduate research in Italian literature at the University of Rome. My thesis is on the affinities between the female characters in Lampedusa and Pavese. I'm sure you're familiar with the subject."

"I hope your research goes well, young lady," Halkidis said, getting to his feet, wanting thereby to signal that the conversation was at an end and also to restrain himself from slapping her across those soft little cheeks of hers.

Rania stayed put in her chair, stubbed out the Camel, returned the gum to her mouth. "I don't want you to get the wrong idea; I assure you I'd much rather use public transport, but Daddy insists on the Porsche. He says it's much safer. Daddy's got a factory that makes tubes and wires and lots of other things I can't remember at the moment," she said in a bid to have the last word.

"I'm sure. And I suppose he also plays bridge with the Finance Minister every second Tuesday, doesn't he?" Halkidis said, his anger having subsided him by now, and the bitterness in his voice actually made me feel sorry for him.

She realized she had crossed the line and shifted to a slightly warmer tone. As warm as she could be considering the abyss that divided their social classes, the gap which those who reject Marxism pretend does not exist anymore.

"You're not far wrong. A few years ago he used to play backgammon with the Culture Minister, but he soon got fed up. Apparently, the Minister never shuts up and would get through week's supply of caviar in one sitting."

"O.K., enough. Thank you for your help. Though I don't see what all that sarcasm was in aid of."

"My apologies. I don't like being taken for an idiot, that's all. 'Simeon's having a bath. He said you should come up. He's expecting you.' It was you on the telephone earlier, wasn't it?"

"I had no choice. This case —"

Rania cut him off in the most charming way possible; she gave him her hand and said, "That's all forgotten now. Anyway, I give you my word – I haven't told you a single lie. Hey – you're going to be late!"

That last was directed at me. Halkidis answered before I had the chance to.

"Not really."

"Is smoking permitted in the bedroom, Mr Wreckage?' she asked me, teasingly, leaping to her feet and grabbing the pack of Camels as she did so, without forgetting to leave a couple on the table first.

I showed her the way and she left us in peace. Neither of us paid the slightest attention to her perfect backside.

"It's a wonder that bird can survive in all this smoke," Halkidis muttered distractedly as he lit up. I followed suit.

"A friend of mine in Thessaloniki had a parrot. Not a parrot exactly – lovebirds, I think they're called. He didn't keep it in a cage so it flew freely around the house. He would cover the entire place in newspaper, the floors, the sofas, tables, bedside tables, everything was protected from the droppings. He had schnapps glasses and little plates of food out all over the place. He smoked more than you do. The bird's still alive."

I decided it was probably a bit redundant to mention that the friend in question had jumped off his fifth floor balcony. Halkidis marched up to the cage and peered in at the canary.

"Perhaps I should get one too," he said.

"Might not be such a bad idea. Have you seen that Alain Delon film – 'Le Samourai'?"

He shook his head.

"You should. Delon plays a professional hit man. He's something of a wolf without a pack. He lives in a hotel. The only things he owns are a canary and a pistol. One day he goes out to work and when he comes back he sees the bird shaking with fear. Delon realizes that someone's been in the room, takes the necessary precautions and escapes. At least for the time being."

"And?"

"Nothing really. I just thought that your line of work, it's dangerous. Maybe you could use some kind of alarm system?"

We stood there looking at each other for a while. I realized that neither of us wanted to be like the man we were looking at. The policeman broke the silence.

"I'll hang on to this insurance policy for a while. For routine reasons, mainly. I'll bring it back."

"Mainly?"

"I'm still not persuaded that you had nothing to do with the . . . arson."

"Why?" I asked, terrified.

"Because I've seen so much in my time. And because I don't believe for a minute that you and Sonia were just good friends."

This time I was not about to let the plain "Sonia" go.

"You knew her too."

"No. I saw her in a play once," he said, and hurried on. "There was more to your relationship than that; you don't just open up your house to just anyone. Did you have an affair?"

"No," I said.

"So?"

"Besides, what is friendship if not an idealized form of love?"

"Bullshit."

"Some great mind came up with that. Can't remember who now."

"Stop it! With your help I might get to these bastards that much faster. So pull yourself together. Unless, that is, you don't want me to find them."

He was that close to losing control. By now it was obvious that I was dealing with someone who was seriously unhinged and that I would have to calm him down again.

"Listen, Mr Halkidis – there was nothing between me and Miss Varika – and even if there were, I would never admit to it. Do you know why? Because at the slightest whiff of anything of the sort those bloody T.V. cameras would descend on this place like a pack of hounds."

"I would never talk to those people."

"You are not the sum total of the police force."

"You have my word."

I believed him, but his volcanic expression unsettled me still. Besides, I was too tired to work out whether it was born of professional zeal or something else.

"Well?"

"I'm telling you the truth; I was a friend . . . and admirer. I was only trying to help out, to let her live somewhere in peace."

"Who brought her to this point – do you have any idea?"

"Drink."

"Tell me: Do you have any enemies? Could someone have set fire to the house in order to frighten you? Have you any debts?"

"I don't owe a thing to anyone."

"Some unstable ex-girlfriend, jealous, obsessive?"

"You'll have to do better than that, Officer. You're barking up the wrong tree."

Halkidis gave up at last, picked up the insurance policy, fished a card from his tatty old coat and dropped it onto the table.

CHRONIS HALKIDIS

POLICE COLONEL

DEPARTMENT OF INTERNAL AFFAIRS

HELLENIC POLICE

"If you remember anything, anything at all, Mr Piertzovanis, I will be at your disposal."

"Internal Affairs?"

"About as internal as you can get," he said, opening the door and leaving as quickly as he could, flying back to his nest, with a look that could be taken as almost anything other than a smile.

"Is our ace card-player having a spot of bother? Is there anything I can do to help?"

Rania had come in silently and was stroking my hair. She had taken off her shoes and I could see the red toenails struggling for breath inside her black fishnets.

"No. Just some misunderstanding. It's not important," I said and asked her if she wanted a drink.

She did. We both did. I went to the kitchen and when I got back I found her rummaging through my record collection. She picked out one, stuck it on the turntable, sat down next to me and took a sip. The voice of Bithikotsis singing Theodorakis' "Axion Esti" poured through the small speakers.

"I'm kidding," she said when she saw the look of astonishment across my face. "My father always played this full blast and would raise his glass to 'Sir Gregory' and afterwards would tell us all about . . . O.K., O.K., I'll take it off."

Deftly she lifted the stylus, put the record back in its sleeve and sat in the armchair.

"Are you going to tell me what's going on or not?"

I did not want to, but the girl's lucid gaze helped me find my voice. Without really trying to, I somehow managed to distance myself from the pain and the grief, carried away by the ease of talking to such a pleasant and willing stranger. I did not even touch my drink. Neither did she. I was trying my best to keep the dead at a distance: the old actor; Morenike; Rosa. When I finished, it was without any sense of relief, just terror at the thought of the night outside waiting to fall, which would soon seep into me. I was extremely grateful to the girl for not interrupting, for not asking me that damned question, for not saying what I could not bear to hear, for not making me admit that I was still in love with Sonia.

Looking back, I was trying to invent a convenient narrative, a story in which I conceived her as the heroine of some cardboard cut-out sentimental trash – an innocent little girl who wants to break down and cry, but doesn't because she is so terribly brave. Either that or she is afraid that if she snaps, the wreck of a man sitting opposite her – a man she has only known for two days and who she is beginning to want more than she should at her age – might not want to see her again because he does not want his sordid life to contaminate her own. Her excursions into the melodrama of Pavese and co. nudge her and whisper that the only way to respect his suffering is to keep silent. And as long as the silence lasts, the only thing that frightens her is the thought that Simeon (who has now closed his eyes) was born too early or that she (who is smiling at him although she knows he cannot see her) was born too late. I imagined her standing on tiptoe, taking off her favourite waistcoat with the Stalin badge on it, the one showing him without his moustache, his lips covered in red lipstick puckered into the shape of a love heart, walking over to the cage and pulling the cover over it. She is not in the least troubled by the question, "What's the difference between Rina and Rania? – Just one little 'a' – that's all." Not only does it not trouble her, she actually gives voice to it, touches the man's hair, bends down till she is level with his ear and asks him in a throaty voice if he wants her to stay with him.

"Do you want me to stay?"

"Where?"

I still had not opened my eyes.

"Here, tonight, with you."

"Better not."

"I'll just hold your hand until you fall asleep. I can do that."

"Better not."

I still had not opened my eyes.

"Why?"

I could not take any more. I knew that I should drain my glass and perhaps whatever was left of the bottle too and pass out. But I also realized that it was too late for that. I knew that the only thing that mattered was Sonia. And that she still needed me. That she was still breathing. But the girl kept insisting, in the sweetest way.

"Should I leave my phone number?"

"You ring me."

"When?"

I was about to say, "in two or three years from now", but the warmth of her touch led to a hollow "whenever you like". I kissed her softly on eyes which were still crying, and heard the lyrics of that old song somewhere far off, "kisses on the eyes mean separation", helped her into her jacket, held the door open and abandoned her to a night she did not deserve. Luckily for her, I had decided to spend the night alone with Sonia.

"Do you look at me when I'm asleep?"

"All the time. Do you look at me?"

"Yes, I do."

"Liar."

"Liar."

Monday, 8 p.m.

Why doesn't it hurt? I close my eyes, the iridescence of the light, whiteness and then suddenly a red rush of different galaxies battling together with the ashes. It does not hurt because of a miracle, a little song which keeps coming back, "my pride and joy, don't be afraid of the night that awaits you" – a lullaby like a cool garland on the head, older even than pain itself, "I'll wake you up myself in the new dawn", the coming of the night has finished, what has become of me, a woman pirate, retired, forced to lick the rust of memory? The only round of applause I ever expect to get is from the eyelids of my two boys, opening and closing, trying to trick their long overdue tears.

CHAPTER 3

Chronis Halkidis Discovers Once Again that Police Work is Dirty Work

26.i–27.i
Monday, 7.30 p.m.

"It doesn't get much more internal than this," I quipped, getting out of there as fast as I could. Something foetid hung in the air in Piertzovanis' flat, the smell of death, like that cheap bachelor's pad I moved to after the divorce. I ran down the staircase as though I were being chased, stepped over a blissfully happy stray dog luxuriating in the warmth of the wicker mat in the entrance hall, jumped into the Golf and ripped open the packet of cigarettes that resided in the glove box. I lit up and started the engine, the heating on full. In Exarcheia a group of about ten youths dressed in black huddled together in the square, drinking beer and trying to get warm. I turned slowly out onto Patission, my hatred for Simeon Piertzovanis burning inside me. But for him, nothing would have happened to my Sonia. I had met her in 1999, July 21, the summer she started drinking openly, beginning in the morning, the summer I started feeling sorry for her. She knew it too. I could tell from the desperate, tender way she would say goodnight.

"You promised you'd try."

"I don't mind if you want to feel sorry for me, my friend, but I do mind that you're leaving me alone at night more and more these days. Don't go, not until the sea water reaches right up to your mouth. Don't leave until you're quite sure you're going to drown."

Three months later, I did exactly that, but I now realize that it was not I who left her. She left me after first trying me out, perhaps because she knew that there was somebody like her waiting in the wings, somebody who was as sick as she was, somebody who now had a name and who was now responsible for her destruction. That somebody was not going to get away from me very easily.

I stopped at Gravanis' petrol station, told the young Albanian attendant to fill her up and walked to the tiny office of the one-armed proprietor. He was sitting inside, playing backgammon with some fat guy with a moustache. My mouth tasted like the inside of an old shoe after all that whisky and those bloody awful French cigarettes. I put some water on and made myself a cup of strong tea with plenty of honey stirred into it. The players battled on, seemingly oblivious to my presence. Ten minutes later Gravanis slammed the backgammon board shut, and exclaimed with a thunderous, "That's how real men play!" and a jubilant "Panathinaïkos! Panathinaïkos!" to assert the superiority of his favourite football team. He pocketed two €50 notes from his opponent, who gathered up the dice and left with his head hung low.

"That shit of a taxi driver always brings his own dice, as if he doesn't trust me or something! But he did say I could borrow his Russian girlfriend for a week if we win the trophy back off those Olympiakos bastards this year," he said, rolling a joint.

"Tell me what you know about a Nigerian, Noni Latouse. Plays in goal for our national team." I had to deflect him quickly before he started giving me a blow-by-blow account of what he was planning to do with the woman in the event of a Panathinaïkos victory.

Gravanis was the king of the Kato Patissia area. His business activities ranged from taking illegal bets on any sport the human mind can dream up to small-scale dealing in finest grade Kalamata weed; from match-fixing in the provincial leagues and selling contraband cigarettes and pirate C.D.s to organizing raffles for large sea bass. He could even perform card tricks using his good arm with greater dexterity than the average able-bodied conjurer. He had lost the other arm when my brother, God rest his soul, in his eagerness to exterminate some innocent woodcocks, drove his pick-up into a tree.

"Don't tell me you feel sorry for me; at least I've got one arm left over, but you don't have another brother," he had said when I went to visit him in hospital. He used the insurance money to buy the petrol station and slowly transformed it into a playground for small-time criminals. Whenever I felt like a traditional cup of medicinal tea with plenty of pure honey, I went to him. Gravanis was my only link with my roots. Thank God.

He looked at me quizzically.

"Noni Latouse? Yes, he does play for Greece. Black chap. Good player. I've never had to approach him, but word has it that he's clean as a whistle. What's he done?"

"Nothing."

"So?"

"I just want to know if he's mixed up in anything."

"Doubt it, Chronis. I'd know about it if he was. Hang on a minute, though."

He put his mobile face-up on his desk among all the husks of sunflower seeds and punched in a number.

"Marilyn, my little darling. Can you talk or is your mouth full?"

He winked at me and put "Marilyn" on speakerphone. A hearty male chuckle came down the line.

"Idiot! Still laughing at that tired old joke? Look, I need some information. Urgently," said Gravanis conspiratorially, as though he were some kind of self-important, provincial secret agent. "Is Latouse, you know, the goalkeeper, the big boy in the national team, is he a member of your darkie association?"

"Noni? No, darling, he isn't. No such luck. And he's totally unapproachable."

"Sure about that?"

"Completely. He's the quiet type. More's the pity."

More loud laughter.

"O.K., sweetheart. You reffing this Sunday?"

"Hope you're ready, Kali, my beautiful goddess! The draw's on Thursday."

"Since when have you relied on a draw to find out what's going on, you little shit? Tell me and I'll even pay your bloody telephone bill."

"I'm only being difficult because I love it when you get angry. I'll be doing the match up in Agrinion, and I'll blow the whistle quite unexpectedly."

"And?"

"A clear 'D'. Can't say fairer than that. You know, they told me not to interfere at all, and just blow fifty-fifty."

"O.K., gorgeous. Good luck with tonight. And you won't forget, will you?"

"What?"

"Always rinse with Listerine afterwards."

Gravanis hung up, cutting off the laughter.

Bathroom salesman; cantor at Aghios Eleftherios; referee; queer. What a combination! If he voted Communist as well, I might have married him.

Another of Gravanis' roles was to distribute vouchers for financial support to the poor on behalf of the Communist Party. He would keep a small amount back in commission. His grandfather's cousin was a partisan in the civil war, and some right-wing thugs had burnt his house down, an incident he would invariably cite as an ideological defence of his own lawlessness. "I voted P.A.S.O.K. once in 1981. And look what happened to me," he'd say, waving his empty sleeve around.

I finished my tea and stood up to go; I could only stand so much contemporary Greek reality.

"Where are you going? Hang on. I need an insider tip on the election results. I'm backing the right: Nea Demokratia five to one. What d'you reckon?"

"You'll win."

"Does that mean you'll be out of a job?"

"Why would I be?"

"How should I know? It's always the decent ones who take the fall."

"Is it? And who told you that I'm decent?"

I left him, laughing, feeling very pleased with himself for having a tough policeman for a friend, and drove off without paying for my petrol. Gravanis made in a month what I made in two years, and nobody dared to take the piss out of him the way that runty lawyer and his sullen little slut had taken the piss out of me.

My flat welcomed me back with open arms. On the kitchen table there was an illiterate message in block capitals from my son reminding me that I had forgotten to leave him his weekly allowance. I took a bottle of water out of the fridge and installed myself on the sofa. The private channels were all having a ball with the fire. These Sherlock Holmes wannabes did not fall for the vague announcement the fire service had made concerning "so-far un-known causes and ongoing forensic examinations" and were talking quite openly about arson. Fortunately there was no mention of Piertzovanis – which confirmed the reliability of Fotini and the team. We were the only ones who knew who owned the house, and the press, used to being fed information from its own friends in the force, obviously had not made the effort to come to us. At least not yet. Anyway, the selling point of this story from their proprietors' point of view was the "tragic fate of a great actress fighting for her life in Intensive Care" and the possibility that the true cause of the disaster was "buried deep somewhere in her past". Of course they could not resist speculating about her strange relationship with the elderly actor, or taking swipes at the fire service and the police, who thirty-six hours after the event were limiting themselves to "no comment"-style responses through a variety of spokespersons. The general interpretation of Morenike was that she was Sonia's live-in help who had moved in with her daughter, and that fitted in nicely with the idea that "the actress depended on this kind of help in the light of her alcohol problem". I turned off the television and phoned Piertzovanis. I had forgotten to ask when Noni was due back from

Nigeria. No answer; it seemed he was seeking comfort in the arms of that girl.

I got out my notebook and tried to organize my thoughts. The only person who could have benefited from the arson was the lawyer. Gambling debts have a nasty habit of mounting up unnoticed and the insurance money was nothing to be sneezed at. Bollocks. Impossible. No-one toasts four human beings alive that readily. He might be a total disaster of a man, but he did not seem capable of taking something like that on himself. He would have evicted them first and then set light to it. Alternative scenario: revenge. But who would be taking revenge on whom? Muslims out to punish the crippled Nigerian woman who had disrespected the Prophet? Too far-fetched. The old man? I would normally investigate that, but the idea that someone would hang around for half a century waiting for retribution was crazy – not even Yannis Maris, our nation's most inventive crime writer, would be moved by that. That left Sonia. What had I learnt about Sonia in the two years we were together? Nothing beyond her achievements in the theatre and that she could hold her liquor. She never talked to me about other men, or relatives, or enemies. The reason she hired me as her bodyguard back then was because of a fear that proved groundless. It did not take me long to work out that those threatening letters, which had frightened the life out of her, were written by her deranged sixty-year-old dresser, a spinster who knew the complete works of Agatha Christie, Coelho and Sappho off by heart and believed that Sonia was the reincarnation of the little sister she never had. Once again I realized that I knew nothing about the woman who could have me on my feet with just a signature arch of the eyebrow whenever she deemed the time right for us to wrap ourselves up in the darkness we loved so much, beneath the sheets. Whenever I complained that she never really talked to me and accused her of only being interested in sex, she would threaten me and say that if I went on like that she would get so irritated with me and my ingratitude that she would take her cue from the "Lysistrata" and then we would see who was suffering more.

The clock in the hallway, a wedding present from a colleague from Kastoria, which I only kept because my ex-wife really hated it, struck 9.00. All those coffees combined with the whisky had tied my stomach in knots. The mere thought of a take-away made me nauseous. I chewed on a few pieces of crispbread and swallowed a Lexotanil. If I did not get any sleep tonight either, I would need something a bit stronger than that to keep me going. I lay down and closed my eyes. For once the neighbour's blaring television did not disturb me, but the tap dripping in the bathroom scared me half to death.

Kavala, Okeanida Hotel, hot afternoon, air conditioning gasping, the weak, exhausted voice on the other end of the mobile imploring me.

"Chronis, did I wake you?"

"No."

"Do something, please, I can't get to sleep with this tap dripping. It's like water torture."

Room 505. Assembled in parade ground fashion on the narrow shelf beneath the bathroom mirror were thousands of tiny bottles, each conscripted to protect a certain part of her delicate anatomy anxious for a little rest before it is exposed to three thousand pairs of impatient eyes. I notice the packet of cotton buds. Quick thinking detective in action justifying his huge salary, I open the plastic, spread the contents over the base of the washbasin and tell Sonia that the problem has been fixed.

"So the tap has stopped weeping?"

"Remember that song which goes something like, 'your noiseless tears'?"

"Go to sleep."

On the roof garden, the male lead is playing backgammon with the assistant director, and the girls in the cast give me a warm, welcoming smile. I blank them out. The only thing I want to do is lie in the arms of the woman in 505, the woman who is tired but cannot get to sleep. And to taste her lips, if only for five minutes.

Tuesday, 9.15 a.m.

My people were waiting for me on the 8th floor of G.A.D.A., Police H.Q., in the office used by Internal Affairs in exceptional circumstances. They were leafing through the newspapers, which had all decided that the fire was most probably down to arson. Fotini was outraged by one particularly sordid piece of gutter journalism, which hinted that the house had operated as some kind of rising sun establishment, hosting orgies for the stars.

"Who believes this trash, anyway?" she mused, to which Dedes, anxious to prove that he did not have a social sciences degree for nothing, launched into a monologue on the subject of the manipulation of the popular consciousness on the part of the media moguls.

I cut him short with a snarl, just before he got on to the curse of the two-party state, and we settled down to work. Thanks to Fotini, (who had interviewed various members of the national team by posing as a journalist from a women's magazine anxious to do a feature on black athletes modelling designer clothes) we discovered that Noni Latouse was due to fly in at 8.00 that evening.

I phoned the head of Intensive Care, who reassured me that Sonia's condition was stable. If there was any change in the next 48 hours, he might be able to say more; if not, well . . . The doctor clearly saw little point in finishing that sentence. Fotini rescued me from bleak thoughts by announcing that we had visitors. The new assistant to the Police Press Officer suffocated the office with her heady perfume and Kourkouvelas, who had no time for anybody in the force under thirty who had not got their hands dirty oiling machine-guns, stood up to open the window but was stopped in his tracks when I caught his eye. He offered instead to make her some coffee. The woman, known in the corridors of this building as "the advertising executive", politely declined the offer, sat down on the edge of a seat, put a plastic folder down on the desk, and smiled at the pile of newspapers.

"This is the very case I've come to discuss, Sir."

"At your disposal, Androniki."

"Our supervisor told us that the Chief said he thought some kind of press release might be necessary and we at the Press Office agree, so the minute we get the report from the fire investigator, we'll be able to decide on a statement."

She delivered all that in a single breath. I would have clapped, but was put off when I noticed what she was wearing. Her uniform, in other words. If Androniki had been in jeans and a sweater she might have borne some resemblance to that vanishing breed known as a normal woman, but the combination of bleached hair, painted eyes, lips and nails and that absurd blue jacket left me colder even than the parrot-like fashion with which she communicated the orders from her superior.

"We too believe that a clear statement from us will be necessary. Why don't you come back in an hour or so?"

"I'll see to it, Sir," piped up Dedes, throwing his female colleague a predatory look.

"Just send me a summary of the report and I'll write it up, Mr Halkidis," she answered, ignoring Dedes.

I told her that we would have the final say in the matter and signalled that her time was up. In her haste to get out of office 817 she left her folder behind. I opened it and saw that it was full of blank sheets of paper. Fotini was instructed to implement plan "Mr Halkidis is out of the office and has left his mobile behind" and I announced that our morning meeting had formally begun.

Dedes and Kourkouvelas had been working on the case with great zeal; it had been a while since they had been able to get their teeth into some real police work and it made a change from investigating corrupt colleagues. They had made a commendable effort searching the area with a fine-tooth comb, interviewing everyone in the neighbourhood down to the last stray dog, but had come up with the square root of nothing at all.

I gave a summary of my exchanges with Piertzovanis and shared my conclusions. We were all agreed that he would not have started the fire. A lot of time then went into trying to establish a motive: old debts of Sonia's, or of the lawyer? Perhaps Morenike's brother had got mixed up with the criminal underworld? A burglary gone wrong? Other, more far-fetched scenarios were suggested and not one of them held water. Kourkouvelas was sure that the answer lay somewhere in Piertzovanis' circle. Dedes wanted us to look into the possibility that the arsonist was some kind of psycho-stalker of Sonia's who could not cope with her departure from the theatre. We could not reject that line of enquiry out of hand, but the problem was that there was no evidence to support it. Everything was burnt.

After an hour we were reduced to the conclusion that we would have to get out and about if we wanted any answers. The work was divided up: Kourkouvelas was to find the title deeds for the house and would go through them with someone from the legal department, after first looking over the statement from the press office; Dedes volunteered to interview the locals again, in case someone might now remember something, and after that he would pay Piertzovanis' partner a visit; and I was to have one more word with the Fire Captain before going to the airport to wait for Latouse to land.

The minute Kourkouvelas left, Dedes started complaining. "Why didn't you ask me to do the statement, Sir? I can handle documents pretty well, you know."

"Right now the only thing that interests me is how well you handle people. And I was not impressed with the way you were looking at Androniki."

"What do you mean?"

"She is not the right kind of woman for you, Manolakis. You're a cultivated sort of fellow. You need someone sensitive – an artist, a dancer, a hairdresser . . . or at very least one of those alternative types that hang around Exarcheia."

"You're not serious."

"Perfectly serious. Anyway, after the elections, that little madam will be out on her ear. She's P.A.S.O.K.; one of Laliotis' protégées to boot. I bet her idea of a perfect night out would be going to the bouzouki clubs with that journalist Pretenteris. So what does a nice lefty like you want with a woman like that?"

He smiled. I liked the kid. After he graduated from Panteion University with a degree in social sciences, he spent a couple of years doing not very much in the Refugee Department. He came to my attention after someone made a complaint about him to Internal Affairs. It was his boss up there – apparently Dedes made too many recommendations in support of asylum applications for his liking and the stupid tosser concluded that Dedes must be some kind of agent of Islam. I looked at his file and less than a week later I had made him my assistant. The combination of a good education, competence and honesty is all too rare in our little police family. His only defect was that like most confirmed bachelors, he was determined to fill his address book with as many female names as possible.

He unwrapped a piece of chewing gum and looked at me suggestively. "I do wonder what she's hiding under that uniform?"

"An impressive set of abs and a dolphin tattoo she had done at high school and now regrets. That's all. Sorry."

"Do you know why dolphins are some of the few mammals that have sex all the year round for recreation?"

"No. Why?"

"Because they're so intelligent." He winked at me and was gone.

I could just see him riding his lovingly polished two-stroke M.Z. and singing Savvopoulos songs to help him forget that he did such a filthy job. I have been tone-deaf all my life so sadly that doesn't work for me. I called Fotini.

"Has anyone called?"

"The Chief and the Chief, and oh, did I mention the Chief?"

"And?"

"He's coming back from Patras this afternoon and would be grateful for a word."

"That's great news. But right now I want to hear something cheerful."

"Cheerful?"

"Yes."

"The sun's come out. Draw the curtains."

*

The Fire Captain was leaning against the fence in front of the burnt house when I arrived. He was in a dark green tracksuit and clutching a yellow envelope. Curled up at his feet was a cocker spaniel with huge ears, like slippers. They both looked at me with big sad eyes.

"I took the day off, and thought I'd bring him up here for a run-around in that dried up river-bed. Blow off a bit of steam, you know."

"Do you hunt?"

"No! I hate guns. My brother gave him to my son as a present. He found him abandoned somewhere. His name's Juan. He's a good dog."

I patted Juan on the neck. He greeted me with a bored sort of bark. The captain handed me the envelope.

"I've set it all out as simply as possible. The official report will be released tomorrow, from my office. I don't think I can be of any more use to you than that."

I opened the envelope and gave the three pages of double-spaced text a cursory glance. The Fire Captain was focusing all his attention on his worn-out running shoes.

"I'd be grateful if you didn't show that to anyone else. That is to say . . . I never gave it to you," he said, zipping his tracksuit top up to the throat.

"Everything alright?"

"Please, don't put me in a difficult position. I asked around about you and heard some good things. If you need me, my number's in the book. Iraklis Kakkaris. Larissis 16, Ambelokipi."

Before I had a chance to ask him to explain his strange behaviour, he shook my hand, whistled to Juan and began walking slowly in the direction of a dusty 2.C.V. with its sunroof pulled back. The dog made itself comfortable in the back seat as the captain started the ignition. The old banger spluttered into life with a jolt. I lit a cigarette and started reading:

CASE OUTLINE

We were alerted by the Centre on Saturday, 24 January, 2004 at 11.43 p.m. Three fire engines were dispatched and arrived at the incident at 11.56 p.m.

The fire was brought under control after approximately thirty minutes, by which time it became apparent that the property had been completely destroyed. Initially the charred remains of a man and a woman were removed from the property. The following day the body of a child was discovered inside an iron trunk, also dead.

ASSESSMENT

The seat of the fire was in the exterior of the property, most probably inside a motor vehicle (Hillman), situated in the garden, approximately 3.5m from the main entrance to the property, after which a fir tree and an almond tree ignited, enabling the fire to reach the veranda, where the shells of three two-litre jerry cans were found, the combustion of which contributed to the force of the fire.

(It is important to note that even in the absence of

an accelerant — the jerry cans — the fire would have spread, although at a slower rate.)

The windows at the front of the house were open, a fact that exacerbated the fire on account of renewed oxygen. The following were burnt in turn: wooden furniture; wooden floors; the fire almost instantly reached the wooden ceiling which by the nature of its construction is highly flammable. The time needed for the property to have burnt to ashes is estimated to be twenty minutes.

FINDINGS

The destruction of the house was complete. The few metal objects which were found were handed over to Forensics: the frame of a wheelchair; two metal trunks; a small marble-topped table with cast-iron legs; two candlesticks; an aluminium vanity case containing make-up.

HYPOTHESIS

The discovery of a beer bottle with traces of petrol close to the property together with small pieces of broken glass inside the vehicle lead to the conclusion that the fire originated with the combustion of the above accelerant (Molotov cocktails).

QUESTIONS

1. Why did the tenants, particularly the black woman, not notice the fire? Why did she make no attempt to escape with her child, who, inevitably frightened, shut herself inside a trunk?

2. As above re. the male occupant. It is possible that
   he had mobility problems (see the wheelchair)?
3. Why did the surviving woman not try to save the other
   tenants?

CONCLUSIONS

The discovery of the bottle, which had contained petrol,
in combination with the fact that the fire started in the
garden and later moved inside the property, suggest the
possibility of arson (ninety per cent certainty).

It was apparent that the captain had written this up as he went along and was probably used to having other people draft his reports for him. That, however, was the least of my worries. I wasn't particularly concerned about his questions relating to the reactions of the people inside. Morenike Latouse was disabled by her illness and the ancient actor was most likely blind drunk. He would not have stirred from his stupor until the flames had actually reached his head, and the fumes would have poisoned him anyway. Sonia was luckier, possibly because she was in a part of the house where it was possible for her to notice the fire and get out. The basic question that came out of this report was whether or not the people responsible for throwing the Molotovs were intending to kill the people inside. And what worried me was that they themselves were the only ones who could answer that question.

I stuffed the envelope into a pocket and went into the house.

After half an hour of wandering through hell I had not come up with a single useful thought. My mind went back to the strange behaviour of the Fire Captain. The only thing that could explain it was that there was some kind of internal feud going on in the fire service, stopping him from getting too involved in the case. This chain of thought was broken by the shrill ring of my mobile. The word "Captain" flashed across the screen. That was my name for the Chief of Police because of his pathological dislike for the sea and his fear of any type of vessel.

"Chronis, it's me. I've been trying to get hold of you all day."

"I've been busy."

"Listen: I'm on my way back from Patras; I'll be on the Attiki Highway in a minute. I've got to see you."

"When?"

"Where are you?"

"At the crime scene."

Silence.

"Yannis – can you hear me?"

"Yes, I can hear you. Let's say, half an hour, shall we?"

"Fine."

"Do you remember that *ouzerie* in Plateia Halandriou – the one I took you to on Good Friday?"

"Yes."

"Be there in thirty minutes."

I managed to get to the centre of Halandri using only first and second gear. Armies of 4×4s that besieged the roads and pavement were blocking out the sunlight. It did not even occur to me to look for somewhere to park. I left the Golf at a petrol station and asked them to give it a thorough valeting and check the oil. I walked into the small *ouzerie* and sat at a corner table and lit up. A young man with an earring and ponytail spread out a paper cloth over the table and asked me what I wanted. I ordered a coke and he gave me a genuine smile, which struck me as a surprising yet optimistic note for such a silent restaurant. The only other customers were three old men, each at a separate table, studying the contents of their glasses in great concentration. In front of the industrial refrigerator, which doubled as a bar, stood a tall, white-haired man in an elegant beige raincoat. He was holding a cat and stroking it tenderly while he chatted to a man in a bright white apron. He had straight grey hair and a clean-shaven face. I recognized him at once. He was the owner.

Good Friday, last year. The Chief had suggested the three of us went out: he, his Moldovan girlfriend and me. He had it on high authority that there was a working-class *ouzerie* which opened every year after the Epitaphios procession, and the entire church choir would transfer there after the service, and so the consumption of several tonnes of prawns washed down with sundry litres of ouzo would be accompanied by their wonderful hymn singing. His Russlana was devout orthodox and like most reformed whores, very pious. Every now and then, the Chief would have to grit his teeth and take her off to some remote church or other where she could discharge her religious obligations. On one of the rare occasions we got together off duty he confided in me: "She's on my case, Chronis. Wants me to go to confession. Just imagine what a shock the priest would get if he had to listen to some of my sins." There was nothing very holy about that particular evening, however. The choir kicked off with a couple of hymns, possibly for appearance's sake, but they quickly departed from strictly liturgical music. When the songs of Kazantzidis started to dominate this night of official religious mourning, we knew that despite the noise of all the glasses colliding in a toast and the loud voices, that they were people just like us, wounded by disappointments and mistakes. I remembered vaguely the stories of road sweepers, journalists, employees at the water board, commie painters and decorators, kiosk owners, overlooked artists, and neglected grandfathers, all united by the common thread of ingratitude that runs through the world. We left as soon as Russlana started to crumble under the ouzo and the bitter memories of the various alcoholics she had comforted in her time. We left the owner to dance in that traditional macho style, almost without moving, to Epirot songs. It was a perfect family for orphans, a thousand times more useful than the most luxurious old people's home, with Russlana singing "*agape, agape, agape,* this is what love means" in her native tongue. And me thinking how much Sonia deserved to experience an Epitaphios like this one.

The white-haired man finished his drink and left with the cat secreted beneath his raincoat. The Chief arrived in due course, accompanied by one of his bodyguards, who was getting on for fifty. He always chose experienced men, usually from his own part of the country, who instead of going in for bodybuilding down at the gym tried to exercise the mind. The one with him today pretended not to recognize me and sat two tables away from us and got stuck into his paper, the *Ethnos.* The Chief took off his jacket and hung it over the back of his chair. He looked down at the cigarette burning in the ashtray with displeasure. "I'd like to see what you're going to do when the ban comes into force."

"I've thought about that. I'll just put my pistol and my I.D. on the table next to the packet."

He looked worn. He loosened his tie and nodded to the waiter.

"I'm hungry as a whore. What are you having?"

"Order what you like. I'll pick at yours."

He ordered anchovies, prawns, fried squid, two salads and a beer. "When did you last eat, Yannis?"

"We're expecting company," he said, without trying to hide his displeasure. "Let me just have a sip of this and I'll explain. First tell me what your interest in this case is. The truth, mind. Don't throw me that close relative line or any other crap like that again."

He wasn't wearing his stern face; in fact he was pretty friendly, but even that did not stop the cramp in my chest. Something serious was afoot.

"Yannis, it is personal, I give you my word."

"Whatever you say will be strictly between you and me. Come on, we haven't got much time."

I decided to tell him. Not because he was my friend; it had not taken me long to realize that in this job you cannot have friends. I had to talk to him because he was my boss and in this case I needed him onside. The Chief was one exhausted technocrat, handpicked by the Prime Minister himself, a dull, negligible character, who, for the last three years, had been failing to keep the ship afloat, a ship sailing under too many different flags. A ship that in its hold concealed some very good intentions, as well as bad ones, incompetence, corruption, hard work, bureaucracy and, above all, personal ambition. He had spent quite some time on the other side of the Atlantic, and was in all likelihood, in the pay of the Americans. Perhaps that was why he moved with such ease through the huge, worm-infested, third world sewer the Hellenic Police was still fed on. However convinced he was that the police were dealing heroin, he was just as convinced that the situation would never change in a million years. Besides, Zorro had never been a particular hero of his. He preferred to proceed with caution and settled for small improvements. "The police force is never going to change society, get used to that," he would say when we had been knee-deep in shit on various cases.

We had met in the U.S. on a course of seminars led by the F.B.I. in some hole of a mid-Western town. He was deputy Chief at the time and I was working at the Directorate for Crisis Management. He took a shine to me, possibly because I had not wanted to tag along with our colleagues in their beer-drinking sessions in those depressing rustic saloon bars and stayed in at the hostel studying English instead. He would try to quell the boredom by watching black and white films on television and going for walks in the nearby forest. One evening he knocked on my door, his eyes were red as anything and his nose was streaming. He begged me for a backrub with surgical spirit and admitted that he could not stand being bunged up or having catarrh because not being able to breathe brought on something like claustrophobia in him. After the massage we talked for about an hour. Today's conversation took me back three years to the moment he announced to me that I would be taking over the Internal Affairs Division:

"Mr Halkidis, after our brief acquaintance in the States I realized that you, like me, would never take a bribe from anyone. For this reason, and also because of your qualifications and your undoubted abilities, naturally, I would like you to take up the post. Do not imagine that I am expecting some kind of historic watershed; all I expect from you is that you make sure things don't get worse. And in time, we might even be able to modernize. But there is no big rush, no need for fireworks or T.V. appearances. Discreetly does it, remember that."

After that our relationship chugged along quite happily and was strictly professional. We recognized that what interested both of us was above all the maintenance of our dignity. And one way or the other we had been successful. Until today at least.

"Don't worry at all, Chronis. Spit it out. And pronto."

I did.

"In the winter of '96, shortly after we got back from the U.S., my wife and I divorced. Not the most amicable of divorces at that; the boy was eight, lots of expenses: new house, maintenance – the usual shit. I had to find a second job to pay for it all. Tried various things like taxi-driving, selling insurance, even working as a bouncer at some bar. In the summer, a colleague told me about an actress who was looking for a bodyguard to protect her while she was touring the provinces and also Cyprus. The money was good, so I took all my leave in one go and went off to be her bodyguard. That's how I met Sonia Varika. She was the actress."

"Why did she need a bodyguard? Was she that big?"

"She was, but she wanted someone to look after her because she had been getting threatening letters. Nothing serious – turned out it was some mad old woman sending then – took me less than a week to track her down."

"But the lady kept you on. I see."

"I fell in love with her. It was the happiest summer of my life. She was an amazing woman."

The Chief tapped the table three times with his fingers.

"Don't tempt fate, Chronis. She's still alive, you know."

"Yes, I know."

"So what happened?"

"She loved me. So she said. And she meant it. It lasted two years."

"Did she leave you?"

"I left her. I couldn't take it any longer. She had a massive self-destructive streak. She drank too much – hopeless alcoholic. Towards the end she was off her face most of the time. I couldn't get through to her at all."

"But how did she manage to perform in the theatre like that?"

"Oh, she managed to work around it, I don't know – somehow she timed her sessions so that she was never too wasted on stage. Or at least not noticeably so. What does it matter now, anyway? The point is that I left her, but I could have tried harder. Maybe. But I was terrified. It wasn't easy, you know."

"Did she take drugs too?"

"No, never. She was too frightened of them."

"That's unusual in those circles."

"She never did, Yannis. I'd stake my life on it."

"Was she mixed up in anything?"

"What do you mean?"

"I wish I knew. Mixed up in anything, you know, prostitution, protection rackets, terrorism – whatever."

"Sonia used to get up at noon, drink coffee, pour her first drink at about 2.00, read, drink, eat some bread, cheese, fruit, phone me, drink, have a bath and then leave for the theatre. Around midnight I would pick her up after the show and we would argue about whether we should go to a restaurant or a bar. Not that it made much difference because wherever we went, she would put away as much as she could. Then home to bed. Twice a week she played cards. Never high stakes and never anywhere unsavoury. I checked them out myself."

He took a couple of sips of beer and looked at me thoughtfully.

"When did you last see her?"

"After we separated, I would only ever see her when she was in something. I used to go along on the sly. Until 2000. That's when she chucked it all in and vanished. Never saw her again."

"You had no idea where she was living? Didn't you go looking for her?"

"I did know. But I didn't go looking for her. There was no point."

The young waiter brought us the salads, took away the empty coke bottle and asked if I wanted anything else to drink. I did not.

"Chronis, tell me – hand on heart – was your only motive for wanting to take on this case the past? Guilty conscience?"

"Word of honour."

He pushed one of the salads towards me, looked at his watch and planted his elbows on the table.

"As far as we're concerned, the case is closed. The fire was caused by carelessness on the part of one of the victims. Cigarette, candle, camping gas stove they had forgotten to turn off. That kind of thing. Take your pick."

"Why?"

"Why does anything happen? How should I know?"

He was clearly angry, but not with me.

"Light one of those for me," he muttered, draining his glass.

He took a drag and then stubbed it straight out, and drew his face close to mine.

"Something strange happened this morning. I got a call from the minister's office asking me to go down to Patras for a meeting with him. When I asked what it was all about, they hung up. Quite politely. Then I phoned him back, but it was switched off. So I went. The meeting was in a hotel in Rio. He was waiting for me with some pretty boy he introduced to me as Pavlopoulos, a trusted but invisible government adviser. What a load of bollocks. He never once opened his mouth. Anyway, the long and the short of it is that our esteemed civil leader told me that he had received requests from on high that we close the case. The official line is that the fire was an accident, and that a senior officer in the fire services would personally deliver the report to me. When I told him that our information pointed to arson, he simply smiled; they both did, then got up and left. I got our man on his own and whispered that we were not about to quit the case, and the people in the fire department could say what they liked. And do you know what the stupid sod said – I used to look up to that man – he said that if that was the case, he would have no difficulty accepting my resignation."

"I don't get it."

"Chronis, I've been thinking; thought about nothing else all the way back. Something's obviously going on, something we don't know about. And I fear we may never find out."

Another cramp shot through my chest, sharper this time.

"What do you mean?" I said in a whisper.

"I mean that I have no intention of resigning."

The heat from my burning cigarette scorched my fingers. I put it out, cursing. I needed time. But I didn't have time. I had to find some.

"Who are we waiting for?"

"A Major General from the fire brigade. He's going to deliver the report, and will probably take over from here. I know him; he's harmless enough, and has no experience of these kinds of intrigues. He can be relied on to do what he's told."

The Fire Captain's report was burning a hole in my pocket. Time, time, time. I had to buy some, and I would only be able to do so if I kept my head.

My sweet young Chronis – the theatre's a cerebral affair. Don't be fooled by the crying and the shouting on stage. Have you ever seen an actor just before he goes on? He might have his mind on the pools or the stock market, or be sending a text to his girlfriend and then have to dart on stage with moments to spare, pant his way through his lines, while all the time he had you thinking he was consumed with jealousy over Desdemona. You have to learn to control your mind if you want to trick the audience. You can't let yourself get distracted by something you cannot control. Of course there are some interesting exceptions to this. I'll tell you about them sometime, when I manage to remember the madness of my youth.

I got up and went to the toilet, leaving the Chief picking at his salad. I took my time washing my hands and even longer drying them. In the end, it did not take long to make a decision, not even three minutes. The plan was simple. A few reasonable questions to kick off with, a few low-key protests, after that, silent acceptance of the situation. And that would be the end of it.

I emerged from the narrow cloakroom to find the Major General sitting down at our table sticking his fork into various dishes, dripping oil onto his bushy moustache in the process. The Chief was reading from a folder. He handed it over to me and introduced us. It was the report from the fire investigator, concluding that a malfunction in the stove had caused the fire. I executed my plan with precision: acting seemed to me child's play, but then I did have the benefit of an excellent teacher. He fell for it, and after half an hour of talking in low voices, I admitted that I lacked the expertise to comment on the conclusions of professionals. I cannot be sure whether I fooled the Chief, but it wasn't that important to me right then. I tried a few of the fried entrées on the table, playing the part of the hungry bear while listening with exaggerated interest to the two of them discussing the likely outcome of the March elections and allowed them to argue about who was going to pick up the ridiculously low bill. When they got up to leave I said goodbye in a suitably respectful tone and told them I was staying in the *ouzerie* until my car was washed. I ordered a soda water and sipped it slowly. The situation was tricky, but not so tricky that it could frighten off a man who was on his own and who had very little to lose. I thought about my son and how embarrassed he was that his dad was a policeman. Perhaps the little shit was right after all.

I went and stood at the counter while the owner coated some mullet in flour and tossed them into the frying pan with the tired skill of a magician at a children's birthday party. The burn marks on his hands betrayed a lack of care, probably due to daydreaming. When he finished I asked if I could hire the restaurant for a night.

"Sorry. We don't do that," he said politely.

"There's a woman. She might die. I just want to make sure that I can bring her here before she does. But we'd need to be alone. Just the two of us. No-one else. Except you, of course."

He produced a cigarette from behind his ear, lit it and drew on it heavily.

"I remember you. Last year. Good Friday."

'That's right. It was wonderful."

"Yeah, sure. Same thing year in, year out," he said glancing across at the fish. He turned over two fillets of cod with care and wiped his hands on his apron. All the while he was talking to me, he did not look at me once, as though he was shy. "Sunday evenings we're closed. Give me a couple of days' notice, O.K.?"

"Thank you." I left as quickly as I could. I had my work cut out.

An hour and a half later, I folded the few notes I had into four and stuffed them into my inside pocket. Dedes, Kourkouvelas and Fotini had tried in vain to work out my take on why the powers that be had decided on a cover-up. I had restricted myself to a dry "they must know something we don't know". I registered the discontent in their faces. Up to that point our cooperation had been based on mutual trust and now my stance had shaken them. They could not believe that I did not know more that I was letting on. Kourkouvelas was the first to get to his feet, say goodbye perfunctorily and leave. The rest of them just sat there in silence until Fotini tried to lighten the atmosphere.

"Well, back home tomorrow. Pity, the pollution was beginning to grow on me. I'll start packing up the household effects." By that she meant the kettle, Kourkouvelas' green tea, Dedes' miniature espresso maker, my emergency stash of cigarettes and the icon of Aghios Christophoros which, for reasons that have never been made clear, was a permanent fixture on Fotini's desk.

"Beer's on me across the road," I said in a tone that left no room for argument. They looked at me strangely, but they followed me without a murmur.

The place across the road was something between a bar, café, disco and a television showroom. It was full of people who had nothing to do all day, lounging around in armchairs and on sofas, screaming at the top of their lungs just to be heard at a distance of half a metre, forking out for one cup of coffee what it took the average cleaner half a day to earn, living proof that our homeland was prospering. The only advantage was that none of our poorly paid colleagues ever set foot in it, while our better paid colleagues were lining their pockets in the early hours of the morning with a cut of their takings. A washed-out looking twenty-year-old dressed like Heidi plonked our beers down on the table along with a bowl of nuts well past their prime.

We did not say much. In half an hour, Fotini and Dedes had agreed to give up their free time to help me to find a way round this. I explained that the reason I had not invited Kourkouvelas along to this founding meeting of our chapter was that I was sure it would put him in a difficult position. His impeccable ethics and his almost compulsive love of procedure would not permit him to operate on the margins of official state mechanisms, but at the same time his respect for us would throw him into turmoil. Besides, he did not have a lot of time on his hands, what with the wife and kids.

We swore an oath of secrecy, agreed to equip ourselves with pay-as-you-go phones to ensure safe communication, left the beers half-drunk and stepped out onto the joyous avenue.

By the time I got to the hospital, it was already dark. Of the twenty or so people hanging around in the corridor outside Intensive Care, all were friends and relatives of patients, except one. Sitting on the chair at the end reading a magazine was a young man with a skinhead and a gold sleeper in his ear, keeping watch. I turned round and ducked behind a pillar before he could see me. A couple of weeks back that same young security officer had appeared at my office on Syngrou to deliver my new revolver, part of the policy to renew the stock of unused weapons carried by senior officers and to support certain undeserving industrialists. If he had not been wearing that ridiculous earring, it is quite possible I would not have recognized him. That is what comes of trying to emulate big screen American cops, I thought, and cursed those fuckwits I did not know who always turned out to be more intelligent than I expected them to be. Obviously they were not sure whether I was going to drop the case and had taken measures. Maybe they were worried that if Sonia woke up, she might start remembering things and tell me things I should not know.

I slipped into the toilets and lit up. Visiting time was due to start in five minutes and would last an hour, but I was sure they would have someone posted there around the clock. The very moment I was about to let fly at the toilet bowl, I heard a cough which sounded like the terminal stages of T.B., accompanied by a "fuck this". Recognizing Simeon Piertzovanis' voice, I tossed my cigarette into the bowl and stepped out into the corridor where the lawyer, wiping his hands on a paper towel, soon joined me.

"Swimming with germs in here, Mr Piertzovanis."

His surprise was swiftly replaced by an attempt at a smile.

"Tell me about it. I'm terrified of hospitals. Don't know why. Maybe it's because I've never stayed in one."

He binned the paper towel and stuffed his hands into the pockets of an expensive but worn jacket.

"Have they opened the doors yet?" he said, desperate for something to say.

There was mint on his breath. I was wise to that trick from Sonia: every time she drank she stank of mint afterwards.

"Not yet. But she's only allowed one visitor. What are we going to do?"

He turned his back on me and started walking, but I pulled him back by the arm before he turned the corner.

"You didn't answer my question."

"I'm not interested in a *bras de fer*, Officer. Do you want us to toss for it? I'm sure the rules don't apply to you lot. I'll go first and then you can use your badge to get in afterwards. That way we'll all be happy, though I'm not sure that happy is the right word to use round here."

His sarcasm, added to my stress, would in normal circumstances be enough for me to clock him one, but I adopted a measured tone instead.

"Look, I know you don't like me, though I can't imagine why. I also know that you're keeping things from me. I can live with that too, for the time being. But I will ask you one favour. Go in and see Miss Varika, talk to the head of Intensive Care, and then come and find me outside in the canteen."

"Could you try to relax your grip on me? I'm not about to do a runner, you know."

I let go of him.

"Is something the matter?" he asked, rubbing his arm.

"I'll tell you in a minute. I'll be waiting outside. And make sure you have a word with the doctor."

"Yes, Sir."

I looked at my watch. Noni Latouse would be landing two hours from now. I reckoned the lawyer could be useful to me out at the airport. Perhaps the lawyer could be useful, full stop.

The canteen wares reminded me that I should eat. I bought a cheese pie, which I binned after the first bite, and switched to the chocolate taste of a bar of almond Ion, which in forty plus years had never once disappointed me. I turned up my collar, sat down on a rickety old bench, lit up and abandoned myself to the delectable torments of guilt and jealousy.

"How many men lovers have you had?"

"Are you asking how many men I've had sex with?"

94

"If you like."

"Including you?"

"Not including me."

"You dear little boy, it's not just the number of partners that counts. Frequency's important too. After how many times can you say about a man, or, in the interest of fairness, a woman, after how many times of having sex with, or, forgive me, sleeping with a man or a woman, do they earn their place on the diva manquée's golden list?"

"You are a diva."

"Only a provincial diva, darling. But don't forget that out there, on the other side of that door today Larissa is waiting for me, tomorrow Ioannina. A provincial diva, but a diva nonetheless. Right, where were we? Don't try to wriggle out of it. After how many performances does a stud get his certificate of sexual prowess?"

"Two."

"You and I have only done it once, haven't we?"

"So far."

"Back off. We're having a conversation here."

"Sorry."

"I don't want you to apologize. I want you to concentrate. Tell me – what about kisses?"

"What about them?"

"How many times have you kissed me?"

"A lot. I can't remember."

"Possibly. Though I'm quite sure they were given carelessly, as a formality, out of some ancient notion of male duty to be forgiven by the mother they disdained. That's right. And that's why you remind me more of hands and kisses."

"From now on I'll remind you of anything you like."

95

"Undress me. Kiss me properly. I'm drunk, but I'll manage."

The lawyer sat down next to me on the bench.

"No change. She was sleeping. The consultant was not there, but I spoke to his assistant. It's still too early for them to say anything. Maybe tomorrow. Or the day after. Her chances are still fifty-fifty, apparently. The good news is that there is no post-debridement infection."

He pulled out a cigarette, toyed with it briefly before sticking it in his mouth, where it remained unlit.

"Two beds down from her was a man whose hands they had tied to the bed rails with strips of cloth. I asked one of the nurses what was going on and she said he had got A.I.P. Any idea what A.I.P. is?"

"Acute Interstitial Pneumonia. Smokers' disease."

"Oh, right."

"But why was he restrained?"

"He wakes up now and then and starts pulling at his tubes and tears his oxygen mask off, goes wild like some kind of caged animal. He wants to leave."

"And go for a fag?"

"He gave up twelve years ago."

"How about you and I try quitting, Mr Piertzovanis?"

"Hmm. It's just talk. It helps me forget the other thing."

"What other thing?"

He didn't answer. Instead he returned the cigarette to the packet and stood up.

"Sit down. I want to tell you something."

He did as he was told.

"Noni Latouse is landing at Venizelos at eight tonight. Can you come with me?"

He was clearly not expecting this and buried his fingers in his hair, muttering something I did not catch.

"Please. It would be a great help."

He scoffed loudly. "For who?"

"All of us."

He sighed and walked with me as far as my car without saying another word. On the way to the airport I brought him up to speed, and he listened without interruption, his head glued to the window. When I told him I was determined to find whoever it was who had started the fire, he just laughed.

"Are you going to take on the establishment with your bare hands, Officer, because you've been humiliated by your bosses? Congratulations! I suppose you're going to appear on Trianta-fyllopoulos' T.V. show and expose the lot of them too?"

I let that go, along with the tanker that had been on my back for some time.

"What does Sonia mean to you? I'll bet she's more than just another high-profile case to you. Something more serious is going on."

"She helped me out once upon a time. I owe her a lot."

"Of money?"

"Let's just say I owe her a lot," I said, more for my own benefit than his.

"I see."

"I don't think you do."

"Anyway, that's your business. What do you want from me?"

"Whoever did this is either moving in the victims' circles or your own. I don't see who else it could be. You and Noni are the only ones who have seen her recently."

"So?"

"So nothing. That's all I've got to go on at the moment."

"Who do you think is trying to hush the whole thing up?"

"I wish I knew."

Piertzovanis eventually decided to light that cigarette. The stench of the French tobacco was too much for me.

"What makes you think you can trust me, Officer? Aren't you afraid that I might run off and squeal to some interested journalist?"

"Why would you want to do that?"

"To expose those who don't want to find the murderers that killed my friends."

"And what would you stand to gain from that?"

"My balls. Exactly what you stand to gain from all your heroics and conspiracy theories."

"Are you afraid?"

"No, but I don't hold out any hope that anything will come of this. Why, if a great big head of division like you can't go about this in a legit way and has to sneak around playing Inspector Callaghan with an alcoholic prick for a sidekick, then I'm thinking that perhaps it won't be long before the flat I'm living in will be burnt to a cinder too."

"Or that the insurance money you're due will help you forget your friends, and you can spend the rest of your life drinking and playing cards to your heart's content."

"Fuck you."

"Come again!"

"Go fuck yourself."

"Why so tetchy?"

"Because if you think that you can apply that pseudo-psychological bullshit they teach you to get some poor old fucker to crack up under interrogation to me, you must be stupid," he raged, violently stubbing out his cigarette in the ashtray.

We sat in silence until the airport. It was 8.10 by the time we got there. The Milan flight would have already landed. Piertzovanis grabbed me by the elbow, stopping me on the way in to Arrivals.

"Look, I'm telling you this not because your opinion matters to me but because your insult does. This morning I got a call from the insurance company telling me that on the strength of a clause in the contract, I'm not entitled to any compensation. Something to do with the fact that I wasn't living there myself and hadn't let it out legally. You know, the kind of bullshit they always stick in the small print. So smarten up and try to understand why it doesn't bother me at all that I won't be making any money out of the ashes of my friends. Arsehole."

Noni Latouse was the last person to emerge through customs pushing his trolley. I was leaning against a pillar, ten metres away. Piertzovanis nodded at him and the man looked surprised to see him. He was tall and thin, wore a woolly hat, an orange waterproof, jeans and trainers. He went up to the lawyer and they embraced, for a long time. The lawyer's lips were almost touching the young man's as he whispered to him for what seemed like hours. Piertzovanis started shuddering and sobbing. Noni lifted his head and fixed his gaze on nothingness, lovingly patting the back of his devastated messenger. There was only a small peppering of passengers waiting and he shot them furtive glances. Then came a sugar-coated announcement over the public address system about the Olympic Games and Zeus, god of hospitality. The image of the two men, cumulative tiredness and the anger of the day blurred my vision. I wiped my eyes on my sleeve and lit up, ignoring the myriad signs threatening eco-terrorists like me. My mind needed an escape and found it in the image of a man who had given up smoking twelve years ago and who was now lying strapped to a hospital bed in Intensive Care. I wished him strength and headed out for the car park.

As we drove back into Athens the only thing that was audible in the car was a long drawn out melodic mumble. Noni was grieving the dead in a magical tongue. We dropped him off outside a block of flats near the Kallithea metro station. He flatly refused the lawyer's offer of a bed for the night. Piertzovanis helped him carry up his suitcases and came back down twenty minutes later. He bent over and wished me goodnight through the window. He was wearing the perfect mask of neutrality. I offered him a lift home, but he said no.

"I'll handle the formalities. Noni wants to have the girls buried here. I don't suppose we'll see each other again – can't see any reason to," he said slapping the car roof before turning and walking off down the dimly lit road, his back stooped.

I caught up with him and grabbed him by the arm.

"Did you tell him his sister and niece were murdered?"

"No."

"Why not?"

"Couldn't bring myself to."

"Why?"

"I'm off."

"Simeon."

"What?"

"Think about it."

"Think about what?"

"What we're going to do."

"Too late."

"Think about it."

"Tomorrow. Right now I'm going for a walk."

I pulled up about a kilometre and a half away from my flat, but as soon as I reached the main entrance, I turned round.

I was shattered, but somehow didn't dare take the key out of my pocket, because I knew that a panic attack was waiting for me on the other side of the door. The very idea of sleep terrified me.

"What do policeman dream about?"

"They mostly have nightmares. What do you think?"

"Chronis, are you a lucky man?"

"Why do you ask, Sonia?"

"Because if you are, the day that's breaking will always be better than the night that's just passed."

*

The walk down to Haroula's club cost me twenty minutes and a minor sprain to the ankle. At the entrance to the strip club the small but eye-catching neon sign – composed of the name *Hara-kiri* spelt out in various arrangements of oriental swords – was still flashing. Rumour had it that the name was a combination of the owner's name, Hara, and somebody called Kyriakos who had, apparently, been her first. I pushed the heavy door open and walked down the iron staircase very carefully, mindful of the fact that it creaked even more than the only swing in our school playground. Haroula was sitting on a bar stool behind the cash register reading a magazine. I smiled at her, lifted the magazine delicately out of her hands, making sure I did not lose her page, and then took a look at the cover. An Alack Sinner spinoff: *Joe's Bar*. A comic.

"Any good?"

"I like it because the protagonist, even though he's all macho cop, has a soft spot for whores."

"We don't use the term 'protagonist' when we talk about books, we refer to the 'hero'."

"It's not a book. It's a comic, sweetheart."

She slipped off the stool, came out from behind the bar, barefoot as usual, and threw herself at me. She smelled of soap.

"Since you started chasing policemen you hardly come here. Are we too common a class of criminal for you to bother with?"

"Ha! Only the Anti-Terrorist unit would stand a chance against you lot."

She gave a throaty laugh, tugged at my cheeks and flashed me a bit of bare leg before moving back behind the bar.

"I'm going to have to put something on my feet. Haven't had time for a pedicure this week and they look terrible. The usual Martini, Mr Bond?"

"Tap water, Haroula," I said, blowing kisses to the three half-naked girls who were huddled round a kerosene heater whispering to each other in some Slavonic language, and went to sit down at a table.

The place was empty; things never got here going till after midnight. I was just lighting up when Saravakos, Haroula's guardian angel, emerged from the toilet doing up his flies. Saravakos was his nickname, after the legendary Panathinaïkos striker. Nobody, including I suspect the man himself, knew what his real name was. When he saw me, he stopped in his tracks. He had always been afraid of me and I never knew why. I doubt he did either. He made as if to raise his hand, perhaps in a greeting, thought better of it, attempted a smile, abandoned that too. I winked at him and he fired a look of panic at Haroula, hesitated for a few seconds before scuttling back into the toilets. It occurred to me that despite his fears, he was probably in for a quieter night than I was.

"Does he still sleep here?" I asked Haroula as she sat down next to me.

"Yes, on the floor behind the bar."

"Tell me, honestly now, why do you keep him on? Doesn't he put your clients off?"

"He works out cheaper than an alarm." She tried to make light of it, possibly in an attempt to disguise some kind of sob story or other, one that she knew would not move me at all.

I studied her closely. She was looking younger than the last time I'd seen her. Which was when, exactly? She read my thoughts.

"It's been three years, tough guy. And you've gone grey. Why don't you use one of those special shampoos? They work wonders."

"Is that what you've been using then?"

She was flattered, and leaned in towards me, whispering in my ear, "No more booze, no more weed, only five fags a day, gym three times a week, and . . ."

"And what?"

"Love, my darling, love. Do you know what it feels like to walk along the harbour at Rafina hand in hand, watching the boats leave and hear the words, 'Which one shall we catch this summer? Andros, Tinos, Mykonos – you choose.' Takes years off you."

"Anyone I know?"

"No. He's a retired banker. He's not in the business. We met at the gym."

"Any good in the sack?"

"You perv! Watch that tongue of yours! Anyway, in case you're wondering, I don't let him near those little blue pills. He's got low blood pressure."

I could not help myself. She was almost sixty and had spent most of those years out of the sunlight. But she had been lucky. At thirty she got knocked up by the superintendant of the Kypseli station, told him she had got rid of it, transferred herself and her bulging belly up to Larissa and lived off her savings. She was rumbled in her ninth month. The cop's initial reaction was to slap her round the face, but as soon as he saw the baby, he melted and rose to the occasion. He made her a partner in one of the clubs he looked after. It was known as Hawaii back then. Two years later the owner gave up his share and Haroula took over; in exchange, charges for possession of ten kilos of hash were dropped. The cop, like the mild-mannered junta boy he was, was promoted after the restoration of democracy and carried on looking out for Haroula, discreetly mind, and their little treasure was brought up wanting for nothing. I only knew about all this because the father of her darling little boy happened to be my boss in the early days of my glorious career, and expertly applying the art of listening-attentively-to-my-drunken-interlocutor, I had spent many a night down there in the basement and Haroula had always liked me. I never tried to get freebies from her girls.

"So to what do we owe the pleasure?"

"I need a favour."

"Favours."

"I need ten grammes of coke, about thirty Benzedrine, and about twenty tabs. I'll pay, of course."

She let go of my hand and looked at me, thunderstruck. "What are you planning to do with all that?" she asked sternly.

"It's a long story. Let's just say, they're not for personal use."

"Sure?"

"Promise. Some prick of a colleague of mine pinched a whole load of stuff, and now someone else, who's totally innocent, is in deep over this. It's all got to be back at Alexandras first thing tomorrow."

"Are you sure you don't want it for yourself, you crazy idiot?"

"Why the hell do you say that?"

"Because you look like shit."

"Haroula, get real. Do you really think that I'm about turn into some kind of geriatric junkie?"

"O.K., but surely you lot have your own suppliers? Even the traffic police have their pockets bursting with the stuff."

"It's a bit complicated, sweetheart. Come on, get on to it now. I can't wait."

"Now I'm going to have to owe that shit Maragkos."

"I'm paying, so what's the big deal?"

She walked over to phone, shouting "*Aghia Eleousa*! Fuck, fuck, fuck."

Shortly before midnight, I slapped the package down on the worktop, opened it cautiously and sorted the contents. I emptied out all the vitamins I had into a mug and shared the other stuff among the empty bottles. The powder stayed in the packet. I ran a hot bath, threw on my son's dressing gown, gathered up the drugs, a glass and a bottle of water and went into the bedroom.

I never did find out if Sonia realized that during those difficult moments towards the end of our affair, I would try to treat my wounds with chemical compresses. Back then, of course I believed that I had been blinded by love. I needed time. And a way to improve my stamina.

It looked like that was exactly what I needed as I filled up my water glass. I put it down on the bedside table, next to the hope that Haroula had given me, saying, "This is the last time – and if I hear that you've been doing anything bad, I'll never forgive you". It seemed that I also wanted to make another promise to Sonia, a final promise perhaps, that I would punish those who had destroyed our past.

Or perhaps it was after I had swallowed the first hope?

Tuesday, 11.55 p.m.

Is nobody ever going to hold me? I hear noises, engines, I've never lived close to engines, something's wrong with me, and something's been taken from me. I can remember, but I remember, but don't, a flame, that's for sure, Morenike's asleep, Rosa will be playing in that old bone-shaker, and Manthos will be clapping enthusiastically, trying not to spill his wine. Morenike can't embroider anymore, she doesn't really mind, she says, but she's sad she won't see Rosa grow up, I feel like screaming at her when she talks like that, I want to make her stop talking like that, I want to tell her that Rosa will remember us and will always love us, and will always look at us with those big dark eyes of hers.

CHAPTER 4

Simeon Piertzovanis Decides to Get Involved

Wednesday, 28.i
Tuesday, 11.55 p.m.

Shortly before midnight I ordered my last drink of the day. 16 was full of people I'd never seen before. Over the last few years the night-time population had changed and the average age had gone down noticeably. It wasn't simply a case of natural wastage from sudden death, liver cirrhosis, strokes and blackened lungs. Without its owners lifting a finger, this tiny bar had become the in place. Glossy magazines ran pieces on this "classic Athenian watering hole" advertising it among the 4×4s and millionaires' wristwatches, lauding its no-nonsense drinks and its "British atmosphere"; the broadsheets were devoting several column inches of their culture pages informing their readership that 16 would have been the ideal backdrop for the likes of Joyce, Dali, Bukowski, Rimbaud and Jack

Nicholson to sit up till the early hours in heated debate. Only the Athens Academy had yet to define the part 16 should play in the cultural development of the country.

Aristides put down my drink in front of me and squeezed my hand.

"How are you, Simeon?"

"Never better."

"It's been a while."

"I've been away."

He laughed, watching my gaze as I scanned the room, tore off a piece of paper from his wall of photographs of happy, drunken party animals, and handed it to me. I held it at arm's length, squinting to make out the writing.

Customers used to get together to drink
Nowadays they compete to see,
And be seen. KK

"Tell your poet friend that he needs to work on metre."

"Oh, we don't see much of him now. Something's up with his heart."

"Serves him right. Bet he's spent most of his life in love."

"The morning and afternoon crowds are very different. It's hard to impress a date in the middle of the day, and besides, there's a limit to how much you can put back on an empty stomach," said the grey-haired barman.

He retrieved the piece of paper and pinned it back in its place, where it would sit for the next hundred years, and went back to work. The man sitting next to me, a bald man in a jacket with a loosened tie, a ring on his little finger and one of those astronaut watches on his wrist, was trashing some poor singer to his friend, because she'd refused to appear on the Mega Channel breakfast show. "Who the hell does the stupid slapper think she is anyway, playing the quality T.V. card when she hasn't even shifted a thousand units? I bet she's forgotten all the times she went down on me in her dressing room at that sleazy bar when she wanted me to get her a recording contract. Little slut thinks she's too good for us now."

That was too much. I could not stand there and listen to this filth any longer. I grabbed him by the shoulders and pasted my smile all over his face, trying desperately not to breathe in his repellent after-shave.

"The young lady you refer to happens to be my niece. One day soon, I'll bring her round here for a drink. And when I do, I hope you'll be here and I'll stand you an Alexander House speciality. Our barman here sources the sperm himself from the best bank in the country."

I left the little creep in a state of confusion and my drink untouched. I said goodnight to Aristides, crossed the dimly lit arcade and went head-to-head with the sly snugness of the cold on Stadiou. In twenty minutes I was inside my flat, dripping with sweat. The light on the answer phone was flashing away. I tossed my coat onto the sofa, wrapped a towel round my neck, lit a cigarette, found a piece of paper and a pencil and made a to-do list for the next day.

No alcohol
Laundry
Bath
Shave

Nails

Clean out cage

Bank – money

Bills – building charges

Nexium – Lexotanil

Office – Achilleas to arrange funeral

Call Noni

Buy newspaper

STAY DRY TILL I SEE SONIA

I got undressed, swallowed a Lexotanil and went to bed, leaving that little red light on the answer phone to flash. I was not expecting any good news.

*

I stuck to my list religiously, bar the fact that I cut myself shaving and mixed up my woollens with my underwear.

My partner, Achilleas, agreed to deal with the funeral director and volunteered to take on the horrendous church bureaucracy. The funeral was going to be a civil affair, and to get that organized quickly, it was necessary to make a contribution towards a new table for holding candles, to the tune of €500.

I had lunch with Noni at a place in his neighbourhood. His team had offered to put up the money for the funerals on condition that he would be available for Sunday's match. We kept off the subject of Saturday night; he did not want to know the whys and wherefores, did not have the stomach for needless reconstructions, and I wasn't sure whether I should tell him that someone had murdered his girls. I let him think that the broken heater was responsible for the disaster.

But we did talk about other things. We talked a lot about the past, about his home town, a small place called Giamini, about the first time he was taken to the birthday celebrations of the Prophet at the Kano mosque and how he had çried, about the soil, the rains, and the water which always reached up to your ankles in the streets, and then about the big city, Oshogbo, the harsh training regime, the provincial stardom, suffocating Lagos with its noisy markets, the tender-hearted whores at the harbour and his first love, coke-addict managers who sent him to Belgium and from there to Sweden before finally dumping him in Greece, their cuts filling burgeoning wallets as they threw him a few crumbs. I had heard it all before but it was as if I was listening to these stories for the first time. We had never spent any time on our own together, just the two of us alone; the beautiful females we used to take care of were now someone else's responsibility.

We talked a great deal about the past. The future would have to wait for another occasion.

*

Back home, the little red light on my answer phone was going berserk. Six messages, five of them from young Rania, serial pleas for me to call, each with "I'm worried about you," appended as an after-thought. The sixth was from Chronis Halkidis. He wanted to see me urgently. I pressed delete, lay down on the sofa and opened the news-paper.

The full spread front-page headline made me smile: "Fire Spreads to Parliament". No mention of my fire, of course. Ten or so government M.P.s had been fired because they had accidentally signed on the correct bottom line so that the money in question ended up exactly where it was intended. The story of the burnt house had been relegated to the middle pages. The brief statement made by the fire services pointed the finger at the broken heater and at the negligence of the victims. The injured actress was stable but critical, her mentor's funeral was taking place tomorrow; the devastated Nigerian goalkeeper did not wish to make any statement regarding the deaths of his sister and niece. There was also a photograph of Sonia on the arts pages, with a statement from the Actors' Union beneath, expressing the sense of loss felt by her colleagues. Next to that was a comment by some smartarse, explaining that this was a sublime instance of tragic irony because several years ago Sonia had done Beckett's "Embers" for the radio and, desperate to show off his refined cynicism, concluded with a cliché about self-destructive impulses and the curse of the artist. I tossed the paper to the floor and closed my eyes. The tape with Sonia's youthful voice recorded on it was sitting very close to me, but I could not see any reason to play it. Why should I recall the night when she spoke to me with borrowed phrases to disguise her despair? How were those tired old words going to help me, the broken lines, the hypnotized voices, the fear of the end, the hope that I would ever hear the poor woman's voice again?

That sound you hear is the sea . . . I say that sound you hear is the sea . . . I mention it because the sound is so strange, so unlike the sound of the sea . . . I usen't to need anyone . . . There before the fire. Before the fire with all the shutters . . . no hangings, hangings, all the hangings drawn and the light, no light, only the light of the fire . . . looking out, white world, great trouble, not a sound, only the embers, sound of dying, dying glow . . . Stories, stories, years and years of stories, till the need came on me, for someone, to be with me, anyone . . . to be with me, imagine he hears me, what I am, now. Did you hear them? . . . Galloping? . . . You laughed so charmingly once, I think that's what first attracted me to you. That and your smile . . . I thought I might try and get as far as the water's edge . . . Are you afraid we might touch? Calm yourself . . . The hole is still there . . . The earth is full of holes . . . The time comes when one cannot speak to you anymore . . . You will be quite alone with your voice, there will be no other voice in the world but yours. I can try and go on a little if you wish . . . No? . . . Then I think I'll be getting back.

The phone rang, catching my freefall into the past just in time. The machine swallowed yet another message from Halkidis.

"Simeon – pick up. We've got to talk. Please."

I erased it, made a cup of coffee and sipped it slowly. I emptied the washing machine and hung the clothes out on the balcony, staring at a group of students sitting on the steps of the block of flats across the street drinking funny-coloured fizzy drinks. I put on my jacket, wound a scarf around my neck and stepped onto the street, wonderful Eressou, exchanging wishes for good health with the peripatetic Albanian accordion player as I tossed him the loose change from my pocket. The three Makrydimitris brothers, the irrepressible owners of the shop on the corner of Arachovis and Zoodochou Pigis streets, gave me some sesame seed bars to chew on, after which I hailed a taxi, jumped in and crashed out along the back seat, my hands stuffed deep in my pockets so that the driver would not see how much they were shaking from too much coffee and too little alcohol. I decided that from tomorrow, I would go back to the tried and tested recipe of green tea with a few drops of brandy in it.

The waiting room at Intensive Care presented the selfsame picture as it had the day before. The same stationary figures, the same empty looks, the same stolen glances at the clock in the corridor. I sat down between an elderly man from out of town in a drill jacket and woolly hat and a young man with a shaven head and an earring. The latter smelt of aftershave; the former of mould.

"Hey, lad, can you come with us a moment – go in there like, help me get me bags up on me knees, seeing as I can't bend, what with the arthritis and all," said the old man, shoving his gnarled fingers in my face by way of illustration.

"Of course. Whatever you want."

"There's a good lad. Got the old lady in there with pneumonia, don't we?"

I gave him a sympathetic look, which only encouraged him.

"You know what drives me mad, lad? I got three big strapping lads of my own, and all three of them's up and left the village and gone to the city and got their selves sorted. Two of them with the phone company, and the youngest fits car lights. Sent me up to Athens to get their mum sorted. Can't take a day off work, can they?"

"I wouldn't worry about it. The doctors will take care of everything here."

He looked at me, seeming not to understand what I was talking about. And then he lowered his gaze.

"I'm a broken man, lad, all worn out. And I don't understand what them doctors tell me. Not one word of it. If the old girl's gone and got herself pneumonia, why have they got her tucked up in just a sheet? Doesn't pneumonia need the warmth? I brought in a blanket the day before yesterday, from the hotel, but they wouldn't let me give it to her."

"They know what they're doing. Don't you go worrying yourself."

"Only the good Lord can know, only He knows," mumbled the old man, clutching a cloth bag on his knees.

Our conversation was interrupted by a nurse calling out names from the door to Intensive Care. I got up and went in with the old boy, helped him into his green robe, slipped the plastic coverings over his shoes and watched as he dragged himself across to his wife's bed. I put on my own hospital issue and went in to see Sonia. She was asleep. I slipped my hand under the sheet and found hers. I stroked it gently, taking care not to dislodge her tubes.

"You can talk to her, you know," whispered a nurse who had appeared silently next to me.

"Can she hear me?"

"Who knows?" she said, smiled sweetly and walked off.

I did not follow her advice. In times of stress, Sonia always preferred physical contact to words.

The head of Intensive Care was poring over a thick, leather-bound book. He was in his early sixties, with a bony face and stark white hair. Long-sighted, he raised his glasses to look at me.

"Simeon Piertzovanis. Here to see Miss Varika."

"Take a seat. Have you spoken to me about Miss Varika before?"

"Not you personally. I spoke to a colleague of yours yesterday."

"I see. And how are you and Miss Varika related?"

"Used to be married."

He shook his head and slammed the book shut.

"Is there any news?"

"Her situation is critical, but her chances remain fairly good. As you can appreciate, we can only speak in terms of odds. The patient has suffered forty-three per cent third-degree burns. The statistics in these cases are both with us and against us. They're calculated on the basis of the age of the patient and the extent of the burns; in this case that comes to fifty per cent. They put her on a drip inside the ambulance and that probably saved her life. Fortunately there was no poisoning."

"Meaning?"

"No carbon monoxide poisoning."

"So what's the main danger at this stage?"

"Her body's in shock. It's in a state of confusion. We're trying to encourage it to regain equilibrium, but as always, there's a concern about possible complications. But we're prepared for that."

He must have noticed something about the expression on my face and smiled reassuringly.

"You're a smoker, I see. I can tell from your breathing. Much as I'd like to, I cannot allow you to smoke in here."

"Don't worry. You were saying something about possible complications."

"Infections are one concern. All of the vital organs could theoretically present problems, from the kidneys to the heart. As I said, we're prepared. It's the liver that worries me. Did your wife drink?"

"Yes."

"I see. That explains why her liver isn't too healthy."

"So what will happen if . . . I mean, what can we do about it?"

"Don't panic. Do you believe in God?"

"No."

"Pity. If you did, I would recommend prayer. It would save me the more pedestrian option, where I explain to you that the human body is a machine, with a highly complex mechanism that we barely understand, but a machine nonetheless. A machine that carries out its own repairs, and as you know, production plants vary in standards, as do technicians. Of course, time is a factor too. Do forgive me if I come across as a vulgar materialist, but so far the only ones I've seen performing miracles and saving lives have been doctors and nurses. God has never once put in an appearance, not even to stitch up a simple eyebrow."

"He's been replaced by the medical professionals, has he?"

"How can something that does not exist in the first place be replaced, Mr . . . er?"

"Piertzovanis."

"What do you do for a living, Mr Piertzovanis?"

"I'm a lawyer."

"A man of few words. Most unusual for a lawyer."

"It's the production plant that counts, as you pointed out, doctor."

He smiled.

"One last question, doctor. Is she in pain?"

"Yes. A little."

"Is she able to think?"

"Only she can answer that."

"When can she speak to me?"

"When she's ready."

I thanked him, stood up and opened the door. His voice was friendly.

"I thought she was unmarried. That's what the T.V. was saying."

"We married in secret." I thanked him again.

In the small lobby outside the office, the old man was still standing up, clutching his cloth bag. He was probably too embarrassed to sit down on the brown sofa, no doubt the most luxurious piece of furniture he had ever seen.

"Go right in. The doctor's inside," I said, encouragingly.

"She looked better today, our Golfo. Opened her eyes and looked me for a long time."

"Is your wife called Golfo?"

"No! Her name's Antonia. I call her Golfo for a laugh. For a bit of fun, you know. We had some laughs we did, till her health failed, that is."

"Ah, yes!" I said, enjoying the literary joke. "So I suppose she calls you Tassos, does she?"

"Tassos? Why would she go calling us Tassos when the name's Giorgos? Hatzopoulos, Giorgos. Seventy-eight years old. That's what it says." He tapped an imaginary nametag on his lapel with pride. "If you ever come to be passing through Dyrrachion in Arcadia, be sure to come and find us in the *kafeneion*."

Winding my scarf around my neck, I walked out of the main building and made my way to the hospital gates. As soon as I found a low wall, I sat down and lit up. The doctor's words were reeling inside my head: Shock, infection, complications, kidneys, liver.

I have no idea how long Halkidis had been standing there watching me in his gloves and woolly hat, just a few metres away. I was on my second cigarette before I noticed him.

"I'm surprised you haven't frozen to death, Mr Piertzovanis."

"I was about to leave."

"Your taxi's waiting," he said, nodding across at his Golf. We got in and set off.

"Did you get my messages?"

"What exactly do you want, Officer?"

"What the consultant told you will do for starters."

I told him everything I had been told, down to the last detail. He would pipe up with the occasional question I was unable to answer. When I finished, he lit up and drove on for a while in silence, giving me the chance to study the face of a small boy glued onto a tiny magnet bearing the warning, "Slow down, Daddy!" When we got to the Psychico interchange, he turned right into the Kifissias slip road and parked behind a fleet of diplomatic number plates. He switched off the engine and turned to me, his arm around the back of my seat. There was a strange glint in his eye.

"What's going on?"

"I hardly slept last night."

I pointed to the magnet with the little boy's face on it.

"Does your little boy worry about you?"

"He's sixteen. He lives with his mother."

He removed his arm from the passenger seat and intertwined its fingers with the fingers on his other hand, which was beating out a rhythm on the steering wheel. My patience was wearing thin and I told him as much.

"If you loved this woman, even just a little, you've got to help me. I've left you ten messages, but you, not a squeak. What's the matter? Do you even give a damn or is all this beneath you? Do you think I'm beneath you? Why, when I've explained everything to you, when I've begged you?"

I opened the door and stepped out into the freezing air. I needed a drink like nothing else on this earth. I leaned against a stone wall for support and looked down at the wonderful avenue beneath, remembering a time when there were only two lanes and very few cars, and those buses with the long snouts and surly conductors, the low buildings lining both sides. And then I remembered yet another time, more recent but much more remote.

"Do you like that hum, my love?"

"The traffic never lets up on Kifissias."

"I prefer Alexandras; it's friendlier, more accepting."

"One night I'll take you to the cinema down the road, the Astron. It's the only cinema I know with the balcony under the stalls. And the only one that has an outside balcony. The balcony doors are always open, and you stand there looking down at the avenue and it seems so far down, yet right next to you at the same time. You know, the cinema in "Cinema Paradiso" had a balcony like that too."

"No, it didn't."

"It did."

"No. It was just a very large window. Like this one here."

"Whatever you say, Sir. But may I humbly request permission to stick with Alexandras. And Ippokratous as well. Ippokratous more."

"Ippokratous is a street, not an avenue."

"Yes, you're right. But what about Stadiou? Where do you stand on Stadiou?"

"Stadiou, yes. That's an avenue."

"Marvellous. So you'll put me to bed one night in that old hotel at the beginning of it?"

"The President? Isn't that a bit of a come-down for a diva like you?"

"What – that dump is called the President*?"*

"That's right."

"Oh, no, I don't like that. I'd feel as if I were in Tokyo. Too many tourists taking photographs."

"You should see an analyst. That's the only way you'll ever be free of your irrational fear of cameras."

"Whatever you say, doctor. But afterwards you'll put me to bed in the Grande Bretagne, won't you?"

"Of course."

"It's cold. I'll go and say goodnight to the competition and turn in."

"I'll be with you in a minute."

"Goodnight, wonderful Kifissias."

"I like it more now," I said to the policeman standing next to me.

"Like what more?"

"Kifissias. I like the noise, the colours, the traffic. One of my worst nightmares is finding myself walking down a deserted avenue."

"You have nightmares?"

"Doesn't everyone?"

"I don't know," he said, walking over to the car.

I stopped him, calling after him with his first name for the first time ever. He swung round.

"I need a drink. Have to have a drink. Then we'll talk. I'd prefer somewhere closer to home. Is your passport valid in Exarcheia?"

He got into the Golf and started it up. It's just a matter of time before the exhaust gives out on him, I thought.

*

I chose a quiet place on the paved part of Themistokleous. Halkidis ordered a juice, I asked for whisky and a bowl of ice. Out of respect for my damaged oesophagus, I was frequently forced to water down my poison. We spent the first few minutes of this tender *tête-à-tête* smoking and listening to a peculiar mix of Tibetan monks chanting through the speakers against the noise of builders frantically working on installations in time for the Olympics. The waitress set our drinks down on the table and cheerfully agreed to turn the racket down. Apart from us, there was only one other customer – a middle-aged man buried inside a horse-racing magazine – and a fat cat fast asleep on the deep red bar. Halkidis tasted the juice and then pulled two pieces of paper from his pocket.

"Read it. Take your time," he said, getting up and making his way to the toilet.

It looked like some kind of report, written in quite bizarre Greek, describing in disturbing detail the destruction of the house, and reaching the conclusion that the fire was the result of arson. Halkidis came back, took two sips of his drink and started rubbing his nose nervously.

"Must have caught a cold," he said.

I folded up the report and pushed it across the table to him. He put it back in his pocket, started to say something, deliberately avoiding eye contact with me. Very drawn with bloodshot eyes, the man clearly had not slept for days. For the few seconds that he let his cigarette rest and burn away in the ashtray, he fiddled with the cocktail stirrer in his juice. It did not take much to convince me that there was something very suspect behind this arson attack. The evidence that the report had amassed was overwhelming. Despite his obvious agitation, he was precise in his choice of words and his explanations were remarkably lucid. Here was a rational policeman, an experienced policeman, an intelligent policeman. What he failed to conceal were the cracks in which something was festering, something dangerous for whoever might come face-to-face with it. It was the way that he almost spat out some of the words he used: murderers, bastards, that shithead of a Chief of Police, three innocent victims, I won't rest until . . . In the end, he did not ask any very much of me, nothing more than the day before.

"Try to remember. Just that. Rack your brains and try to remember what might be the motive. I've got a mental block and I haven't got much at all to go on at the moment. I can't even go and see Sonia. They're watching the hospitals. My hands are tied. I want you to visit her every day; she might come round and talk."

It was not an unreasonable request. Visiting Sonia was something I would have done anyway. My problem was something entirely different, but I did not think it was the right moment to explain.

"Alright, Officer."

"Call me Chronis, for fuck's sake."

"All in good time. I'll go to the hospital every day and try to remember anything that might have a bearing on the case. I cannot promise any miracles; I've got a memory like a sieve and don't forget I've been away for the past few months and haven't had anything to do with anybody for a while."

"Away? You never mentioned that to me."

"You never asked. After Easter I left for Marseilles. Don't ask what I was doing there – suffice it to say I wasn't there to take delivery of a heroin shipment. I was back in Greece at the beginning of January. I didn't go and see Sonia as I wasn't feeling my best and I didn't want to upset her. I didn't even call."

"I see. Noni would have seen her regularly, wouldn't he?"

"Absolutely. I'll have a word with him tomorrow, after the funeral."

"Good."

"Have you considered the possibility that the fire was started by some wacko racist because there were immigrants living in the house?"

"It has occurred to me."

"And?"

"Do you really suppose that the Prime Minister's adviser and the chiefs of the security services would go to all this trouble to cover the backside of some random psycho?"

He was right. We sat there in silence for a while. I ordered another drink and lost myself staring at the horse-racing fan stroking the cat.

"Why don't you want to tell me what you were doing in Marseilles?" he said in a low voice.

"Because we're not exactly best buddies yet, are we?"

"True."

"But you're dying to know, aren't you? Because you're a detective, and a good one at that, as far as I can tell. And you're thinking, something's going on here; the man's out of the country for eight months and the minute he's back, his house gets burned down. Am I right, Colonel?"

"You're a natural."

"Funny thing is I can't stand crime fiction."

"Oh, I love it. Always take a good one to bed with me."

It was as if he had suddenly relented. He reached for his lighter, unaware that he already had one cigarette lit. He stubbed it out quietly as I smiled at him. The second whisky and the anticipation of a third confirmed my passage to Lethe.

"I'll tell you about Marseilles on one condition."

"Go on."

"That you tell me the truth about you and Sonia."

"What's that got to do with it?"

"I can't believe that you'd put so much on the line for the sake of your professional good conscience alone."

He relaxed back into the chair, scrutinizing my face as though he were trying to impress every last wrinkle on his memory.

"O.K., sharp lawyer, you're on."

I took a solid slug of whisky and began telling the story of the last few months of my life. It took all of sixty seconds.

"Nine years ago I fell in love with a woman. A good woman. Seventeen days; that's all the time we had together. Not together, exactly. Just the one night and a few other occasions. Then she left, because she had to go into hiding, mourn two men and raise her little girl when she was not much more than a girl herself. Last April I got a letter from her asking if I wanted to come and live with her in Marseilles. Her daughter was now twenty-one and at university somewhere else. She believed that we owed it to each other, and should at least give it a go. That's how the letter ended. So I went. And we tried. We had a glass of red wine in the evenings, went on trips, read, cooked, swam, laughed. We tried everything, tentatively, tenderly. It failed. So I came home. If you want to see if my story checks out, her name's Daphne Kyprianidis, and the address is rue Jean-Claude Iso, number 7."

Halkidis was coughing. He ordered a bottle of mineral water from the waitress, poured himself a glass and downed it in one, put the glass on the table, filled it again to the half-way mark and cupped it in his hand.

"What is it: half full or half empty?"

He threw his hands up.

"Science throws its hands up at that one too," I said, combining this gesture with a nod to the waitress, because virtually the only thing that had been of any interest to me these last thirty years was making sure that my glass was always full. "Your turn."

"Yeah, sure," he muttered and fixed his gaze on the glass. All the time he was looking at it as though he were willing the level to rise.

After a good half hour of telegraphese, significant-sounding dates, towns that he never wanted to visit again, conversations with Sonia he recalled almost word-for-word, sketchy descriptions of happy moments and empty days, Police Colonel Chronis Halkidis made me realize that only two kinds of men are of interest: those who are destroyed because they love too much and those who are destroyed because they are loved too much. Halkidis was the classic example of the latter. Sonia loved him deeply, so much so that in order for him both to bear it and to go along with her, he had to cut off all ties with his own world, the real world. Her uncompromising "all or nothing" was incomprehensible to him. He took fright and made his escape. He was still young, not yet forty, and believed that by leaving her he would escape her. But like everyone who has fought hard to make something of their lives, he refused to be dragged into her sweet defeat. I was convinced that every night for the last five years he had been kicking himself over this decision, but he had not dared do anything to reverse it. He could not bring himself to screw up that little plastic flag into a ball, the one representing all his beliefs and principles, which he summed up in his last sentence.

"I watched her going under and knew that if I stayed with her, she would take me down with her. Life is a gift, Simeon. We don't have the right to toss it on to the rubbish heap."

The waitress filled my glass and replaced the ashtrays. Halkidis wiped away the sweat on his brow with the back of his hand.

"Have you got a temperature?"

"Maybe."

"Get her to make you a hot drink."

He stood up, said something to the waitress and disappeared behind the door to the toilets, leaving me to down my whisky and take stock of the jealousy raging inside me. He had left her; she had not left him as she had left me. I knew that it hardly mattered anymore, but I was jealous, encouraged perhaps by the first stages of drunkenness. But I could neither overcome this grievance nor banish images of them together from my mind. The first girl I was involved with left because she was scared of having to spend the rest of her life living with the guilt of the suicide of a friend of ours who we had betrayed; the second one left me because she did not have the nerve to follow through at the right time, and Sonia left me because she had chosen to die alone. I was wondering whether I drank because I wanted to feel like the hero of some kind of popular melodrama – the perfect excuse to drink – when Halkidis came back and sat down again.

"What's on your mind?"

His hair was wet; he'd probably just stuck his head under the tap. He pushed two schnapps glasses containing some kind of pink liquid in my direction.

"What's this?"

"On the house. Have mine too; I don't want it."

"Just pour them onto that plant next to you. Discreetly."

"You surprise me."

"It must have been early in 2000 when I managed to persuade Sonia to have her liver looked at. The tests were not encouraging. I remember the doctor telling her, 'Miss Varika, you must stop drinking. Completely. Not a drop of alcohol – not even communion wine, Miss Varika.' She promised me she would take care of herself. Then one evening she asked me to go to a taverna with her. She was meeting someone in the theatre business and two young actors about a job and she wanted a lawyer with her because she was usually taken for a ride in these deals. She was drinking soda, the others had wine and I had ordered beer. We ate, chatted and she promised them she would get back to them in a few days. When the desserts came, the restaurant brought us gum mastic liqueurs on the house. Nobody touched theirs apart from me. When we got outside Sonia pretended she had left her gloves inside, and went back in to get them. I watched her go inside. She drained all the schnapps glasses and whatever was left in the wine glasses into my beer glass and drank it. Down in one. I said nothing, and I've never touched schnapps since. You can understand why."

"Yes."

"Good. Can we pay?"

"I already have."

"Shall we go?"

"In a minute. Tell me something."

"What?"

"Why won't you admit it?"

"Admit what?"

"Your affair."

"Comrade Chronis, alcoholics don't have affairs. They just find excuses to drink."

"Now, why don't I believe you?"

"Because you're jealous. Because it drives you crazy when you think that you'll never be free of your guilt. Maybe, just maybe, if the lady dies, you'll grow up and get your life together."

"Want her to die, do you?"

"About as much as I want to die myself."

"Are you in analysis as well?" he said maliciously, rubbing his nostrils impatiently.

"You do coke, don't you?" I asked casually.

"Bullshit."

I drained my glass and took his hand over the table.

"You shouldn't have left a woman like that," I whispered, and threw him on the mercy of the cruel night.

*

I found a note stuck on my front door with some chewing gum:

If you don't call, I'll cry. R.x

I called. Half an hour and two whiskies later she arrived, threw open the balcony doors, fed me some cheese on toast, chatted to Rina, shaved me carefully, brought in the washing, forced me to brush my teeth, shut the balcony doors again just before I froze to death, and accompanied me to bed.

"Grandpa, I'll do your ironing and then I'll get on with some work in your dusty old study. I've brought my laptop with me, and I hope that beautiful woman looking down from the wall at me will inspire me. Who is she, by the way?"

"Romy Schneider. She was an actress."

"Cool. I'm sure that'll help. I've got to unravel the mystery of a note Pavese wrote. What did the poet mean when he wrote in 1941, in the thick of war, 'I don't know what to do with other people's wives'?"

"Make yourself at home," I said, forcing a smile.

"Thankfully this dump will never be my home. And thankfully you're never going to fall in love with me, but if you do wake from some horrible dream – you know, cockroaches, reptiles, falling off a skyscraper, that kind of stuff – don't be shy. I always carry condoms."

She kissed me on the forehead and ruffled my hair.

"If you are you, then I am I, which means that I don't know how to behave. Pavese again. Night night, grandpa."

She closed the door behind her before I had a chance to tell her that the iron had not worked for years.

28.i.
Wednesday, 11.30 p.m.

Closed game of poker, three switches, a pair of jacks leads, the man opposite me has been getting consistently good hands all night. I've never seen him before, he could be a pro. He doesn't seem to recognize me. He has probably got more interesting things to do than go to the theatre. I am sure his evenings are more exciting than mine . . . Let's see – two nines, an eight, jack, queen . . . I'll hang on to the nines and change the other three – or maybe I should get rid of one of the nines and try to get a run. That man still hasn't asked for any new cards, he'll have a flush or something better . . . either that or he's bluffing . . . the rest of them are thinking. I couldn't care less about the others. I'm only interested in him.

"What did you say your name was?"

"Simeon."

He had a good look.

"New cards."

He has kind eyes. He is standing pat and not holding back on the bets. *I admire the run on my hand, the queen. Lucky little Sonia got rid of that nine and got a ten. That's a nice run on the queen. "Kolofardi Sonia": kolofardi – wide-arsed; what a horrible word to describe a lucky person – vulgar and phallocratic. But it's the first word that comes into my head. And I,* kolofardi *little Sonia, am betting everything. It's not so much that I want to beat him as to kiss him, just like that, as he sits there looking at me and smiling and counting his chips and lighting a Gitane and listening, convinced he is going to win, hearing that the other players are going to pass, the others but not all the others. There's that Fiat dealer – or M.P., or son of an M.P. – here too, dressed expensively, following the bets carefully and collecting chips shamelessly from the entire table because he's got three aces, and as everyone knows, three aces beats a run quite spectacularly.*

"We lost quite a bit tonight, Mr Piertzovanis."

"Never mind. Tomorrow is another day."

I should not have put my coins out on that strike, I should not have gambled everything that night just because of the man whose smile announced that he hated losing as much as I did; I should not have gone with him to that bar in the arcade, I should have remembered that another man was waiting for me in the warmth of my nest, his deep embrace trembling.

That's good . . . that's so good, things are beginning to come back to me. I can remember much more now . . . but I don't just want to remember. . . I want to live a bit longer too . . . just a tiny bit . . .

CHAPTER 5

Chronis Halkidis in Action

I got to Syngrou around 10.00, greeted Dedes and Kourkouvelas, who were having a heated debate about the ramifications of the forthcoming Olympics, asked Fotini for a coffee and shut myself in my office without taking off my sunglasses. I had not managed to get to sleep till about 7.00 that morning, and the dream I had had was still spooling through my head like a film: a black-and-white documentary narrated by a little boy in a country village whose friends were taunting him because he always screwed his eyes shut when his father slit the throats of their aged cockerels. I knew that the pills and cocaine would only get me through one week tops, and after that I would need a different kind of help, something along the lines of a steady hand or a voyage to a magical land inhabited exclusively by nice people, the land I always hide out in when the going gets tough.

Then I remembered an old hooker, a "mature" lady, who had taken care of me for a few sleazy weekends. She told me that her greatest fear was there would be a power cut during the weather forecast. "It's like my lucky charm. When I know what the weather's going to be like the next day, I know that I'll wake up in the morning, and I won't miss the sunshine or the overcast skies. But the thought of dying in my sleep makes me crazy!" she said, and swore at me because I was bent double with laughter. I tried for a minute to remember her name, but couldn't so I set to work instead. Before I even finished my coffee, I had managed to pick out an old case file, which had been gathering dust in the bottom drawer of a filing cabinet in Internal Affairs. The superintendent down in Argos had been accused of aiding the escape from justice of a bouncer at one of the local night-clubs. The bouncer in question stood accused of assaulting a waitress who had refused to hold hands with a seventy-year-old citrus producer punter of theirs. My esteemed colleague happened to be on excellent terms with all the local politicians and fat cats in that beautiful town, and was coming up for retirement in two years anyway. The nightclub owner eventually persuaded the young woman to drop charges against the bouncer, but by then the thug had fled, so the file was still with us, open. It was a classic case, one in which Sherlock Holmes himself would have had trouble digging up any hard evidence. I opened my office door and stood there watching Kourkouvelas and Dedes at each other's throats still. Kourkouvelas was accusing Dedes of undermining the national interest, so I decided to interrupt them before I got too depressed by the inanity of their argument. I gave Kourkouvelas a squeeze on the shoulder and asked him if he felt like taking a trip down to Argos for a bit of muckraking and got the answer I was expecting, knowing full well that my subordinate was always up for a chance to hit the road, anything to provide relief from the stifling atmosphere of a stale marriage. As soon as he walked out of the building, the file tucked under his arm and a huge grin plastered across his face, I explained to Dedes and Fotini that it was a good idea to get him out from under our feet for a few days. One of the advantages of being head of division is that you are answerable only to the Chief of Police and the prosecutor from the Court of Appeal who oversees interrogations. I can give priority to any case I choose, tail anyone I choose, go A.W.O.L. "on police business", no questions asked – precisely what I intended to do over the next few days. Both the Security and the Anti-Terrorist divisions had been swamped in the run-up to the Olympics, and what is more, on the friendly instructions of the Americans and the British, a fact which possibly minimized the chances of anyone causing me grief if I strayed into their territory. And I was determined to do just that without delay.

After Kourkouvelas' ecstatic exit, Dedes called the rest of the team together for a scheduled meeting and told them vaguely that for the next few days he and the boss would be out of the office a great deal on work related to the Olympics and took a seat opposite me. I had given him the short version of what had been going on since yesterday, when we last spoke: about Sonia's condition; about the officer with the earring keeping watch in the corridors of Intensive Care; about my exchange with Simeon Piertzovanis. He listened intently.

"I don't know if the Chief is . . ."

He stopped, pulled a stick of gum from his pocket and unwrapped it, very slowly.

"One giant testicle of a man?"

"I wouldn't put it quite like that."

"How would you put it?"

"You know how I feel about labelling people. I just wonder why he didn't believe you, seeing that you had given him your assurance that you would not be concerning yourself with the case anymore."

"It told you – because he's one giant testicle of a man. And an ungrateful one at that."

"What about something a bit milder? Something along the lines of 'the Chief is under the thumb of his political masters'?"

"For brevity's sake, you mean?"

"Precisely."

"Any idea who did it?"

"Not really. I can't see who would stand to gain from that fire."

"Not Piertzovanis. That's for sure. He won't even be getting the insurance on it. He might be a wanker, a freeloader and a drone, but he hasn't got the balls to step on an ant. Washed-up old alcoholic. Let's just hope he remembers something useful."

"Mr Halkidis —"

"Please. As long as we're breaking the rules, use my first name. It's Chronis."

He looked at me in bewilderment. I did not have the reputation of being the big-hearted boss who would go and let his hair down with his subordinates after work, gossiping about women and watering his plants with the saliva collected from his closest associates. Something inside me forever told me I was in the wrong profession and that mixing with my colleagues could only make the situation worse. On the rare occasions I had not been able to say no to meals and dinners, I had regretted it. But I also realized that it was not my profession alone that was wrong; I had the wrong wife, the wrong child, came from the wrong village, lived in the wrong city, and the wrong face stared back at me in the mirror.

"*Seriously, young man – you surely don't avoid looking in the mirror? You're such a handsome man. Hasn't anyone told you?*"

"*I'm not crazy about what I see.*"

"*Why don't you try to look at it differently?*"

"*That's the luxury of your profession.*"

"*Do you want me to tell you how? Do you want me to let you in on the big secret of the acting profession?*"

"*I do, yes.*"

"*Bring over the tequila and lie down next to me.*"

"*Just a minute.*"

"*You don't have to take your clothes off.*"

"*Not even my shoes?*"

"*No.*"

"*The lady's wishes are my command.*'

"*Excellent! Turn round and look at me. That's right. What do you see?*"

"*Your eyes.*"

"*And in my eyes. A handsome man?*"

"*Your eyes are too cloudy.*"

"*Cloudy?*"

"*Very cloudy. Too much tequila.*"

"*Fuck you.*"

"*Sonia!*"

"*What?*"

"*They* are *very cloudy.*"

"*Sorry, young man. You don't know what you're missing.*"

"Mr Halkidis . . ."

"Yes?"

"The red phone."

I had not even heard it. The red phone was meaningfully red. An unwieldy device, one of those that had been so fashionable in the '80s. A New Year's gift from Fotini and Dedes; a wretchedly unfunny joke which I bore stoically. They had connected it up to my direct line to the Chief. I decided, not unreasonably, to stuff it into my middle drawer. It hardly ever rang anyway.

"Good morning, Chief."

"How are things?"

"Quiet."

Dedes was frantically waving to me to get me to give him permission to leave the office. I signalled that he should stay and lit a cigarette.

"When are you going to give up that junk, Chronis?"

"Any minute now. I've read about some nicotine patches that you stick on and they give you an aversion to it."

"Excellent. Why don't you give them a go?"

"How are you?"

"Oh, forget it. The Americans are keeping me on my toes. But I'm not going easy on them either. I was over at the Embassy and I said to one of the F.B.I. bigwigs, 'Look, mister – we send so many billions your way, what could possibly go wrong? We will host the perfect Olympian Games, so take it easy, let us in peace, and let me buy you an ouzo to help forget your worries'. And do you know what the little sod said to me?"

"What?"

"'So why is it that the Porto Carras scandal has broken just now?' Christ, Chronis – the old hood even knew the name of the hotel!"

"They do read newspapers, you know, Chief."

"Anyway – so I said to him – 'What are you so worried about, mister?' And he says, 'Gas canisters – we don't want gas canisters being thrown at banks and at McDonald's.' So, I said to him, 'Don't worry, mister. Everything's under control.'"

"And?"

"Nothing. 'Everything's under control.'"

"Same here. Quiet."

I took a long drag on my cigarette and looked at Dedes, who was enjoying his gum. Then the Chief decided to get to the point.

"Really? What about your girlfriend – the one in the fire, the actress? Any news? Have you been to visit at all?"

"Oh, Yannis – when do I get the chance to . . . ?"

"According to the papers she might pull through."

"The doctor told me the day before yesterday that they should know in a few days. It's a tough call."

"What a shame. She was a great actress too, I'm told."

I stubbed out my cigarette and pulled out a new one from the packet. Dedes looked at me reproachfully. I ignored him and enveloped the filter between my lips.

The Chief's voice was heard over the flick of the lighter flint.

"Chronis – do me a favour. Don't spend any more time on this business. It's all under control. I'll see to that. I'll explain everything soon. It was an accident. Believe me."

"Yannis – all I care about is that the woman recovers. Nothing else."

"She will. And you know what – anything she might need later on, any treatments, medication, plastic surgery, we're here. We'll take care of everything. Even if she needs to go abroad – that won't be an issue. You have my word."

"Understood."

"Excellent. And you and I must get together some time. Russlana will cook. One of those lethal dishes her lot likes so much."

"Just name the day – you know what a packed social calendar I have."

"Don't worry about a thing. What are you working on at the moment, anyway?"

"I'm not. I'm busy finishing up our annual report to the parliamentary commission."

"When can I have it?"

"In a week – ten days at the most."

"Good luck with that."

I replaced the clumsy red receiver, stubbed out my cigarette, put on my jacket and instructed a puzzled Dedes to wait for me. I threw a casual "back very soon" at Fotini and climbed the stairs, trying to ignore my heavy breathing. You can see the sea from our roof terrace. Today the sea was beautiful. And even more beautiful if you looked at it through two lines of magic powder. You could blank out the grey parts and concentrate on its more refined promises.

*

The rest of the morning was spent searching databases looking to dredge up something on the Prime Minister's advisers, because we believed our Chief when he said that it was one of those pen-pushers who had put pressure on him to close the case. This was Dedes' idea, and I thought it was interesting. A year ago, Parliament had decided to make Internal Affairs responsible for crimes relating to the wider public sector, which is why we had access to all these civil servants' files. At the point where we found ourselves, this was our only lead. We found eight names; obviously we could hardly bug all eight of them or monitor their mobile phones. Fotini suggested we start with the government adviser on public order. This seemed reasonable to me, and I passed the job on to the Department of Special Cases. I trusted their man in charge, only because he was right-wing. Wouldn't he just love to go after the adviser to the enemy? Round about 3.00, we abandoned the computers and wolfed down some of those monumental "builders' sandwiches", as Fotini, who made them for us, liked to call them. She always used fresh crusty bread, feta from Limnos, and organic tomatoes, but always made do herself with a couple of green apples. About a year ago, when Kourkouvelas announced to us that his cholesterol levels had hit the roof, Fotini issued a blanket ban on all take-aways and deliveries. One morning she had found the remains of a pizza in Dedes' office and didn't speak to him for two whole days afterwards. As for beer – forget it. Even asserting our right to drink Diet Coke came at a price. I was having my only cigarette of the day (which even in her view could do me no harm) when my new secure mobile rang. It was Piertzovanis, ringing from a pay phone and sounding stressed. I told him so.

"Stressed? Maybe. I haven't had a drop to drink; that might be why. I've bought a pay-as-you-go thing, but had to leave it at home to charge. That's what they said in the shop; it takes twelve hours."

"Congratulations! Did they show you how it works as well?"

"Yes, they did, Colonel. Now listen. I'm in a hurry. I won't manage to see Sonia today; I've got to go to the funeral. And after that I was thinking of telling Noni the truth. He might just think of something, I don't know – something that may have happened at the house while I was away."

Predictably, he had no idea what the number of his new mobile was, so he promised to ring me later – and to keep off the booze. I finished my cigarette and told Fotini and Dedes to go home, locked myself in a toilet cubicle and swallowed a pill. When I got back, Dedes was waiting for me, chewing away on a piece of gum.

"Mind if I come with you to the hospital?" he said to me hesitantly.

"Why?"

"I might be useful, Mr Halkidis."

I parked my backside on his desk, and to his bewilderment asked for a stick of gum.

"There's a first for everything, Comrade Manolis. And if you don't drop this 'Mr Halkidis' crap when the two of us are on our own, I'll start calling you 'comrade' in public. Not that I'm entirely confident that you young pink socialists even know the meaning of the word."

"But I'm not . . ."

He stopped and looked at me as though he wanted to see whether he should open up any further. I waited.

"I'm not – I mean, Mr Halkidis, I'm not . . . I've never tried to hide the fact that I do hold certain views and I try to do my job without compromising those views. And you yourself have helped me do this. Anyway, I'm sure there are people everywhere who . . ."

"Please! I was only joking. Don't rise to every bait, Manolis."

He relaxed a little, and even tried to force a smile. I don't know what got into me; maybe it was the dope, messing with my head and making me rant incoherently.

"Manolis – remember this: we're still policemen. Just plain old policemen, a negligible minority, perhaps, searching for the truth.

But our job is not to prove that capitalism is the root of all evil. Every pre-schooler knows that. I discovered it around about the time I was weaned from the breast. Three months from now all our bosses will be replaced. I don't give a damn. I only voted for them the once – back in 1981. By 1982 I was already regretting it. I haven't a notion where I'll be this time next year. And you know what? I've just turned forty-five and I don't owe a thing to anyone. Eighteen years with the force and I only let myself get bribed once: I had no choice. You know that I have nothing but respect for you. I'm even a bit jealous of you sometimes. Not because you're young, but because you hope that you'll be able to change things. That has nothing to do with age. It has everything to do with the way you are; what you're made of. Do what you think best – just don't go mixing police work with Marxism. The two things have nothing to do with each other. I'm sure you've already worked that one out. How does that old song go? Remember it? 'Governments they come and go but the police are here to stay.' And as far as this bloody case is concerned, the only thing that matters is finding out who killed those three people."

He looked at me, dumbfounded. I gave him a mock thump on the shoulder and told him to meet me at the hospital entrance at 6.00.

"Yes, Mr Halkidis," he said in a whisper.

"For fuck's sake, man! It's Chronis!"

*

Dedes was standing out of the drizzle under the canopied hospital entrance. As we walked towards Intensive Care, I explained how he should present himself to the doctor: he was Sonia's cousin and he had just arrived back in the country after a trip abroad. I left him outside the unit, turned right and dived into the toilets. I pulled my tobacco tin from my coat pocket. Inside was my powder and a telephone card with the monstrous figures of Athena and Phoebus, our Olympic mascots, printed across it. I had a line and rolled a cigarette. So far I had been in complete control of my doses. The night before I had even managed to steal myself five continuous hours of sleep, and the two Maxalt tablets I took kept the midday migraine at bay. I focused hard on the thin red second hand on my watch and waited till my pulse was back to normal. Very delicate work for someone in my condition. A mobile phone number was scrawled across the door in thick marker pen, and underneath it, the announcement, "Tommy! Blowjobs – and much, much more!!! Special rates for doctors." I flung my cigarette end into the toilet bowl and walked out, bumping into an old lady in a wheelchair, who was being pushed along by a titanic nurse whose voice was only marginally softer than Pavarotti's.

"Right, grandma. Listen carefully. If you know what's good for you, you'll do it this time. I can't push you up and down to the toilets every five minutes," she said sternly, hoisting the old lady up by the armpits and kicking the door open.

"If only I could, my love," said the sick woman submissively, supporting herself on the doorframe in her attempt to get to the toilet.

"This is the ladies', Sir." The harridan sister shot me a look so murderous it would have stunned a rabid dog at ten paces.

"I beg your pardon," I said hurriedly, biting my lip and imagining what fun I could have shoving her into that wheelchair and sending it hurtling down the stairs.

I paused at a filthy window with cracked panes and tried to calm down by watching globules of moisture dripping off a pile of rusty old metal, which had been piled up in the courtyard outside. Very soon the nurse was back out again, the rolls of fat that had usurped the position once occupied by a face now red with rage. Sonia's image suddenly flashed across my mind, replacing the face of the old lady. The fear, that pressure on my chest, the smell of the hospital, the rain, and the coke came together in a mixture which would have been the envy of any young yob high on ecstasy. I made sure that my Beretta was safely nestling in my pocket and started walking down the corridor towards Intensive Care. About a dozen relatives were sitting waiting on plastic chairs. Dedes was not among them. He would have gone in and would be talking to the doctor. But the officer with the earring was there, bent over a water fountain at the rear of the room. I walked up to him briskly and noiselessly, and gave him a gentle whack on the back. He stepped back, muttering something, then looked at me, holding his bloodied lips. I waved my police I.D. under his nose, grabbed him by the arm, and opened a door marked LINEN. A young doctor was inside, cigarette in one hand and a plastic coffee cup full of stubs in the other. Still clutching my I.D., I waved it under his goggle eyes and asked him to step aside.

"I caught this punk having a piss in the corridor – he's under the influence of restricted substances. No need to make a big deal out of it and go upsetting the patients. I'll have him out of here in five minutes."

The poor little doctor managed a limp, "But he's bleeding!"

"I'll just check his identity and I'll take him across to Accident and Emergency myself if necessary."

I tossed a pillowcase at the casualty, who caught it and stuffed it into his mouth. I communicated to the doctor by way of a meaningful nod that his time was up, thanked him for his cooperation and locked the door. When the policeman saw me pull out my pistol, he turned the same shade of the pale green as the hospital issue pillowcase.

"Look, you little shit – do you know who I am?"

He shook his head with difficulty, not for a second taking his eyes off the Beretta.

"I don't hear you, shithead."

I ripped the pillowcase out of his mouth and watched the blood spatter across his light blue shirt. Something that sounded like a "yes" seemed to be coming out of his reddened lips, which had already started to swell.

"Are you following me everywhere I go or just here?"

"Just here."

"How many of you are there on each shift?"

"Three."

"What's your brief?"

His hands were shaking and his eyes were turned towards the floor. I leant back against a cupboard plastered in photographs of the singer Giorgos Dalaras and looked at my watch.

"We're under instructions to report any – I mean, if we see you go into Intensive Care."

"Whose instructions?"

"I . . . I don't . . . I don't know."

"What's your name? Or don't you know that either?"

"Karavidas – Konstantinos Karavidas."

"Where do you serve?"

"Narcotics."

"Have you any idea what I could do to you, Karavidas? Maybe not, eh? So you'd better listen. One morning, you'll be unlocking your car and my men will just happen to be there. What kind of car do you drive?"

"Audi."

"What kind of Audi?"

"Quattro."

"Nice. And that's registered in your name, is it?"

"No. It's . . . um, my sister's."

"Far-sighted. Now, where were we? Yes – my men, who aren't really very nice at all, will find you, show you their I.D.s and then they'll open up your lovely Quattro and right there, inside the reservoir that other law-abiding citizens keep filled up with fluid for their windscreen wipers, they'll find a nice half-kilo of heroin, which makes . . . ooh, twenty years! You'll serve at least half of those, and when you finally get out, you might find that your sphincter's a little on the loose side. You must have seen those American films – what a lovely time ex-cops have of it inside! Well, things aren't any different in our prisons, only we have Albanians instead of blacks."

He was on the brink of collapse. I checked my watch again.

"A name. That's all I need, Karavidas. And then you can relax."

"Are you serious?"

"I am. On condition that this stays between you and me. Got it? Because I'll find out at once if you go and blab."

"Of course."

"And you'll carry on as normal with your shifts; besides, I'm not intending to come back."

"Of course."

"Spit it out, then. Who are you reporting to?"

"Berios. Police Captain Evangelos Berios."

"Football Information."

That was the last thing I expected, but I left it at that. I put the Beretta back in my pocket, unlocked the door and grabbed his shaven head, bringing his ear right up to my mouth.

"Now all you have to do is pray that you never see me again, arse-hole," I muttered and left.

The little doctor, two grey-haired men with the faces of cardinals and three security guards had congregated outside.

"He'll be fine. Just make sure he has access to the appropriate counselling services," I said in my sweetest possible voice, flashed them my best smile and walked off.

The security guards caught up with me at the end of the corridor. It wasn't very hard to pump them for information because the minute they saw my I.D. they started treating me like a celebrity. I turned up my coat collar and walked out into the rain and ducked under the refectory awnings. Two cigarettes later Dedes turned up, his face the perfect complement to the black cloud that had descended overhead.

"Is she still alive?" I asked him flatly.

"Yes. Course."

"And?"

"She's doing well. I mean, she hasn't deteriorated."

"Did you see her?"

"Yes, I did. She was asleep."

"What did the doctor say?"

"He said that the consultant thinks that if there aren't any complications, she can move to a regular ward. They'll let us know – either us or Piertzovanis."

He plucked the gum out of his mouth and tossed it far away.

"Can I have a cigarette, boss?"

He struggled to get it lit and then sat down on the edge of a wet seat.

"She's very calm . . . very beautiful. I remember seeing her in an old film. I must have been a student at the time; I'd gone to a screening at the film club in Komotini. It was a difficult film, slow but good. I've only just realized who she was . . . is. Those pictures in the papers make her look somehow too made-up and, I don't know – different."

"'Windows'."

"Come again?"

"The title of the film, 1986."

"Oh, I can't remember. It was such a long time ago."

"I saw it in '99, on video. Do you remember that bit at the end when she's woken up by lightning and opens the window, sees the flashes, and goes barefoot out into the garden, a garden without any trees or flowers, to water the soil before the rain starts?"

"Yes, I think so."

"What a load of old crap! Bullshit symbolism: we create filth only to roll around in it later. How naïve can you get?"

He coughed, got rid of his cigarette and looked at me expectantly, as though he was waiting for some kind of confession, perhaps the truth he had guessed at. I decided to leave it for another, more difficult occasion and told him instead all about the Western I'd just staged in the linen cupboard with Karavidas. Something told me he did not entirely approve of my methods, but mercifully he kept his opinions to himself.

148

"Have you ever heard mention of a Police Captain, an Evangelos Berios – from the National Football Information Office?"

Before he got a chance to answer, my mobile rang. An unfamiliar number flashed up across the screen.

"Inspector Chronis Callaghan? We must meet." It was Piertzovanis.

"Where are you calling from?'

"From my new acquisition," he said sarcastically.

"Where are you?"

"With Noni, a small bottle of zero-star brandy and a twelve-year-old waiter who wants to chuck us out because he's expecting a large funeral party any minute. So everything's wonderful."

"How did it go?"

"Everything was fine – I slipped the right amount of money to the right people and we managed to get the small coffin next to the large one."

"How much have you had to drink?"

"Two bottles times zero stars equals zero. Don't worry. My African goalkeeper friend here will drive me back to his house, throw me into the bathtub and I'll be as good as new. I'll meet you at 9.00 – there's a business meeting at the Migrants' Centre in Exarcheia – the loveliest neighbourhood on earth. After the old lake at Marseilles, that is. Never mind – the big news is that Noni does actually remember something that you might find interesting."

"Are you out of your mind? I'm a police officer, remember; we're not exactly welcome in places like that."

"Don't worry. I'll look after you; I won't let any of those darkies hurt you."

The familiar feeling of despair which always overwhelmed me

whenever I had to deal with drunks seized me by the throat. The image of Sonia after yet another wasted evening.

"Simeon, that's not what I meant. Besides, the place is under constant police surveillance – both the Anti-terrorist lot and the Aliens lot watch it for at least twenty-five hours a day. Someone's bound to notice me."

"Wear a disguise!" he shouted and hung up. I looked at my watch. Two-and-a-half hours. Dedes was impatient for me to say something.

"I'm heading back to Syngrou to do a search on that Berios character. You go home, get some rest and I'll meet you outside the Vox in Exarcheia at 9.00."

"Is something wrong?"

"Piertzovanis has some information from Noni Latouse, the brother of the woman who —"

"What kind of information?"

"Didn't say. He was drunk. Not surprising really; he had been at a funeral after all. Have you ever had brandy at a funeral?"

"Oh, many times. At the kind without coffins."

"Funerals of the future."

"Something like that."

The rain had stopped. I nodded to Dedes, signalling that it was time to leave.

"It's time for us nice policemen to make a move, Manolis. Leave your gun at home; this is Exarcheia we're talking about."

"I thought I might stop by Syngrou myself and see what I can turn up on Berios. I think we need to get some rest now, don't we, Sir?"

"Oh, do we?"

He smiled.

"Yes, *you* do."

I left him sitting down on the edge of his sodden chair, deep in thought, wishing the profession he had chosen, or rather, had been forced into, could ever cohere with his vision of a better and fairer world. It would not take him long to realize that the enemy was already counting out its spoils.

"*Shall I tell you something that will make you jealous, tough guy? I was in love with a woman once.*"

"*In love?*"

"*Yes – Isabel Adjani. It was the summer of '80, or just before. Can't quite remember – at the Vox. I saw her in some Polish guy's film, half-mad, he must have been. She was playing a woman possessed, and I realized then that I would never get to be as good as her.*"

"*Possessed?*"

"*No, no. Not possessed: disturbed. That's a better word – sounds better, doesn't it?*"

"*So what does Isabel spend her time doing in this film? Looking sultry?*"

"*No. She was looking. Looking you in the eye. She's divine. What a goddess! The film itself was rubbish – trying to prove that we can resist Stalinism, that we can make better thrillers than the Americans, with that extra European je ne sais quoi. Are you listening, country boy?*"

"*I can hear your heart beat – very clearly.*"

"*Lucky you.*"

★

Dedes was outside the Vox, his head stuffed into the hood of a snow-white padded jacket. His computer search had not turned up anything useful about the police captain who had put his sniffer dogs on our tail. Berios: forty-one years old, had served for a while in the protection unit of some slimy, state-fed publisher of a P.A.S.O.K. weekly, and after our stunning victory against terrorism, was transferred to the National Football Information Office, the perfect job for a layabout, judging by the way they dealt with the phantasmagorical ceremonies at matches, regularly laid on by the armies of fans in the pay of various club owners. Dedes found shelter in a small café, and would wait there for news from this urgent meeting with a Nigerian goalkeeper I had been summoned to by a drunken lawyer.

The Migrants' Centre was housed in a two-storey neo-classical building with dark green shutters and a newly painted facade. On the marble steps leading to the front door sat a black man, feeding *souvlaki* to an emaciated dog. The two lines I had had a little earlier in the car heightened my self-confidence. I turned up my collar, took a quick look at the deserted streets, smiled at the African animal-lover, and made my decisive entrance into enemy territory. The small entrance hall was choked with posters, condemning the Olympic Games and warning of the disasters they would bring. I went up the broad wooden staircase and found myself in a large room full of bistro tables with a small bar at the back. Manning the bar was a young woman with a short boyish haircut, who was rummaging through a box of C.D.s. Rap music throbbed out of the speakers in a language I could not quite identify. Two Asian guys were talking at one of the tables over beer and crisps. I went up to the bar, and asked the girl for a Fanta. She opened a small domestic fridge and fished out a small bucket.

"Where's this song from?" I said, producing a €10 note.

"Algeria. Good, isn't it?" she said brightly, opening a box to find me some change. "Don't suppose you've got two euros, have you?"

"Don't worry. Think of it as a donation."

She flashed a pearly white smile at me and went back to the C.D.s. Before I had a chance to open the can, my mobile rang.

"It's Simeon. Where are you?"

"Inside a terrorist safe house."

"Get yourself something from the bar and tell the girl to bring you here."

"Here" was an upstairs room with a huge wooden table in the middle of it, and the surrounding walls resembled a map of the world. Posters which had incited millions of people from all corners of the earth to rise up in pointless outbursts, colourful pictures dominated by stylized roses, stars, clenched fists; brief accounts of colourful movements which struggled with unbelievable naïvety to resist the inevitable progress of the world. I never did have any time for activists – products of petit-bourgeois families, who would stand up in front of the television cameras, selling their smartly packaged indignation over the slaughter of innocent civilians in Gaza and then spend their evenings downing cases of whisky, drinking to the health of psychotic terrorists, and planning their holidays in Anafi or Koufonissia, all the time dreaming of nothing more than getting stoned and laid.

I stood there looking at a black and white poster raging against police brutality and remembered an architecture student about two years ago who reported two policemen who had grabbed him outside his house, pushed him to the ground and kicked the shit out of him. They were drunk at the time and apparently his ponytail and black clothes had provoked them. I told him that I would sort them out on condition that the press and television news did not get hold of the story. He gave me a ten-minute lecture, concluding that "you pigs are all the same". I told him that of all the creatures of the animal kingdom, the pig was the one I loved the most, took a detailed statement from him and commended him to the devil. The two policemen got a three-year suspended sentence and are still leaving me threatening messages on my answer phone for ruining their brilliant careers. After the trial I paid the revolutionary a visit. He opened the door and looked at me as though he had never seen me before; he was clean off his head and in the heady sweetness of it all, failed to recognize me.

"My name's Halkidis. I'm the officer to whom you reported the assault you suffered at the hands of two former colleagues of mine. They were sentenced the day before yesterday. Now perhaps you'd like to apologize to me for calling me a fascist."

"O.K., big guy – cool it!" he said, grinned broadly, turned his back on me and flopped down onto the designer sofa to resume his trip. I left, realizing for the thousandth time that you cannot sort people into categories of "good"and "bad"; only "sort-of-worthwhile" and "utterly worthless".

Three men were sitting round the wooden table waiting for me. Simeon, Noni, and a twenty-five-year-old with thick wavy hair, a bushy moustache and glasses with thick lenses. I put my Fanta and my cigarette on the table and sat down opposite him. Simeon made the introduction – he was a little pale but he did not seem to have been drinking.

"Chronis is in the Internal Affairs division of the police and is as interested as I am in finding out who is responsible for the fire.

Chronis – Stratos is one of the main board members of the Refugee Support Network. We've had a chat, and he wants to help. Obviously, nothing we say will leave this room."

Stratos smiled and stretched out his hand. I squeezed it and lit a cigarette. Piertzovanis followed suit and took a couple of swigs from a water bottle. Noni looked at me intently. He was still in the suit he had worn to the funeral: black jacket (a bit tight around the shoulders) and white shirt, no tie. He tried, without much success, to return my smile. Simeon was about to say something but I motioned him to wait.

"I have to ask you all to turn off your mobiles and leave them in another room. For obvious reasons."

Stratos raised his eyebrows, smiled, collected up everyone's mobiles and left the room.

"Very sophisticated," remarked Piertzovanis.

"Not really – but you can't be too sure."

As soon as Stratos was back, Simeon began.

"Noni has remembered a few things that might just lead us somewhere. I called Stratos, told him a bit about what was going on and we agreed it would be a good idea to get together and talk, all of us. You'll soon see why. Noni, I'll do the talking, but interrupt me if I leave anything out."

Noni nodded. His eyes were red-rimmed and he was fiddling with some sort of woven lucky charm. I could picture him at the stadium, defending his goal, not so much from the attacks from the other team as from stupid abuse from the stands.

"When I mentioned the possibility of arson, Noni remembered that as soon as I left the country last April, some really strange things started happening. Young kids on mopeds started chucking rubbish into the garden, cars with speakers on the outside would stop in front of the house late at night and leave as soon as Sonia or Manthos turned on the lights. They would smash the street lights. One night in late summer Morenike phoned him in tears, begging him to come over.

"They dumped two dead dogs and a dead cat into the garden. Then at the beginning of October they plastered racist slogans all over the fence: *Blacks Out – Fuck Africa – Make Your Own Soap: Melt Down a Junkie Today – Say No to Pollution – Keep Greece Greek.* Stuff like that."

"Did anyone sign this graffiti?"

Simeon looked at Noni. Noni looked at me. He stretched out his long arm, picked up my packet and lit a cigarette.

"Just one a day," he said.

His voice was trembling.

"Chronis is a good man. Seems good," he said, exhaling without actually inhaling first.

The compliment I had just received from this broken young lad intensified the awkwardness I felt in those surroundings.

"Thank you, Noni."

"Only the last one, it had a signature. Something like signature. A cross and . . ." He traced the outline of something, using his finger, in the air.

"A cross next to a lightning flash," Stratos said.

"That doesn't mean anything to me, but I can easily —"

"We'll explain – let Simeon finish first. He won't take long," interrupted the activist.

"Sonia went to the municipality to complain about the broken street lights. Manthos went to the local station about the dead animals. They reassured him, saying that there were a lot of young gypsy kids in the area as well as junkies, and promised they would keep an eye out. They didn't say anything to me about it. I phoned them from Marseilles once a week and they said everything was fine. One Sunday night in November – Noni went round every Sunday to cook them his speciality, this weird fish soup with peppers —"

"*Obe eza tutu*, it is called."

Noni's clarification was delivered with a bitter laugh that froze us all. Simeon cleared his throat and went on.

"That Sunday, while they were eating, there was a power cut. Noni went to check the fuse box round the back of the house. Someone had forced it open and stuck a piece of paper inside saying, 'It's over – get the hell out NOW'. Sonia filed a complaint with the police. Your people came along and took some prints, but never came back."

"Come on, mate – drop the 'my people' routine. I'm in the job I'm in precisely because I want to catch 'my people'."

"We all make choices in life, Comrade Policeman – we all chose to belong somewhere," he said, having fun with my aggression.

Noni then surprised everyone around him with the sobriety of his contribution. "Simeon, stay cool – O.K.? We agreed. The policeman is a good man."

Then it was the turn of the curly-haired revolutionary to show off his organizational skills.

"Let's form a group with definite aims; I don't think we'll need to —"

I stopped him, apologizing meekly, explaining away my outburst as a consequence of exhaustion. I did not think it wise to explain that coke sometimes made me oversensitive. Piertzovanis took over.

"As soon as Noni told me all this, I immediately suspected some neo-Nazi group and got on the phone to Stratos, who's got a lot of experience in this area. The Network here collects all kinds of information from the statements of migrants relating to violence they've suffered at the hands of these types of gangs. He looked through the records and discovered that there is a group that operates in this area and uses the symbol of a cross and a lightning flash."

"Yes," Stratos broke in. "The organization operates in the wider area. Its base is in Aghia Paraskevi. They call themselves the Black Wave and consist mostly of Olympiakos and Panathinaïkos fans. Every Sunday they fight at the stadiums, and trash each other's offices, but they've drawn up this contract of joint action against migrants. One of their favourite games is going after street sellers, Filipinos and Africans selling pirate C.D.s. Their boss is someone called Agisilaos, who declares his allegiance to a Berlin club that uses blue and white colours – Hertha or something like that – and he owns a karate academy."

"How do you know all this?"

"There are people in every neighbourhood who are worried about all this, Mr Halkidis, people who try to resist it as much as they can."

He wasn't being sarcastic. Not at all. He tried to make me see the obvious. Even so, I got annoyed.

"I'm worried too, young man. And I try to resist too. And I put up with unspeakable shit each and every day so that I can defend all these bloody institutions. But I don't go smashing shop windows. I don't go robbing banks, and I don't burn down —"

Piertzovanis saved me from the worst.

"Chronis, calm down. Remember, this is about Sonia, after all.

You've driven yourself crazy trying to understand what's going on. We – all of us – we only want to help. We have lost people too – don't forget that. If you don't like it, leave. But if you do stay, don't insult anyone else."

I apologized for the second time in fifteen minutes and excused myself. In the toilets, I took my dose, cursed my reflection in the cracked mirror, saluted a sticker bearing the image of Che staring down at me condescendingly and went back to the chamber of revelations. Noni had taken off his tight black jacket and Piertzovanis had drunk his water bottle dry. The activist was relaxed and cheerful.

"I can understand why this confuses you, Officer. I can understand your difficulty in accepting this bizarre alliance. It's also feels strange for me, sitting here talking to a senior police officer. But look, in three months I'll have finished my thesis in Thessaloniki on the thermodynamics of black holes. Seriously. I am an astrophysicist, or rather hope to become one. I've applied to an American university. They might just overlook my principles and take me. It'll be such a pleasure to go to the capital of capitalism. I'll learn a lot about the world there. Maybe when I get to your age I might start saying, 'what an idiot I was in my youth'. I don't know. But I do know that I haven't smashed a single shop window, never thrown a Molotov cocktail. I'm not saying I wouldn't if it came to it. But there's one thing I'll never be able to get out of my head. As far as violence goes, the only people who are not to blame are the weak."

"If you're trying to recruit me, you'll have your work cut out for you."

"Not really, Officer. We belong to the same party – the N.G.P."

"The N.G.P.?"

"Yes, the Naïve and Guilty Party."

I had to admit it, he was quite a good bloke. I just wished he would stick to science and leave out the professional consciousness raising. We made a truce and got to the point. This violent gang frequented a billiard club on the Halandri–Aghia Paraskevi borders. The owner was the son of a former officer of the junta, Papagiotis, who had maintained an excellent relationship with absolutely anyone who had any sort of local or regional power. Their leader Agisilaos would prove his mental and physical strength before a small court of subjects. They in turn let him win at the billiard table in exchange for protection at football matches, strip joints and other seedy venues. In addition to migrants, they regularly went after homosexuals, transvestites, whores and junkies, not only with the blessing of local policemen but also the support of clubs, iron bars, knuckledusters, kitchen knives, and daggers. They cut quite a figure in the well-to-do northern suburbs, going around on enormous motorbikes, in 4×4s and cabriolets with crosses hanging on their broad, hairy chests, and vacuous girlfriends with their signature elongated vowels, trying to emulate their idols at expensive private colleges.

As I listened to Stratos' speech, I tried to form a plan of action and was grateful for the little white friend who was helping me stay decisive and in fighting form.

"I've said as much as I know. From now on it's up to you. Naturally, this meeting never took place. I have complete confidence in Simeon, but . . ."

"But not in the police, right? I approve absolutely, Stratos, my friend. Just as you'll come to realize over the next few days, that I don't have much faith in them either."

He laughed benevolently.

"Yes, I approve absolutely. I have to leave you now. I have to go down and set up the microphones. We're expecting three of our Italian comrades, accordionists. They're from Bologna – really fantastic. Should be a good little party – why don't you stay?"

"Duty calls, comrade," I said, shaking his hand.

"When did you last hear the accordion, Colonel?" Simeon asked as soon as he left.

I offered Noni a cigarette. He did not take it. I lit up and let my eyes roam to a poster across the room from me – it was a snail with its fist raised aloft, announcing "Planet Earth is our homeland". Bullshit. The only "homeland" I have ever known was Sonia's burnt flesh, and I fully intended to go and play a game of billiards with those bastards who had plundered it. Simeon was onside without a second thought. Noni was off home: his dark skin would make it awkward. Dedes, who was waiting patiently in the bar across from the Refugee Centre, Fotini, who was willing to relinquish her solitude, Simeon and I were going to pay a visit to the billiard club and make the acquaintance of Agisilaos – or at least discover where to find him.

"Chronis – I've got a serious suggestion, one that improves on yours, as well as maximizing the impact of the group."

Piertzovanis had walked Noni out and was back caressing a glass of whisky.

"Let's hear it."

"It's not that clever if we three louts walk into that place with just one woman – what's her . . . what did you say your secretary's name was?"

"Fotini. Thirty-five, bit on the chubby side, but a fine woman."

"What about your assistant – he's young, isn't he?"

"Thirty-two."

"O.K. – the trick is I walk in there with young Fotini, seeing as I'm the oldest. Your assistant comes in holding hands with Rania – remember the young woman who wasn't at all impressed with your tough guy act the other day in my flat? I'm supposed to be meeting her soon."

"If you think that was my tough guy act, my lawyer friend, you haven't seen anything."

"Brrr . . . Just a minute. Listen, what we need is a little parliamentary democracy round here. O.K., so in the formation that I have just outlined, we will walk in there as two well-matched couples. You'll arrive ten minutes later. Your assistant will casually start asking about Agisilaos, and —"

"Bravo, my legal eagle, nice idea, but don't exert yourself unnecessarily. Go and ask the young girl if she can get herself up to look really slutty. You know, put on something a bit minimal, at least a couple of metres above the knee. What are her legs like?"

"I really couldn't say."

"Never mind. Tell her to slap on the make-up and do whatever I tell her. The situation's under control. And no more drinking tonight. We're not going to a children's playground, you know."

Piertzovanis looked at the glass in his hand and then across at me, acknowledging defeat. He drained the liquid gold in one gulp and left me by myself in this multicoloured terrorist hideout. The accordions had already started their lament downstairs. I phoned Dedes and Fotini and explained the plan to them, winked at the snail that was still shaking its fist in the air and went down the wooden staircase. The ground floor was packed out with young men and women who were persuaded that the future belonged to them. Three dark-haired types with shiny accordions were playing songs, a hybrid, it seemed, of children's songs and revolutionary battle cries. The audience was singing along, miming the foreign lyrics with adolescent uncertainty. They were happy. I hated them. I ducked quickly into the toilet and snorted two fat lines of powder, confiding my sinful thoughts to the Che Guevara sticker: Everyone lives in the world they deserve, and my particular world cannot take any more accordion music.

"Do you like the accordion, young man?"

"No."

"Why not?"

"It reminds me of blind people."

"I like it."

"Why?"

"Because it opens and closes."

"So what?"

"And then it opens and closes again. You hear it opening again and again, like it wants to rip through the wind. And together, the same moment, you see it asking for something. You can see it breathing. It struggles for breath, but it's still alive."

*

The billiard club was on the first floor of a shopping centre. On the narrow balcony that ran along the outside was a flashing neon light in the shape of a fox, stretched across the top of some letters in gothic script informing anyone who wanted to know that here was the Black Fox. The wide pavement below was strewn with a dozen or so nicely polished motorbikes, mostly B.M.W.s and Ducatis. We parked our small motorcade opposite them: my Golf, Dedes' police Citroën and Fotini's high-end Cinquecento. The two Aghia Paraskevi couples listened to my final instructions: the beefy Simeon with Fotini, dressed for a full night at a seriously bad nightclub, and Dedes with young Rania, who would have tempted even an archbishop from the path of righteousness in her barely existent mini skirt and her scanty excuse for a top. Our performance would rely on Rania's and Dedes' talents for improvisation. The aim of the first act was to make Agisilaos fall for Rania's charms, or, failing that, one or other of his men.

The lawyer and my secretary were the first to go up, shortly followed by Dedes and Rania. Meanwhile I had a cigarette and a couple more lines, listened to the 11.00 p.m. news on the car radio and tried really hard to persuade myself that that fatty, who in a couple of months would become prime minister, was our saviour and would deliver us from financial ruin and corruption. It didn't work. I stubbed my cigarette out on the seat of one of those B.M.W.s and crossed the threshold of the Black Fox. I counted eight pool tables, two table tennis tables, and about thirty pretty boys with closely cropped hair, each a disgrace to the human race. Two or three of them were wearing combat trousers, and the rest of them looked like dummies in leather shops. The few girls there were ridiculously young and looked as though they were on the verge of anorexic collapse, puffing away on their Marlboro Lights and shrieking each time a ball landed in a pocket.

I sat at the bar, lit a cigarette, pulled out my mobile and dialled 141. The sweet voice on the other end informed me that it was 11.13 and something. I listened as she calmly reached 11.14 precisely and hung up. The barman, a dark-haired man in his thirties whose face announced that he had long since tired of life, waited for my order. I asked for a small beer and redialled 141. As soon as the beer arrived, I angrily shut my mobile off and tossed it onto the bar.

"Not turned up, has she?" he asked conspiratorially.

I gave him the most gormless grin I could muster.

"No, no – she's waiting for me back home. A good friend of mine asked me to come here and meet someone called Agisilaos and give him a C.D. I don't know what this man looks like, and I'm calling him and calling him, but he's not answering. Do you know this Agisilaos? You couldn't point him out to me, could you?"

"He's not here. Hasn't been in for days."

"Just my bloody luck. I've come all the way from Kolonaki. I don't suppose any of his mates are here – I could give it to one of them to pass on to him?" Plan B was now in operation. I produced one of Dedes' C.D.s from my pocket. Bob Dylan covers.

The barman pointed to a group crowded around one of the billiard tables at the back.

"That lot over there, they're really tight with him."

Agisilaos' best buddies were four hulks and two young girls, laden with three tonnes of make-up. I thanked the barman and left him €10.

"Keep the change – but do me a favour, will you?"

"If I can."

"I'll leave the C.D. with you, and you hand it to him when you next see him. I don't want to interrupt those boys."

He nodded, took the banknote and the C.D. and left me in peace. I stood and observed Agisilaos' friends. They seemed to be playing something that looked more like pool to me, but maybe they had agreed that the player who succeeded in shattering the white ball would be the winner.

Simeon and Fotini were sitting at a small table near the door drinking *frappés*. My secretary played her part to perfection. She was on the phone arguing loudly with a mythical friend at the other end of the line about which nightclub on Iera Odos they should end the evening in. I took a sip of my beer, and turned my attention to the other couple. Dedes was pretending to teach Rania how to do a French three-cushion shot while she acted the bored girlfriend, sending longing looks across to the other tables. The success of this plan relied on how brazen she could be and how well she could act. She was doing extremely well already. Her wardrobe choices had resulted in a lot of male as well as female attention – discreet at first, overt as time went on, and the hatred emanating from the painted eyes of the women cut right through the smoky atmosphere. I subtly managed to signal Agisilaos' friends to Dedes. He went up behind Rania, right up close, whispered in her ear and took hold of her hands, ostensibly to correct the way she was holding the cue. She quickly released herself from his grip, tossed the cue onto the baize, strode proudly across to our prey, grabbed a shot glass from the hand of a huge blond man and threw it in Dedes' face.

"You piece of shit! Who do you think you are? Only real men get to touch my arse – not queers like you."

Dedes wiped the drink off his face with his sleeve and started to move towards her. The girl backed away towards the table with the big guys. The blond took her by the shoulder in a don't-you-worry-baby-I'm-here sort of way. The rest was easier than we had imagined. Dedes was approaching the livid-red Rania, rebuffing the pushing and shoving he was on the receiving end of, with lukewarm remonstrations from the brutes who were protecting her. He gave the little tart a hurt look, dropped a €20 note on the table, put on his coat and left the hall with his tail between his legs. He was going to wait for us outside, with his engine running, mobile in hand, keeping an eye on the traffic and the sabotage that was part of the second stage of the plan. Rania said something to her knight in shining armour, who was being congratulated by his friends, took the cigarette he was desperately offering her and made her way to the bar with all the confidence of a catwalk model. She sat down next to me, looked at me ecstatically, flashed me a triumphant smile, which luckily no-one noticed, and then swivelled her stool round ninety degrees blinding me with the sight of her bright white back. Her muscle-bound *chevalier* was by her side in a matter of seconds.

"What are you drinking, gorgeous?" he smiled inanely.

"A shot of Ursus," she said, still wonderfully confused by what had just happened.

"Two Jack Daniels," he commanded the barman, his eyes beginning their descent into Rania's *décolletage.*

I picked up my mobile from the bar and called Simeon.

"Congratulations, my lawyer friend, as you can see our right-winger has already scored. Are you ready?"

"Not quite. I'm busy here with Fotini, analyzing the appalling character of that autocratic boss of hers, which, according to her, is the consequence of a difficult childhood, which —"

"Be serious. I'm leaving the phone on. If you can't hear properly, come up and get a drink."

"O.K., boss."

I put it down on the bar, close to Rania but out of view of her companion. The barman came along with the shots, and said they were on the house. Rania downed hers in one and came straight to the point.

"I met this guy once, it was a really crazy scene, someone called Agisilaos. But I was with someone, a real arsehole, worse than the one you dealt with back there, and we didn't get a chance to talk much. Just enough for him to tell me about this place you all come to here. He was right. It's cool."

"No kidding? Agisilaos is like – we're like brothers!"

"Is he here? I was completely off my face that night, and I don't remember too well what he looks like."

"No. He's not here tonight."

"Doesn't matter. You look pretty cool to me."

The incredible hulk reprised his ridiculous grin, took a sip of bourbon and grimaced like the Marlboro Man. You had to admire the girl, who continued her performance without flagging.

"What about those bikes downstairs? They yours?"

"Mine's the black Ducati, the —"

"Black Ducati?" Rania screamed like a little kid whose letter to Santa has just been answered, making sure the information reached the intended recipient. I looked across at Simeon who reassured me with a rapid wink.

"I'm crazy about Ducatis. The guys own the B.M.W.s, the yellow 1000ccs and the purple 600."

"Wow! Wicked coincidence!" shrieked Rania again. "I knew these twins once who used to ride yellow B.M.W. 1000s! They didn't like 600s. Can't say I do either – especially the purple ones. Can't stand purple – it's the colour of feminists. Did you know that?"

"Yeah. And who'd ever fuck a feminist?"

"Have you ever been with one?"

The blond idiot grimaced again.

"Feminist? Are you serious? I wouldn't let a feminist look at it, let alone touch it."

"Very wise. She might try to cut it off."

Her humour was wasted on him, and he restricted himself to a grunt that evolved into a very shrewd observation.

"We've been talking all this time and I don't even know your name. I'm Daniel. You?"

"I don't believe it. Oh my God! This is too much!"

"What?"

"My name's Daniela! My grandmother's Italian."

The beast stood stock still. I brushed past Rania and dropped a mobile phone into her pocket. She was capable of keeping herself amused all night with her victim's inadequacies. I spotted Simeon out of the corner of my eye, his mobile still glued to his ear. He had to bury his face in Fotini's chest to hide his laughter. Rania realized that her role was almost played out, and signalled to the barman for another couple of shots.

"These are on me – alright?" she announced in a hoarse voice, giving him a quick peck on the cheek.

"Whatever you say," he said, trying to recover from the shock.

Simeon was on his feet, helping Fotini into her fancy coat. He paid the barman for their coffees and left, his arm around his companion's waist. In a minute, he would indicate to Dedes which motorbikes would need to be taken to the nearest tyre specialists in the morning. Rania touched my knee and turned to the blond.

"You know what I'd like right now?"

"Just name it."

"First introduce me to your friends. Then take me for a quick

169

burn-up on the black Ducati. Up to Dionyssos and everything, really lean in on those bends, so that my stockings get shredded at the knee, and afterwards . . ."

She let that thought merge with the smoke in the bar.

"Leave the afterwards to me," said the blond, who, completely hot under the collar, got up from his stool, sliding his fingers through his blond hair and walked Rania over to his friends, who welcomed him with cat calls and macho slaps on the back.

After I had paid, I ducked into the toilets to recharge my batteries before stepping outside into the cold, ready for my second violent encounter in the space of just a few hours. Fotini was waiting in the Cinquecento, behind Dedes' Citroën which was purring away gently. My assistant was standing on the low wall of an empty fountain while Simeon was producing enough liquid to fill the tank of a Land Rover, whistling The Internationale off key as he pissed. The gang's motorbikes were a few centimetres closer to the ground now, thanks to Dedes, who had been using them to sharpen the jagged blade of the knife he used for gutting fish on his camping trips. To me, that was way over the top – excessively cautious, but I didn't want to upset him and spoil the pleasure he had no doubt taken in this symbolic act of castration. I took the Beretta out of my pocket, made sure the catch was on, and hid myself behind the fountain with Dedes.

Rania was the first out. She emerged singing "We are the Champions" without a care in the world. Before he knew it, her companion had my pistol sticking into the back of his blond head as Dedes twisted his arms behind his back, slipped on the handcuffs and sealed his mouth with duct tape. In fewer than ten seconds he was sprawled face down in a heap in the back of the Citroën. Rania dived into the car, pulled his hair and screamed straight in to his ear, "Don't fuck feminists, do you, arsehole? Can't stand the sight of them? Maybe it's time you find out how a feminist would go about fucking you!"

I pulled her out of the car before she managed to do him any permanent damage and led her over to Fotini's car. I said goodbye to the ladies after planting a kiss on each cheek, chucked the keys to the Golf across to Simeon, and sat down next to Dedes, indifferent to the murmurs coming from the bound animal on the back seat. I gave the order to drive off.

The streets were empty. In ten minutes we would be at the burnt house. I reckoned that the worm would wriggle much more readily if we took him to that nightmarish environment, especially if he had anything at all to do with its creation. We heaved the gagged creature into the garden, and laid him on his back across the bonnet of the burnt-out Hillman. Dedes handed Piertzovanis an enormous torch, the kind you use for underwater fishing, and pulled a folding truncheon from his pocket. I lit up, and pretended to release the safety catch on the Beretta. The blond's eyes ballooned to the size of side plates.

"This place hold any memories for you?" I asked him while Simeon shone the torch over the black walls.

Daniel muttered something.

"You're not being clear. I'll take that tape off your mouth if you promise me to talk to nicely, like you do to your girlfriend on the phone. But if you go raising your voice, you lose a knee. Do we understand each other?"

He moved his head up and down. Dedes ripped the duct tape off his mouth with only a modicum of sensitivity. The whine the pain provoked modulated into sobs the instant his cheek caught the palm of my assistant's hand. I was astonished that this staunch defender of civil rights was capable of such violence, but I let it go.

"Didn't we say that causing friction was off limits? I don't want to hear any wild screaming, young man. All I want is a nice little chat. You see, this game has only got one rule: I do the asking; you do the answering. Every time I get a wrong answer, I will hurt you. You won't know how until after you've made your mistake. We might, just for argument's sake, test the resistance of your anus with the help of that large truncheon my friend over there is holding. Or we might suggest to that other gentleman over there, the one holding the torch, that he might like to take a crap on that lovely pink face of yours. Hey! Torchman – what did you have for dinner today?"

The expression on Simeon's face told me that I had gone too far, but, all the same, he let the word *fasolada* escape. Daniel's sobs intensified. I thought of Sonia, imagining her trying to escape the flames, and kicked him on the shin.

"Don't interrupt when I'm talking. O.K. – so I've explained more or less what happens if you give the wrong answer. But if you happen to give a right answer, you get a point. If you get ten points, you'll be a rich man. You see, we do believe in fair play."

"We haven't got much time, boss," Dedes said as he produced a reporter's tape recorder from his pocket.

"First question: What's your name?"

"Daniel Georgopoulos."

"One point! Question two: have you been here before?"

"No, never."

"You lose a point. We equalize. Question three: Have you ever participated in acts of violence?"

He gave me a look that implied that he didn't understand Greek – which he probably didn't.

"Hesitation. Time's up," I announced cheerfully and gave Dedes the signal.

He walked up to him and raised his truncheon. The blond worm was wriggling so much that he almost fell off the bonnet.

"I promise, I've never . . . never been here before."

Dedes looked at me. I pulled Daniel up by the collar. His sweat stank of aftershave.

"Tell us about your friend Agisilaos."

"What do you want to know?"

"Where he is now will do for starters."

"Why . . . why are you looking for him?"

"Listen, you little shit! I do the asking round here!" I shouted and smacked him round the face.

His nose burst open and he started crying like a small child. Piertzovanis was about to say something, but I stopped him before he got the chance. The last thing I needed was to listen to some bullshit about human rights and that wanker was quite capable of laying it on. Luckily he backed off and carried on shining the torch onto the scene. I glanced at my watch and then at the blond.

"I won't wait much longer. It was a simple question. Where is your friend Agisilaos?"

"I don't know. Really I don't . . ."

I threw my cigarette to the ground, stuffed the Beretta back in my pocket, searched his, found his mobile and turned to Dedes.

"Gag him, break his knees and ankles, tie him to the steering wheel of the old banger and leave him here. He had it coming, the idiot. Someone might find him in the morning. He might get lucky."

I motioned to Simeon to follow me and we walked across to the fence, very slowly. The screams of "no!" coming from the young man sounded like tyres braking on wet tarmac.

"Boss – I think the little prick might have remembered something. Do you want to hear what it is or should I make a start?"

"Coming," I said, feigning boredom and turned back. "Get it on tape."

Fear had loosened his tongue. Once the blond confirmed that his statement was freely made and not coerced, he came up with much more than we had anticipated.

After he had described the almost military structure of their organisation, the Black Wave, the nationalistic literature which they were made to read, their belief in the historical continuity of the Greek race, their not-so-covert admiration for the *Führer*, the endless hours they spent keeping fit at the gym, and Agisilaos' conviction about the crucial role they played, fighting alongside the pure elements within the Order, he arrived at what interested us.

On Saturday, January 14, about 11.00 in the evening, Agisilaos left the billiard club with his two closest heavies, climbed into a 4×4, and set off for the old shack, as they were pleased call their target. For a few months now, the head of this gang had been working on a campaign of terror against the tenants. Exactly what Noni had told us. The rubbish and the carcasses in the garden, the offensive slogans graffitied on the fence, the damaged electricity meter. Our thug had agreed to smash the street lights with his airgun. He was not just a pretty face, he was also a member of the rifle club. Agisilaos and his mates, whose names and addresses the blond now had no difficulty recalling, had vanished off the face of the earth the minute it got out that the house had burnt down, complete with tenants. Daniel admitted to talking on the telephone with his boss three days earlier. He was lying low in some monastery until things calmed down. He was fine, if you ignored the sexual harassment he was subjected to by the holy men. The blond did not know where the monastery was, but that did not matter because Agisilaos had phoned from their landline, and the number was stored on Daniel's mobile. By morning Fotini would have managed to pinpoint the hideaway.

I told Dedes to take off the handcuffs and wait for me with Piertzovanis by the cars. The blond looked at me imploringly. I slid the Beretta out of my pocket and said, very calmly, stroking the piece as I did so, "I could easily finish you off and leave your carcass here to rot. It would probably take about a week for the stench to get you discovered. You would be a bit out of shape of course. Rats have an excellent sense of smell and a regrettable weakness for human flesh. But I won't because I don't think I need to. Do you know why I don't think I need to? Because I think you've worked out what kind of man I am, and you realize that if you breathe a word of our little discussion to anyone, I'll find out and I'll come after you wherever you're hiding. Now, go back to your friends and carry on as normal. And you'll forget about Agisilaos. Do I make myself clear?"

A breathless "of course" slipped out of his mouth.

"Daniel – isn't that your name, eh?"

He nodded.

"Daniel – you have no idea how lucky you've been tonight."

I pointed my pistol at his face. He shielded it with his hands and burst into tears. I spat on his lacerated wrists and went off to find the others, not knowing for sure whether Sonia would have gone for that over a warm bullet through his forehead.

Thursday, 11.35 p.m.

I wonder where all those girlfriends, those liars with their fine phrases are sleeping now? They used to help me when I needed them. It's not fair. Why does Virginia have a more robust liver than mine? How can Medea carry on living with all that guilt? And that crazy Electra gets away with it, and they still applaud her, enthusiastically at that. Then there's Lulu, who screws around shamelessly – stupid whore. She's almost chalked up a hundred. Winnie! Smiling idiotically in that ridiculous little rubbish mound of hers. Lyuba grieving with such dignity over a vanished cherry orchard. Not one of them has been to see me – and we were meant to be best friends! Shitty, fair-weather friends, the lot of them. Just as long as they get their tidy little pensions in perpetuity they don't give a damn about their old comrades. Never mind the fact that I spent my entire life taking better care of them than maids, better than sisters. Bitches! How can they leave me imprisoned in a white dream, defenceless in a foreign place, where the cold is the only vegetation. I know, I grew to know them really well. I know that they'll go looking for other fools like me, other youths to destroy. You can all leave . . . queens of deception . . .

I'm getting thirsty again. Simeon – can you hear me? Bring me something to drink, sweetheart, just a sip, one little sip from your mouth. Hot from your mouth.

CHAPTER 6

Simeon Piertzovanis
Goes on a Day Trip

30.i
Friday, 9.30 p.m.

I had just had my coffee and was about to change Rina's water when that infernal device started whining and blinking. Halkidis just wouldn't take no for an answer.

"You're coming with me. The monastery where our man's hiding out is just beyond Karpenisi, not even three hours away. We're very close, very, very close and we can't back off now. Meet me at 2.00 outside the Polytechnic, at the gates the tanks used."

I was not trying to "back off"; I just wanted to give my canary her water, treat her to a piece of apple and force her to take pity on the only creature on this earth who has ever cared for her. Last night had hit me hard. I couldn't deal with it, neither through the punches I threw at the walls, nor with the half bottle I downed in my attempts to pass out. My only hope of cleansing my wretched mind of the violence that had defiled it was a solid afternoon drinking session alone with my bottle, the shutters firmly down, Rina singing away, photographs of Sonia spread out in strict chronological order, that corny English comedy she had done at the beginning of her decline playing on the video, Simeon Piertzovanis a snivelling wreck on the floor, waiting to hear the doctor's voice on the answer phone announcing that unfortunately the 1954 Sonia had been withdrawn, the motor having been destroyed in a head-on collision with an armoured vehicle, and the parts no longer available. I would wait for the announcement, curled up in a heap with the old pictures right in front of my eyes, as though I was entirely innocent. After that everything would be easy. I had a lot to wait for, and I would wait. I would not neglect the canary. Never. I would turn on the television every evening to persuade myself that there is greater misery than mine out there, and I would wait. I'd explain to sweet little Rania that she was a terrific girl who had been born too late, but I would wait. I would let that insane policeman pursue a past he was not equal to and I would wait, just like those cantankerous old men who wait to hear just one spontaneous "Happy New Year!" from their grandchildren. I would wait for one more departure, for the sadness of one more loss, for one more low-key winter funeral.

Rina shouted something at me, something along the lines of "I'm fed up with your whingeing", and began an assault on my central nervous system with noises attributable only to exhibitionist successors of Minkus. I poured water for her, whisky for me, sat at my desk, lit a cigarette and phoned Halkidis.

"Chronis? Simeon. Listen – I can't come with you today."

"Why not?"

"I'd rather see Sonia than yet another criminal."

"I've sorted that out with Fotini. She'll be there at visiting time."

"I mean it."

I could hear something like a fax coming through on the other end. And then a door closing.

"Are you sure you don't want to help anymore?"

"Not today. Maybe tomorrow. We'll see."

"O.K. I'll wait at the Polytechnic till 2.05, just in case you change your mind."

"I won't."

"A pity," he said, and hung up, irritation in his voice.

I hurled the mobile against the wall, narrowly missing my framed photograph of Romy Schneider. Rina started flapping frantically. The whole thing had smashed to pieces. I emptied my glass and let my forehead drop to the desk. It was the shame. I could not be rid of it. It had pitched its tent inside me, and would pop up every time I thought about the events of last night and my part in the interrogation of the blond fascist. The two cops did a professional job, perhaps a little too angrily, but anger is an acceptable emotion in such circumstances. The ever sober Simeon Piertzovanis, however, the longer it went on, was enjoying himself like the classic idiot in the crowd watching the boxer choking on his own blood. I wasn't short of excuses: the exile and torture my father had been subjected to and which had screwed up my childhood; the images of his comrades, who took care of me, and who, to their dying day, honoured lives destroyed by the victors. I remembered something an old man in Thessaloniki, who had never had any regrets, said to me years ago: "Civil wars never end." But most of all it was a woman, a woman who was slowly dying. I was too afraid to admit that if I wanted to keep Sonia alive inside me, I would have to team up with an honourable but ruthless policeman, play the part of an apprentice cowboy, and admit that I envied his unconditional devotion to her. But then again, maybe I would not have to resort to excuses and cheap psychologizing. I am a lawyer and therefore know that there is no legal route to justice when injustice is supported by representatives of the law. But Chronis was not interested in justice: he wanted revenge, a concept that had never meant anything to me, but somehow yesterday I had begun to articulate it. Perhaps because I worried that if centuries later Sonia were to turn round and ask me "What did you ever do for me?" I would want to be able to give her a more convincing answer than, "I waited".

A second whisky failed to clear my head. I threw on my coat and walked out into the freezing sunshine, still dogged by the nightmare image of the loser drunkard and the coked-up cop fighting the forces of darkness.

The wooden door to the Migrants' Centre stood half open. I pushed it and climbed the stairs to the bar. The stools were all inverted on the tables and a tall woman of about thirty with the body of an athlete was mopping the floor and singing something that sounded like a slow tarantella. As soon as she saw me, she interrupted her performance, and without a shred of embarrassment gave me a big smile. She had tied her hair back into a ponytail and I struggled to see her eyes through the large dark circles.

"It's been stuck inside my head since yesterday. We had some Italian musicians over and it went on till morning."

"Yes," I said absently, "I popped in for a bit."

She looked me up and down, as far as her condition allowed.

"Don't I know you from somewhere?"

"I don't think so."

"Are you looking for someone? We're usually closed in the morning."

"No, I just dropped in. I live round here and . . ."

"Are you alright? Do you need anything?"

Apparently my face also had something of the night before about it.

"No, I'm fine," I said and turned to leave.

"Be careful, won't you?"

Her voice was warm. I stopped.

"Careful?"

"I thought I saw you shaking."

"It's the cold."

"Oh, right."

She was leaning on the mop handle, hesitating before she finally came out and said, "The truth. What are you doing here at this time of day?"

"I'm looking for Stratos," I said without thinking. "Do you know where I can find him?"

"Stratos?"

"Yes, the astrophysicist."

She burst out laughing.

"And where would you expect to find an astrophysicist of a morning?"

"I don't know. Where?" I said uncomfortably.

"Think about it: Astrophysicist? Morning?"

She abandoned the mop, grabbed one chair in each hand with admirable strength and put them down in the middle of the floor.

"Take a seat. It's easier to think sitting down."

I sat down, unsure whether she was playing with me or was slightly mad. She straddled her chair backwards and asked me for a cigarette.

"Gitanes! Nice," she said, hurriedly lighting it with a black Zippo she fished out of the pocket of her black jeans. She closed her eyes and took a long, deep drag on it.

"So where can I find an astrophysicist at 11.00 in the morning?" I asked her, interrupting her march towards Nirvana.

She gave me a sly look.

"What do astrophysicists study?"

"The stars?"

It was not a rhetorical question. I genuinely did not know what astrophysicists did.

"That's right, Mr Gitanes. And when do the stars come out?"

"At night."

"And if an astrophysicist discovers a new star one night, wouldn't it make sense for him to continue observing it with his long telescope?"

I was confused. I was never up to much in the mornings. To my relief, this tall woman challenged my intellect no further.

"Stratoulis left with a starlet he discovered last night, here in this hotbed of anti-globalizing debauchery. Who knows when he'll complete his research."

I laughed with what little enthusiasm I had left.

"Do you need any help with the cleaning?" I asked when one of my coughing fits was over. They never missed an opportunity to remind me that my lungs were no longer robust enough for such extreme sports as laughter.

"No. Almost done. It's not like a man to be so eager to help."

"Are you suggesting that the male revolutionaries around here don't lend a hand with the chores?"

"Do I really look like such a helpless little woman to you?" she said, feigning anger, releasing a volley of baritone cackles that left me open-mouthed. "Oh, come on – it was a joke. My real laugh is almost feminine," she insisted, and offered me her hand. "Eva – Independent Lesbian Community."

"Simeon," I whispered, barely able to speak.

"I haven't made you feel uncomfortable, have I? A little, maybe? You're a friend of Stratos', you say. Are you his professor?"

"Do I look like an astrophysicist? I'll take that as a compliment?"

"No – it's just that you're skinny and scientists are always skinny."

"They forget to eat – at least according to the stereotype. So – what do you do?"

"Assistant Director of Photography. Television mostly. I've done a short as well."

"Can I guess what it was about?"

"There's no way you could," she said with a glint in her eye.

"Shall I try?"

"O.K. – one fag for every wrong answer."

"Deal."

She had turned into a mischievous little girl – a very pretty mischievous little girl.

"First guess. I'll have three. Three wrong guesses and you get the whole pack."

"Off you go."

"Short film about traditionally male professions in which gender equality has now been achieved."

"One down."

She asked me for the pack, plucked out a cigarette and slid it behind her ear.

"Second guess: 'We can do what we want with our bodies'."

"Another Gitane, please."

"Of course. Last guess. The poetry of Sappho and its influence on the performance of female athletes of the G.D.R. in the 1980s."

"The packet, please."

I kept one back and handed the rest to her.

"Cheat," she said sternly.

"Tell me what it was about."

"It was called 'We don't bite'. It's a documentary about the contribution made by women on Chios to the island's gum mastic trade."

I lit up and got to my feet.

"Leaving so soon?"

"I appear to have run out of cigarettes."

"Have one of mine."

"I'd rather you gave me an answer."

"Eva's all ears," she chuckled, removing the three cigarettes from her behind her ears, returned them carefully to the packet and waited for the question.

I asked it, without really knowing why.

"If someone destroyed everything that you loved, would you use violence to get revenge?"

"Easy," she said without any hesitation. "If I had the balls, that is. You obviously haven't discovered yours yet, have you?"

"Perhaps not."

"I found mine the minute I realized that life is short and there's no point spending it skulking in your little corner because the bastards are out there doing exactly as they please."

"You could be right," I said and left, hiding my disappointment.

"Good luck," I heard her shout as I walked down the wooden staircase.

*

"*What are you reading, young man?*"

"*One of your old interviews.*"

"*From when?*"

"*1986.*"

"*1986. Wait, let me think . . . Light me a cigarette.*"

"*At your service.*"

"'*Twelfth Night?*'"

"*No.*"

"'*Lulu?*'"

"*No. Something short.*"

"*Röhmer. 'Trio en mi bemol!' It was fun.*"

"*The interviewer is asking you what you hate the most and you say: 'When men give me a friendly slap on the shoulder, tweak my cheek and wish me good luck.'*"

"*Yes. You see – I haven't changed at all in the last fourteen years.*"

"*Why do you hate those three things so much?*"

"*Because I'm not their buddy. Because I'm not a baby. Because Lady Luck is a pig-ugly, swarthy old hag who sits by the side of the road deciding our fate.*"

"*Who says so?*"

"*Our folk tradition, you ignorant lawyer.*"

"You would have made a fine teacher."

"I am a fine teacher. How else do you think you learned how to dress, to drink elegantly and not to fear the dawn, all in one short year?"

"I had Lady Luck on my side."

"You rotten chancer."

*

The newspapers at the kiosk were celebrating the latest Macedonian scandal; our future prime minister, with a huge grin and dressed like a bohemian, was guaranteeing the happiness of the nation's farmers, while his opponent was playing D.J. at a youth radio station with an enormous pair of headphones on his ears.

"We belong to a despicable race," I said to Halkidis, fastening my belt.

"Since when were you a racist?"

"Well, you know whose fault it is?"

"How would I know? I'm only a civil servant."

"The 'Great Powers'. If they hadn't interfered back then, everything would be alright today."

"Which 'back then' are you talking about?"

"The Battle of Navarino. Wasn't that when it all started?"

"Try to get some sleep. We've got more than three hours ahead of us. Open the window a bit – you reek of whisky."

"Martini, actually."

"Do you want anything to eat? I have a sandwich in the back."

"No, thanks, I've eaten. Three, four, maybe five olives."

"Go to sleep. Wind down the window and sleep. We'll stop for coffee at Leventis."

186

"Chronis?"

"You're supposed to be asleep."

"I know you do coke, so get off my back. At least alcohol's legal."

"Go to sleep."

"Goodnight."

*

I woke up with a strained neck, a dry mouth and a survivable headache. Everything outside was white. I cursed the snow under my breath and asked Halkidis for some water.

"There's water in the back, handmade sandwiches and some chewing gum. Eat, drink, chew – take about ten – see if that can't get rid of the stench of booze from your breath."

"You haven't got a beer back there too, have you?"

He gave me a filthy look and carried on driving the Cherokee at speed along the narrow road. I drained a bottle of water and lit a cigarette. The car clock showed 4.30.

"Where are we, Captain?"

"Not far from Karpenisi. Should be at the monastery in an hour at the most."

"Don't suppose you've got any aspirins on you?"

"There's some Paracetamol in the glove box."

The box was sitting between two pistols and a pair of handcuffs. I swallowed two bitter pills, belched and fixed my gaze on the snowy landscape.

"Do you like snow?" Halkidis said.

"Can't stand the stuff."

"Why?"

"I don't know. Ever since I was a child, it's had an oppressive effect on me, a bit like claustrophobia."

"The Inuit have forty-nine different words for snow. There was a documentary about it the other day."

"Fascinating," I said, opening the window to toss out my cigarette and breathe in the frozen air for a while. To the right, in the distance, the bulk of a mountain loomed.

"That's Velouchis, isn't it?"

"Yes. It's a Slavonic name. Do you know what it means?"

"What?"

"White Mountain."

"That's where Velouchiotis got his name from."

"So I've been told."

We crossed Karpenisi and took the road to Prousso. Despite all the bends and my entreaties, Halkidis continued to drive as though he were taking part in the Acropolis Rally.

"I want to get there before five when they close the gates."

"Do we have a plan or are we just going to tie the guy up and toss him into the ravine like a slaughtered animal?"

"Don't worry; we'll be doing everything by the book today. I've got a warrant for his arrest."

He went into long and tedious detail about the progress they had made in the morning while I'd been knocking back Martinis in a student café, celebrating my acquaintance with Eva. Fotini had got everything they needed on Agisilaos: one arrest for disturbing the peace at a Peristeri match and one for dangerous driving on the coastal road. But neither had come to anything. Dedes had broken into his flat in Holargos, but apart from a baseball bat, some pepper spray, a vibrator and dozens of anti-Semitic tracts, he found nothing helpful. Chronis' assistant was at that moment positioned outside the bad cop Berios' house, with orders not to let him out of his sight and to keep his boss posted.

"Congratulations, Head of Division! Excellent work. So can you clear something up for me?"

"Ask away."

"Since you've got your warrant for this man, what the fuck am I being dragged through the snow for?"

"The warrant's a fake. Our Fotini made it. You're needed because I think you'll make a first-rate prosecutor. I can't remember your new name. You'll find your new I.D., a white shirt and a silk tie on the back seat. You realize that this is not a day for things to get ugly. We'll escort the young man down to Athens nice and quietly. And before midnight, you'll be back, describing this breathtaking scenery over a drink with your girlfriend. And don't fail to convey to her our warmest congratulations for last night's performance. Tell her that the doors of the police force will always be open to her. How does that grab you?"

He sounded as if he was asking me my opinion of the outline of some carefree day trip he was proposing.

"How exactly do we find this guy among all those monks?"

"I am hoping that the venerable gentlemen will cooperate with agents of the law."

"What if they're hiding him?"

"They won't be. They're not even expecting us."

"Blondie might have tipped them off."

"Blondie will have been up all night changing his underpants," he said.

A short while later a signpost appeared. We only had three

kilometres to go. I noticed some arrows on the right, painted onto the rock; there were some votive candles below, lanterns, small icons, and other kitsch objects guaranteeing the faithful a ticket to Paradise.

"What's all that?" I said.

"If you look closely, you'll notice some strange shapes on the rocks. That's what the arrows are pointing to. They say that they're the footprints of the Virgin Mary as she climbed up to the monastery."

"You're pulling my leg."

"Not at all. Fotini unearthed the entire history of the monastery on the internet this morning. The place is positively heaving with pilgrims in the summer."

"And you say *I* drink too much . . ."

*

We left the 4×4 in the huge monastery car park. Halkidis slipped his pistol and the handcuffs into his pocket and took a piss against a tree. I took my new clothes from the back seat, and, shivering, disguised myself as a prosecutor. I memorized my new name – Adrianos Spyropoulos – pocketed the I.D., lit a cigarette and admired the monstrous structure built into the rocks. A large church with a high dome, and beside it, two three-storey buildings, possibly accommodation for visitors. I was wondering how easy it would be to track down Agisilaos inside that vast place when Halkidis popped out from behind a tree with a spring in his step, motioning for me to follow. At the gates, a young monk was trying to communicate with an elderly Scandinavian couple. Chronis interrupted them, pulled the monk to one side and asked him something. The monk shook his head, but stepped back at the sight of the police I.D. only a whisker away from his nose and started walking towards the monastery, leaving the tourists at the mercy of the snow. We walked for about 300 metres and arrived at a wing of cells. From somewhere in the distance came the sound of turbulent water. The monk knocked on a low wooden door, stood aside, and shot us a hostile look. We waited a little, and Chronis gestured to the monk. He knocked again. A key turned in the lock and as the door opened another black figure appeared, with a well-groomed beard and round glasses. Dangling from his ear were the hands-free earphones of a mobile telephone fastened to a wide belt. He looked at us questioningly.

"Father Abbot, I . . ." the monk began, but Halkidis interrupted him with a friendly pat on the back.

"Thank you, son, we won't be needing you anymore."

"What's going on?"the abbot said.

Halkidis looked to me. It was my turn.

"Spyropoulos. Prosecutor," I said abruptly, showing him my special I.D., made by Fotini. "This is Police Brigadier Maniatis. May we come in?"

"What is going on?"

"May we come in?" I said again, lowering my voice an octave.

The abbot turned his back on us and walked to the far end of the cell. We followed him, closing the door on the young monk and his questions.

The word cell did not do justice to the abbot's small room. Among all the austere icons was a huge plasma television screen hanging from a bracket on the wall facing a low double bed. A laptop sat on a small, elegant desk, the screensaver a photograph of the Hagia Sophia. Squeezed next to it were a wine bottle, two glasses and a plate of olives. The floor was covered with white *flokati* rugs and from the ceiling hung a light with a yellow glass shade. At the back was a closed door, probably his toilet. The room was unbearably stuffy. We removed our coats almost simultaneously and tossed them onto the bed. The abbot folded his arms around his stomach, trying to look composed.

"Make yourselves comfortable, my children. Naturally, we can't offer you much in the way of luxuries, but . . ."

"We won't take up a lot of your time," I said drily. "We have a warrant for the arrest of a Theodoros Anastasopoulos, who we believe to be a guest of this monastery. We'd like you to tell us where we can find him."

He seemed to relax a little.

"There's nobody here by that name, so I'd be most grateful if you could —"

"Better known as Agisilaos."

The abbot avoided my gaze and looked at Halkidis, who was busying himself with the hangnail on his little finger.

"Agisilaos, you said? I'd have to go through our guest books, and they're in the dormitories. I'm not at all sure whether this lies within your jurisdiction —"

"You can be sure that the entire Greek state lies within our juris-diction," I said, irritated that he should have called my office into question.

He was not in a mood to argue.

"My children, as you know, all of us here have renounced the secular world; the only law we serve is the law of the Almighty. And because secular matters are not my domain, I would ask you to allow me to consult the monastery's legal adviser, and receive the appropriate counsel."

"Regrettably, there is no time for that. I would not like to have to call for reinforcements. You know these officers, they can be a somewhat heavy-handed. They'll cordon off the monastery, forbid anyone to enter or to leave, and it's more than likely that the T.V. stations will get wind of it and that would not bring you the best sort of publicity. I think this should stay between us, don't you? It wouldn't do much for the reputation of this monastery if gets out that you're harbouring a criminal wanted by the police."

His face suddenly grew calm; a gentle smile formed on his thin lips. I remembered Sonia saying to me that a good priest has to be a good actor, and have complete control over his facial muscles and his voice; then and only then would he be able to persuade his congregation that he is bringing them the word of God. The abbot threw up his arms in the direction of his master's dwelling place.

"As you wish, my children. Let us walk towards the dormitories."

I picked up my coat, but before I managed to put it on, Chronis spoke.

"May I use your toilet?"

The pious mask fell from the abbot's face.

"Please tell Agisilaos to come out peacefully," Chronis said, producing the pistol from his pocket.

"How dare you?" the abbot whispered, utterly broken.

"If you don't come out now, you're in real trouble," Chronis shouted, and pushing the faithful monk to one side with minimal tenderness, knocked on the toilet door with the barrel of the pistol, and took one step back.

Within three seconds a man appeared at the door. He shot a desperate glance at all of us and lowered his head. Naked from the waist up, he was a poster boy for anabolic steroids. A sweater and leather jacket were draped across his arm. The abbot buried his face in his hands and sat down at the end of the bed.

"Sir," he said to me, "I promise I had no idea this young man was in trouble with the authorities."

"Of course you didn't, Father Abbot," I said to him. "Your holiness is not in question."

Chronis waited for the body beautiful to get dressed, cuffed him from behind and winked at me.

"On behalf of the Greek state, I thank you for your cooperation and wish you every success with your most holy endeavours," I said cheerily to the black heap on the bed and opened the door.

Halkidis walked out, pushing Agisilaos in front of him. Night had fallen and the small flakes of snow adorning the closed horizon welcomed us in a crazy dance.

*

"How did you know he was hiding in the toilet?"

"Because our black-clad diva in there had forgotten to hide the second wine glass. You're not very observant for a prosecutor, are you?"

"I've never been inside a monk's cell before; the decor took my breath away."

"What did you think?"

"Cosy little nest, wasn't it?"

"I'd settle for a motel any day. That Agisilaos – what do you know? Great strapping lad, Philhellene, successful businessman – owns his own gym, that he should sink so low!"

"May I remind you that everybody has the right to do as they please with their body? Law 1296, 1989 clearly states that homosexuality is no longer a criminal offence."

"You're absolutely right. But I'm not a young man anymore. My memory is not what it was."

"Of course, you'll have to be a witness in court, and your testimony will of necessity include the matter of the appearance of a half-naked young man."

"Naturally. I wanted to suggest that once we get back to H.Q. we contact the medical examiner and ask him to give the accused a full anal examination."

"We'll see, we'll see."

"Think about it," Halkidis said in a serious voice and started fiddling with the radio.

"I told you I want a lawyer. I want to call a lawyer. And I need to piss," came a hoarse voice from the back.

"Where on earth are you going to find a lawyer in this weather, my boy? As for the other matter, you might want to think twice about that. Who's going to undo your flies? Who's going to hold it for you? Who's going to shake it dry?" Halkidis answered in a kindly voice before turning up the radio and singing along to Eleftheria Arvanitaki begging someone or other to stay with her and never kiss her goodnight. I drained the third of the five beer cans I had acquired in Karpenisi, opened a fourth and humbly took my place in the choir. The Cherokee's headlights licked a sign saying ATHINA 81 KM.

*

We got to Internal Affairs on Syngrou at 11.00. The first part of Halkidis' plan had been carried out. The contacts list on the fascist's mobile included the name Berios, which proved a link between the sold-out police captain (we still did not know who he had sold out *to*) and the gang of arsonists. Dedes was still waiting patiently outside his house somewhere in Ilissia. Agisilaos was going to spend the night in a small room in the basement, watched over by a trusted officer, without of course being given the slightest explanation for his arrest. By morning he would be ready to sing our tune – that at least was what Chronis' long experience of interrogations had taught him. Fotini had been to visit Sonia and had spoken to the consultant: barring complications, they would be moving her to a regular ward on Monday. Everything had improved since yesterday. Halkidis was in a state of advanced excitement. I was convinced he was doing coke, but did not refer to it again; it was his right. Perhaps I was not far behind? The beers had done me in and the only thing I wanted was a real drink and some friendly conversation. I thought of Rania. I searched for my mobile, but then remembered that I had destroyed it. I told Chronis, who gave me strict instructions to replace it.

"Don't go thinking this is over. We've got the person who started the fire and hopefully by tomorrow we'll have the person who told him to do it. The fun will really begin once we find out who's behind it – who is trying to cover this up and why."

"We'll see."

He was greeting the guard at the entrance when his mobile rang. "Dedes," he said checking the screen and moving back. When he hung up, he called me over. He was very angry.

"I'm such an idiot. Such a big, fucking idiot."

"What's wrong?"

"Berios has just left his house carrying a suitcase, jumped in a taxi and is heading for the airport. He'll get there any minute. Someone must have tipped him off."

"The Abbot."

"That little creep! How could I be so stupid?" he yelled and started kicking a parked car.

"What were we supposed to do? Bring him along as well?"

"I don't know. We should at least have taken his mobile off him," he sighed, and lit up.

"Where's Dedes now?"

"Tailing him. I told him to see what plane he gets on – if it's a domestic flight, he'll get on it too. If he's on his way out of the country, we've had it."

"Can't he arrest him before he boards?"

"Not without a warrant. Berios is a policeman; he's not going to fall for any cheap tricks."

He walked towards his Golf, cursing both himself and the antichrist.

"Let's just pray that that piece of shit doesn't get wind of Dedes," he said, fumbling for his car keys.

"He's a smart lad – don't worry."

He unlocked the door, sat down behind the wheel and tugged at the wrong seat belt. I sank down next to him. He opened the glove box, found a leather tobacco pouch and took out a pre-rolled joint.

"Don't mind, do you?" he said as he lit it. "It's Dutch, strong but harmless. I need it for inspiration. Have a drink if you want to."

His features were taut with exhaustion. I wound the window down a fraction.

"Close it, Simeon! You're not going to die. Look, I might be in charge of this whorehouse, but I still have to keep up appearances."

I took a drag and spluttered.

"The next one will sort you out. By the way – are you in favour of legalization?"

"Of course," I choked.

"So am I, but don't tell anyone," he laughed. A strange laugh, a slightly demented laugh.

"If they do decriminalize, just think of all those fat cats who'll go into mourning!"

"Yes, and all those police officers too," I said, lifting the joint out of his fingers. He was right; the second time it went down more easily, as did the third, and then all the rest.

"Shall I tell you a secret?"

"Feel free. My lips are sealed, and only open in response to the code words, 'what's new, Simeon?'"

We both laughed, loudly and inanely.

"Did you know that my assistant, Emmanuel Dedes, is a leftie?"

Another fit of laughter.

"What kind of leftie?"

"A left-wing kind of leftie – progressive, parliamentarian, establishment – what do you call it? Not marginal, like the ones you hobnob with in your part of town."

"But I'm not a leftie, Halkidis, old chap."

"What then? A socialist?"

"If you insult me one more time, we're finished!"

"Alright. Where's your sense of humour?" he said, stubbing out the roll-up in the ashtray and turning the key in the ignition. My head was turning pleasantly, and the prospect of the night ahead no longer seemed so grim.

"Chronis – switch off for a minute. I want to tell you something. It's not a long story – I'm not going to bore you."

He turned off the engine and lit a cigarette.

"We're always telling each other stories. Is this a sign of old age?"

I rested my back against the door and looked at him. He moved his eyes away from mine and squeezed the steering wheel.

"I don't mind if you share this story with your leftie assistant – but no-one else."

He nodded.

"Once upon a time, I turned up skunk drunk at my old man's house, asking for money. I had lost a lot in a *kafeneion* in Gyzi; I'm sure the cards had been fixed or something. My old man gave me the money to pay off the debt without a murmur and made me a cup of black coffee to help me recover. 'Is it my fault that you've ended up like this?' he asked. 'No,' I said. 'It's your fault that *you've* ended up like this. We're all to blame for the things we've never done.' He stood up, opened the fridge and got out a bottle of water. It was the thick of winter, just like now, but he always drank chilled water. He gulped it down greedily and then started talking. 'You know when it all went wrong for me, son? I've never told you this, but it won't hurt you to listen. Besides, you'll have forgotten it all by tomorrow. In the early '50s, I was in prison, in Sotiria, the hospital. Ploubidis was with us. When the party put it about that he was a police grass, we said nothing. How were we supposed to know if it was true? Zachariadis knew more than we did. August '53. It was a cool day; his appeal was quashed. They took him, and on the way up to Daphni, he walked past in front of us and said, "Farewell, comrades". He was scared, but still managed to smile. To this day I can remember the look in his eyes. And do you know what we did, son? We looked away, that's what we did. We turned our sorry heads away. Most people thought it was all just for show and that the police would never execute one of their own grasses. Well, that's what happened to that teacher. He didn't get a single word from any of us. To be able to go on living with that guilt, I had to do something. And I did the wrong thing. I kept quiet, got married, just so I could feel like a normal human being, and carried on living like that, hoping the wound would heal. And I ended up punishing myself, just like those Christian martyrs I used to ridicule so much. What a waste of time! Ploubidis had evaporated – hadn't even managed to take one greeting with him. I still dream about him, but it doesn't disturb me anymore. He simply evaporated, that's what I say, and it's just as well because imagine if he could see what we've achieved, we who back then didn't have the decency to give him a proper farewell.'"

Halkidis glazed over. I struggled to light a cigarette, but I couldn't get my fingers to do what they were told.

"Do you see now why I'm not a leftie? The road is full of hazardous bends and my old man didn't reach the end of it. He hanged himself from a tree, fourteen years ago to the day, January 30."

Halkidis turned the key and revved up the engine.

"You should have asked me to put on some background music and hold your hand."

"Go fuck yourself."

"Gladly, but tell me where to drop you off first."

"Stadiou. By the statue of Kolokotronis."

Friday, 11.50 p.m.

Where are you? Don't be angry – our agreement not to ask more of each other than we can give still stands. I know, darling, it still stands, but it's just that the same old demons keep coming back. "Demons are company too," as you used to say back then, or was it yesterday, next to a calm sea, a deep green sea? I did agree, but I didn't know then . . .

I didn't know what it's like not being able to move your lips, not to have a voice, just a weak death rattle, your fingers so heavy that they can't reach those transparent tubes. Those are different demons, new demons I never imagined existed. There was a time when I found comfort in your chest, and you in mine. Just look at it now – buried under all this stuff, come and cut yourself on my dry lips, come and tell me how far my toes have gone, fetch me my small round mirror, I want to see my hair ruffled by your hands one more time.

CHAPTER 7

Chronis Halkidis
Cannot Forgive Himself

31.i

Saturday, 12.10 a.m.

I dropped Piertzovanis off at the statue of Kolokotronis, waited for him to take a piss on it and then lurch across Stadiou, his arm raised to deflect the oncoming traffic; drivers were drowning him in hoots, obscene gestures and abuse, but they spared his life. I stopped off at Syntagma for a packet of cigarettes, a plastic sandwich and some chocolate, sat down at one of the tables outside McDonald's and was soon joined by a stray dog. Eating and smoking, I managed to plan my next moves. If the bad guys find out that we kidnapped Agisilaos, they're likely to suspect that my boss had something to do with it; that officer with the earring who had been keeping watch in Intensive Care could well have complained to Berios about how heavy-handed I had been. I had no idea how far the tentacles of this gang extended, which was why I had to keep my trump card safely locked up in the basement in Syngrou. I called Fotini.

"Did I wake you?"

"No, Sir; I was watching T.V."

"I need a favour, Fotini. Have you still got that country house in Oropos? Is it empty at the moment?"

"Yes. Who'd want to go there in the winter?"

"Can I borrow it for the weekend?"

"Sure, but you'll have to light the fire; there's no heating."

"Don't worry. I'll be fine."

"Is something wrong, Sir?"

"No, nothing. I've got my son staying with me, and something unexpected has come up. You know."

"Yes," she said, sounding dubious. "I'll be expecting you."

I did not want to worry her by telling her what I was planning to do to her holiday home . The less she knew, the safer she would be. I bought another couple of sandwiches, spread them out in front of the dog and went back to the car. Within the hour I had picked up the key, explained to the guard watching Agisilaos that he needed to forget everything he had seen recently, allowed fascist-face to relieve himself, handcuffed him and bundled him into the back of the Golf. He didn't say a word the entire journey, respectful of the duct tape placed strategically on the seat next to him. I decided to take the old National Road to avoid the cameras at the tollbooths. At about 1.00 we drew up outside Fotini's dark illegally built country house. Agisilaos showed no signs of cracking, but beyond an un- certain, "What do you want with me anyway?" he didn't put up any resist-ance. I walked him to the bathroom, cuffed his ankles, and to make quite sure he could move no more than a few centimetres, I used a chain to bind the cuffs around his feet to the pipe leading to the immersion heater. I also ensured that the neighbours would get a good night's sleep by slapping a piece of miracle-working duct tape across his mouth and promised him we could have a nice long chat about anything he liked in a few hours' time. As I pulled the door to his cell shut behind me, it occurred to me that I was in danger of becoming just like him; but I had forgotten all about it by the time I had turned the key twice in the lock. I slid into a narrow sofa and punched out Dedes' number on my mobile. The subscriber I was trying to reach had turned off his phone. I assumed he had followed Berios onto some domestic flight and had complied with the guidelines regarding mobiles. We had spoken about two and a half hours earlier, he was bound to call any minute. I could hear the waves lashing against the rocks in the distance. I took off my coat and spread it across my chest.

"Why didn't you let me swim?"

"It's very dark, young man."

"So?"

"The sea is dark."

"But the moon is out."

"It's yellow."

"Yes, but it is giving off some light."

"The sea is black, stupid. It doesn't want us right now. It's sleeping."

"I'm going in. Just for five minutes."

"And I'll be afraid for five minutes."

"You're always afraid, Sonia."

"You're mean."

"Sorry."

204

"Fine. Jump in, then. But don't go too far out. I don't want to lose sight of you."

"I adore you."

"I adore you too – provided I can see you."

I woke up on the floor. A dim light was fighting its way through the crumbling shutters. I looked at my watch: 9.10. It was a struggle just to stand up. I splashed some water on my face, and drank water straight from the basin tap. Agisilaos was in exactly the same position I had left him in, but the look he gave me was not as terrified as I would have liked. The stench of urine forced me to close the door. I tried Dedes; his phone was still off. I lit a cigarette, heated the powder, snorted a couple of lines and tried to keep my sense of panic in check. It was not easy. I tried his official mobile. That was switched off too. I tried his home number and hung up on the twentieth ring. I snatched my coat and rushed out of the house to the car, intending to drive to the airport. Next to the gear stick, my other phone sighed under the burden of six missed calls – all of them from the Chief. My hands were shaking but I somehow managed to press the right keys.

"Where the fuck are you?"

"I was asleep. I didn't hear it ring."

"Come to Alexandras. Now!"

"What's the matter?"

"Dedes has killed himself."

*

I didn't do more than seventy. I stuck to the right lane and did some thinking. Just outside Varibobi, I pulled over, rolled a joint, and smoked it quietly, trying to come to a decision about my future. It was not at all difficult.

"You're late. Where have you been?"

"To hell," I said, and sat down opposite him.

The Chief Coroner and the heads of Forensics and Criminology restricted themselves to simple shakes of the head.

"What's going on?" I said, lighting up. In the circumstances, none of these four non-smoking colleagues of mine felt able to protest.

Criminology assumed the task of narrating the events, trying to rise to the tragedy of the occasion, to the tragic loss of a policeman, especially one who had always exhibited the requisite seriousness and professionalism.

Dedes had been discovered in a car park off Marathonos Avenue by a truck driver who spotted him slumped over his steering wheel. He knocked on the window, got no response, opened the door, tried to shake him, and as soon as he saw the hole made by the bullet that had lodged itself into his right temple, he threw up. That was at 2.30 this morning. The coroner confirmed that the bullet had come from his duty gun, and put the time of death between 11.00 and 2.00. Forensics had found no evidence to point to anything other than suicide.

"He was a good lad," I said as soon as they had finished filling me in.

"Chronis – were you aware of anything? Was he under a lot of pressure? Having problems?"

"No, he was absolutely fine, Chief."

"What cases had he been on?"

"Our annual report to Parliament."

"Did he have any enemies?"

"I don't know. He was a policeman, wasn't he?"

"Alcohol, drugs, debts, whores?" ventured Criminology's answer to Hercule Poirot.

"My men are pure as the driven snow, Brigadier."

The Chief declared the meeting over, stressing that in view of the forthcoming Olympics it was crucial to keep the matter quiet. He asked me to stay behind; I told him I would be back in two minutes and ran to catch up with Forensics at the lift.

"I want you to bring me his mobile right away."

"He didn't have it on him, Mr Halkidis."

"You're joking."

"We turned his car inside out. We didn't find his phone."

"Where is his car now?"

"In the garage. Feel free to take a look at it whenever you want."

"Fax your report through to me at my office and e-mail me your photographs. Now. We'll deal with his house."

"The pictures might take a while."

"Be as quick as you can," I said, stressing the imperative. Not that it made any difference now.

I went to the toilet and realized I had left my cut straw in the Golf, so I settled for rubbing the powder gently into my gums. When I got back to his office, the Chief was on the phone; I asked his secretary for an orange juice and waited, listening to him exhaust his impressive repertoire of "yes"s, "indeed"s, "of course"s, "certainly"s, and "absolutely"s. He hung up and looked across at me like a dog that had just been kicked.

"Chronis, I've had enough. The minister is interested in one thing and one thing only – do you know what that is? That news of our dear departed colleague is kept out of the papers. As for television news, forget it. He has already been on to the owners. He says we cannot expect to host the Olympics successfully while our police officers are running around blowing their brains out."

I waited for his secretary to leave the juice and biscuits on the table and close the door behind her.

"Chief, Dedes phoned me last night at around 11.00. He was in my neighbourhood and asked me if I wanted to go and have a *souvlaki* with him. I told him I had a more attractive offer than his, and he hung up, laughing. He did not sound like a man who would top himself within the hour."

"Yes, I know, but we've seen stranger."

"Yannis – his phone has disappeared."

"What do you mean?"

"What do you think I mean? Do you really believe that he phoned me, got upset because I wouldn't join him for a *souvlaki*, drove all the way to Mesogeia in the middle of the night and killed himself after carefully disposing of his mobile?"

The shock and then anger writ large across his face convinced me that the Chief had absolutely nothing to do with Berios, or with Dedes' murder. He went up to the window, threw it wide open and left me staring at his back. I drank my juice and lit up.

"Is there something you're not telling me?" he said without turning round.

"Absolutely nothing," I said, innocence personified.

"What do you make of this? Personal differences? Terrorists? The Secret Services, the C.I.A., Al Qaeda? Who the fuck did it?"

"No idea, Chief."

He turned round and flopped heavily into his chair.

"I think I'm going mad," he said.

Over the years, I had come to realize that if there was one thing he could not stomach, it was losing one of his men. My timing could not have been better.

"I'll instruct Forensics to treat it as a homicide. I'm sure they'll turn up something. There must have been more than one of them. If it does turn out to be murder and not suicide, what do you want me to do?"

"I want their heads on this desk," he said quietly.

"I'll need at least twelve men."

"You can have twelve thousand."

"And absolute secrecy."

His mind was elsewhere. I took the crack of the pencil he broke in two with the fingers of his left hand as his scrawl on the dotted line.

I phoned Piertzovanis from the waiting room telephone.

"Buy yourself a new mobile. Charge it and call me from a public phone booth. We have news."

He did not argue.

*

By 4.00 the operation had been organized to the last detail. The prosecutor willingly cut all the red tape to secure the legality of our movements. Someone would be posted round the clock at Sonia's bedside. We did not intend to let Berios out of our sight for one second and we were to bug everything: phones, car, house, and get everything, even the sound of his cistern flushing. A well-equipped team of five was on twenty-four hour alert. Kourkouvelas, who had rushed back from Argos the minute he got the news, was to coordinate everything from Syngrou. Piertzovanis and I were to keep up the dirty work. He phoned. I broke the bad news, and told him to keep calm until we met.

At around 4.30 I got home, had a bath, changed my clothes and sat down to my fifth coffee of the day at the kitchen table with a sketchpad and a black pencil. The time had come for me to draw my thoughts.

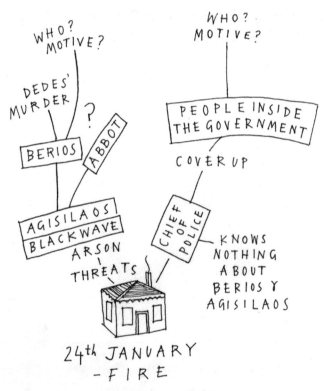

My only leads so far were Agisilaos and Berios. If only I could take the Chief some solid evidence of Dedes' murder – I was convinced it was Berios and his men – I would appeal to his conscience and persuade him to tell me who was putting pressure on him to cover up the arson. At least I would have serious reasons for persuading him. There was no doubt that at the top of the pyramid the activities of Berios and the neo-Nazis converged with those of the big guns who did not want me sniffing around the burnt house. Both kidnapping Agisilaos and tailing Berios had prompted knee-jerk reactions and led to Dedes' murder, to the fatal mistake that untied my hands and put me back in the game. There was nothing on the television news about it. The minister obviously had his means, his ways. Right now Kourkouvelas and our top psychologist would be accompanying Dedes' parents to the morgue. He would be trying to sell them the ridiculous story about the suicide, while inwardly vowing that in a few days from now he would be able to tell them who had killed their son. The two of us had been out to the car park on Marathonos where he had been found, with a bunch of roses. Red, on Kourkouvelas' insistence.

"We might not have seen eye to eye about politics, but he had a heart of gold. He used to give me films to watch, you know."

"No, I didn't know that. What kind of films?"

"Old films: Italian, Hungarian, German. Ones he had recorded from the television. What should I do with them now?"

"Keep them for your kids."

"We'll find them, won't we?"

"Yes, Thomas, we'll find them. You have my word."

It wasn't about revenge. It was about honour. At least that was what it suited me to think.

At 5.30 I pressed Piertzovanis' doorbell. Rania opened.

"He's been in the bath for the past hour, reading. He hasn't had a drop," she announced, anticipating my question.

"Does he read in the bath?"

"Yes."

She squeezed three oranges for me, made coffee for herself and Simeon and knocked on the bathroom door.

"Coming," came a snarl from within.

"He told me you think you know who killed him."

I nodded.

"So what are you going to do?"

"My best."

"Simeon shouted at me earlier, but I don't care. I'm here if you need me. I'll do anything. I'm serious."

I smiled and took a sip of my juice.

She went into the kitchen shouting to Simeon to get a move on. He appeared almost instantly, clean-shaven, neatly combed, and smelling of aftershave.

"What was our lawyer studying?"

He tossed the book he was holding at me. I snatched it out of the air; it almost came apart in my hands.

The Line of the Horizon. I opened it and my eye fell on the dedication:

> *To the man who almost became my friend,*
> *who almost became a lawyer, and who almost got lucky.*
> *Respectfully yours,*
> *C.*

Underneath it somebody had written in pencil:

Do not stop praying as long as, by God's grace, the fire and the water have not been exhausted, for it may happen

that never again in your whole life will you have such a chance to ask for the forgiveness of your sins.
—John Climacus

"I glance through it every now and then when the going gets tough," he said, lighting a cigarette. "I find it very enlightening."

"I've made some coffee," said Rania.

Simeon was still standing up; his eyes fixed on me. I carefully put the book down on the table.

"Chronis, does it occur to you that we might be responsible for what's happened?"

"I haven't had time to think about it; I prefer to . . ."

"That's a very aristocratic way of dealing with things."

"Simeon, I will mourn the loss of my friend as soon as I've finished with the people who killed him."

"As soon as you've finished with them, or as soon as you've finished them off?"

"As soon as I have taken them to the prosecutor. I've been doing everything by the book. Nobody's going to stand in my way."

He burst out laughing.

"What if the prosecutor says exactly what your Chief told you a few days ago: 'Leave it to us – we'll take it from here'?"

"In that case, I won't bother you anymore, and you'll read all about it in the papers."

"'Psycho cop takes law into own hands'?"

"Or 'Mysterious deaths of prominent men,'" Rania suggested, trying to lighten the atmosphere. She was partially successful, which gave me an opening to bring out my diagram and put it on the table. I left them with it while I dashed to the toilet for essential refuelling.

"So what do you want from me now?' Simeon said when I got back. I was now confident that I could talk him into coming on board with me if I wanted to.

"I want you to play the prosecutor one last time. You give Agisilaos some sort of spiel that will persuade him you're not really after him at all but want the man who ordered him to burn down the house – most likely Berios. You promise him that if he testifies under oath we'll only use him as a prosecution witness if the case goes to trial. You'll let him think that it most probably never will because the powers that be don't want their names dragged through the mud by having to prosecute police officers who get too carried away with noble yet extreme ideas. He'll go along with it, we'll take him over to Syngrou, and then you can slip out of role and let the real prosecutor step forward. Don't worry about anything else. If I can manage to connect the arson with Berios, there'll be no stopping me."

"And after that someone will whisper in your ear that if you ever want to see your son grow up, you could do worse than take early retirement and discover the joys of amateur angling."

"Not if I can get Agisilaos' confession, and maybe Berios' as well, into a serious paper first."

"Oh dear! You obviously haven't read your Kafka." Simeon yawned and went into the kitchen. The sound of liquid cascading into a glass was heard.

"Leave off that fucking stuff, will you?" Rania shouted at him.

"You should forget about Pavese and turn to Bukowski, you know. At least he didn't top himself," the lawyer said, standing there caressing the glass holding his favourite liquid.

"Nice promises you make," she said glumly.

"You can't have everything."

"Oh, please, shut up."

"Blood thirsts, it seeks revenge," he said, closing his eyes and draining the glass in three gulps.

I despised him. Rania, a grim look on her face, suddenly jumped up, grabbed the birdcage and shut herself in the bedroom. Simeon wiped his eyes which had started to water and in a hoarse voice said to me, "That was the last one tonight. Let's go, and what will be will be. But I want to see Sonia first."

*

Piertzovanis' voice was steady. "The good news is that there have been no complications. They are going to move her from Intensive Care. The consultant told me that he had received instructions from the hospital administrator to give her a private room. Apparently the Ministry of Health has taken an interest."

"Yes – I told the Chief to arrange it this morning."

"The bad news is that she can't speak."

We were having a cigarette in the hospital canteen. On the bench next to ours, a teenage gypsy girl was trying to soothe the sobs of her barefoot infant. Opposite us, Mt Pendeli was smothered in a black cloud.

"What do you mean she can't speak?"

"It might be shock. One of the nurses noticed this morning. She was changing her drip and Sonia tried to say something to her. She was very animated and appeared to be in touch with her surroundings. Her eyes flickered, but she could not say anything. Then she started weeping silently, and fell asleep. When I went to see her, she was still sleeping."

"Will it come back? Will her voice come back?"

"No way of knowing."

"*Do you ever hear voices, young man?*"

"*What sort of voices? Like Joan of Arc?*"

"*Yes, why not?*"

"*Never.*"

"*Good. You're healthy, then. I don't hear them either.*"

"*So what made you think of it?*"

"*I went to my E.N.T. this morning for my annual check-up on my vocal chords, my tool box, as he calls it. He said they were fine, despite the exertions of the summer. But then he suddenly started saying all sorts of daft things. I forgot to tell you, he's a great theatre-lover, and he treats all the big names in the business, T.V. presenters, opera singers too. What was I saying?*"

"*That your doctor was saying all sorts of daft things.*"

"*That's right. Just as I was paying my bill, he started saying that we artists have got two voices, one that's audible to mere mortals, and another one that only we, the divine artists, can hear and he advised me to take care of my second, secret voice.*"

"*That's the second bell.*"

"*O.K., I'm ready. So I said to him, 'That's bullshit, doctor. I've been waiting to hear my first voice for the last thirty years, and haven't heard it once, and you want to lumber me with a second one?' What's so funny?*"

"*Didn't we agree that there'd be no drinking in the morning?*"

"*I swear on my life, I've only had one miserable glass of milk.*"

"*Don't swear on anything; in approximately two hours from now, the playwright will be killing you off.*"

216

"And in three you'll be lusting over my dead body?"

"Third bell."

"Have we got a full house?"

The minute I had left Kifissia and these memories behind me and pulled out onto the motorway, I realized that I was being tailed by a green Polo.

"What the hell?" I said, slowing down.

"What is it now?" Piertzovanis was telling the worry beads on a string Rania had given him as a peace offering.

"Someone wants to know where we're going."

"Let's pull up at a car park," he said in a voice suggesting he'd been raised on dangerous missions in war zones, and turned round to take a look at our pursuers.

"It's a green Polo," I said. "Middle lane, five, six cars behind us."

"Is that girl completely out of her mind?"

"What girl?"

"You're quick, aren't you? Rania, who do you think?"

I slowed down even more and let the Polo approach. The lawyer was right. Rania had tried to disguise herself with a pair of dark glasses and a cigar between her teeth.

"What do you want me to do? I don't want to get involved in your personal life."

"More to the point, what do you think *I* should do?"

"Looks like she's in love with you."

"She can't be that stupid. It's a game. She's fooled herself into believing she's in love and now she's playing the part. Just pretend you haven't seen her. I'll get rid of her later."

"What did you say her father did?"

"Piss off, Halkidis."

I got to 120, and managed to lose her. Simeon tuned in to Radio Avlida: "What have you done to me? / What will I do to you? / Passion always leaves us unsatisfied." I shot him a filthy look. He ignored it.

"Are you considering a serious relationship with her?" I said just outside Oropos.

"Does she really strike you as the sort of girl who longs to change bedpans for an old man?"

"No, but . . ."

"Just drive then. And make sure you change that exhaust tomorrow. I'm getting high sitting here."

"I'd give it serious thought if I were you."

He changed stations, turned up the volume to drown out my useless advice. The green Polo was back on my bumper. Rania was moving her head rhythmically, possibly in time to the same music we were listening to, vintage Bob Marley.

*

Agisilaos was in a semi-comatose state. His eyes were bloodshot from crying, his lips cracked from thirst, his wrists purple where the handcuffs had cut into his flesh. Piertzovanis gave him a kick and relieved himself of the water he had drunk on the journey into the toilet, at the same time criticizing me in no uncertain terms about the treatment of prisoners. We carried the young man into the sitting room, put him down in an armchair and sat opposite him. The "prosecutor" ordered me to remove the handcuffs and pulled the curtain back a fraction. He admired the landscape and turned to look at me.

"Right. This shouldn't take long; after all it is Saturday night."

Mozart's *Eine kleine Nachtmusik* interrupted him. He searched his inside pocket for his mobile, put his finger up to his lips to command silence and said conspiratorially, "Hello, Mr President." He listened to the caller for a while, contributing the occasional "of course", "there's no question of that", "no, we won't be put in that position", "we are in complete control of the witness" by way of reassurance. He wound up his call with a servile "I'll definitely be following your speech in Komotini next Sunday." I had my back to Agisilaos throughout the conversation so he couldn't see my face. I knew it was Rania on the other end. She obviously thought that a call from the "president" would bolster our attempts to be convincing. We had told her to wait outside, which she did under protest, whining like a ten-year-old. She did not have much faith in our deranged-police-officer/alcoholic-lawyer combo, but Simeon managed to reassure her with the promise of a long weekend in Thrace. She was thrilled and I crossed myself: obviously I did not have a clue what appealed to young people these days.

Piertzovanis turned off his mobile, sat down in a chair and watched me position a camera on a tripod opposite Agisilaos. I set the microphone up on its base, put it down on the table and after the necessary tests, watched over by the little fascist with a glazed look, sat down and declared everything ready to go.

Simeon once again played his part to perfection, finely balancing the formal stiffness of the lawyer and the lightness of someone who knows that they are holding all the cards. Agisilaos responded stoically to his questions, and after three quarters of an hour, we were confident that we knew as much as he did.

The gang had formed in 2002, after Agisilaos had been arrested at a football match. Apparently he had broken the arm of some stoned fan of the rival club, and Berios, who had questioned him, realized that it would be easy to manipulate this brainless pretty boy for his own ends. He let him go, gave him some pocket money (out of secret police funds) and helped him recruit the hard core of the gang. They called it the Order of the Black Wave and drew up a list of sickening rules that defined its strict nationalistic principles. From what the astrophysicist activist had told us, together with everything the blond had blurted out at the burnt house, this was just one aspect of the Black Wave's activities. Agisilaos mentioned about ten kiosk and mini-market break-ins, car thefts, small-time coke deals, pimping for the wealthy of all genders, and even selflessly aiding the police in their efforts to break up student demonstrations. It was always Berios who determined the targets and gave the orders. The siege of Simeon's house had begun in the spring of 2003. They had given the job to some kids, as a kind of trial run, their qualifying exams before they could be admitted as full members of the gang. The Saturday before, Berios had called Agisilaos and told him to chuck a few Molotov cocktails into the garden, because the "bloody blacks" who lived in the house had had the nerve to go and complain to the police. He said that he would love to join the party, but had to go and supervise security arrangements at a match up in Thessaloniki. The young bloods carried out their mission and only discover- ed what had happened the following afternoon. Berios phoned Agisilaos and very calmly set out an escape plan for the four arson- ists. The three kids who had helped their boss turn the house in to a blazing inferno, he could hide. Agisilaos would be taken care of by a trusted police friend of his who would drive him to the monastery.

I asked him to describe that officer: forty-five, strong Macedonian accent, well-dressed with a white tuft in his black hair, drove a white Lexus. He had dropped him off with the abbot and vanished. Since then, Agisilaos had not had any communication with any of them. Two days ago, when the eccentric life of the monastery started to get to him, he made the fatal mistake of phoning the blond.

I switched off the camera and went to the toilet for a quick snort. When I got back, Simeon was standing over Agisilaos, who had hidden his face in his hands.

"I swear to you, I regret it now. We didn't mean to harm anyone. I can't understand how it happened. It was an accident."

Piertzovanis kneeled down, leant in towards the worm and said to him in a fatherly tone, "Look here, son. I'll stick to my side of our agreement. You go along with the Police Brigadier so we can get the formalities out of the way, and tomorrow you'll be a free man."

Agisilaos took his hands from his face and looked at me in terror.

"I don't want to die," he snivelled.

Simeon laughed.

"Now listen and don't interrupt me again. We might not be on the same side here, but unfortunately this is a delicate situation. It would be really easy to have you up on three counts of premeditated murder, which means that you're talking thirty years, and that's with a really nice judge. With a not so nice one: life. Now I know that it was an accident. I believe you, but the judge and jury, the jury mainly, are not going to be half so open-minded. Do we understand each other?"

Agisilaos nodded. Simeon drew everything to a close.

"Young man, I'd like to thank you for your cooperation. You can sort out everything else with the brigadier here."

Simeon signalled that he would be waiting for me outside and swaggered out, full of pride. I put the camera away, put the cuffs back onto the penitent Magdalene, locked her in the bathroom after reminding her to be good, and walked out in to the freezing cold. Simeon was inside the Polo talking to Rania. I stuck the camera in the boot of my car, lit a cigarette and tried to listen to the waves. They sounded too remote to give me the least comfort. I carried on smoking, trying to think of a reason why I shouldn't rid the world of the murderer sitting snivelling in the bathroom. I could not think of one – apart from my own tiredness. I stubbed out the cigarette in a pot with a dead plant in it and squeezed into the back seat of the Polo.

"Happy, boss?" Piertzovanis said.

"You believe him?"

"Yes. You?"

"Yes, I do. But that's not reason enough not to kill him."

Rania looked at me in the mirror, obviously alarmed.

"You don't mean that, do you?"

"No," I said and asked her for a cigarette. She lit one and passed it back to me.

"When are you going to nab Berios?" Piertzovanis said.

"Monday. I'll be in Crete tomorrow. I can't possibly miss Dedes' funeral."

The windows had steamed up from all the smoke and breath. After a while, Rania wound her window half way down and turned to me.

"From what little Simeon has told me, it seems this bloody gang hadn't done their homework properly and burned those four people by mistake."

"Something like that," I said.

"So why do the big bosses want to hush the whole thing up?"

"Probably because they were aware of the existence of the Black Wave, and in fact found them to be rather useful. I find it hard to believe that Berios would have acted completely independently, without telling anyone. It's very handy having some idiot thug at your disposal, who you can arm and control from the sidelines. It's quite something. Have you any idea what it means to break up a demonstration just like that by sending in a dozen trouble-makers in balaclavas to burn a couple of banks and a few cars? Or to cause havoc at a football match and let the public gawp at the destruction on the T.V. later?"

"Or publicly burn all the books you don't approve of?" came the trembling voice of Simeon.

"Go easy on the sermons, will you?"

"And disposing of irritations like Dedes?" he went on, still buried in his overcoat. "It comes down to fear, Chronis. Being able to frighten the little people like us. That is what it is."

"Well, I can't believe that the Chief of Police is protecting gangs like that. I just don't buy it," Rania said stubbornly.

"Who told you he knows anything about it? There are cells, my dear girl. Whoever gave the order to cover up this crime might be the last person anyone would suspect."

"Like a politician, you mean?"

"No, they're too frightened of getting their hands dirty."

"Unless money is involved," Simeon said.

"No different from the rest of us, if you think about it."

"I'm tired."

"Tell me about it."

I left a €10 note with a policeman to get the famished Agisilaos something to eat and told the guard in charge not to allow the prisoner to come into contact with anyone else at all. After locking myself in my office, I had a couple of lines before phoning Kourkouvelas. He told me that Berios had not left the house at all, but that he was on duty at the Aigaleio stadium the next day. I told him about Agisilaos' confession, and was very happy to accept his offer of a lift to the airport in the morning. We were flying at 8.00; Dedes' village was just outside Siteia and the funeral was at 3.00. We would return to Athens on the first flight out on Monday. I lit a cigarette and unlocked the bottom drawer of the desk. Why did I keep all these relics of Sonia hidden here instead of at home? Perhaps deep down I was scared that they might suddenly come to life at home and get out of control, sneak into my bed, dirty the walls and break the windows, count the five floors separating the balcony from the street below. I picked up one of the notes she would leave me at the reception desks of the many hotels that we stayed in that long summer of '97. It was a game she played. "When I'm a big Hollywood star, these little words will be worth a small fortune! Make sure you don't throw them away – you'll be ensuring a comfortable old age for yourself."

Nineteen envelopes tied together with a thick purple hair ribbon she had chosen at the start of the "Electra" tour, at some dismal fair in Grevena, together with a clockwork hare, which she gave to a D.J. at a seedy nightclub the same evening just to make me jealous. The envelope I chose bore the hotel stamp, Rhodes Beach, and the note inside was written on a paper handkerchief.

I'm giving an interview this morning to some big-shot local journalists. Then I'm planning a spectacular drowning in the filthy swimming pool. Are you going to be there to save me or are you going to take those washed-out little girls from the chorus down to the beach? Either way, if I haven't seen you by noon, I'll break into your room and I'll sit there and wait for you, and then I'll fire you! Understood?
Sonia

I pulled out a second note from the New Hotel, Sparta. And a third, the Filoxenia in Kalamata. I stopped at the ninth. That was what I was looking for. Hotel Akti in Siteia.

And what am I looking for?
What am I looking for?
A chance to get to heaven . . .
Please don't come to my room tonight. I've got an anniver-
sary I need to celebrate alone. I love you,
Me x

However hard I tried, I could not get her to tell me what that anniversary was.

I called Fotini and asked her to book me a single room at the Akti, locked the forbidden fruits back in the drawer and left.

I got home at about the time most people are getting ready to leave for an expensive night out. I rolled a joint, put half a packet of spaghetti into boiling water, had a warm shower, ate a plateful, rolled another joint and smoked it lying on my back. I closed my eyes and soon came under attack from a kindergarten kid with brilliant white curly hair who was pointing my Beretta at me. I drifted off nursing the hope that he would not find the strength to pull the trigger.

Saturday, 11.35

Who's that young man? A nurse? Most probably. What else could he be? What's he been doing here all this time? Probably fell asleep. He's – it's funny; it's as if he's been covered up by the book. What's he reading? Stolen Time. What an old-fashioned title. Probably sentimental. But the cover's a bit strange for a sentimental book. When he wakes up I'll ask him to read me the opening passage. You can get the sense of a book from the first words. Wrong. How am I supposed to ask him to read? With my voice? Right. Fuck it. I'd never realized before that the voice is like a breath. Don't panic. Keep calm. Play the game. Let's play our game now! We have to play our game now, the magic list now. Only the magic list will free us from the worst. Do you have breath? You still have a bit. Let's go! Sonia, in position! The merciless enemy is waiting for you. He's waiting for your first question.

*   At him!*

SONIA: *What's the use of a voice? I, dear enemy, find it utterly useless.*
ENEMY: *For ordering drinks.*
SONIA: *You lose, enemy. You could just show the bottle to the barman.*
ENEMY: *True. You can use your voice to sing. There you go!*
SONIA: *Anyone can sing. Do you want me to be like everybody else? Do you?*
ENEMY: *To say, "I'll love you forever!"*
SONIA: *It's wrong to tell lies.*
ENEMY: *To sing a child to sleep.*

SONIA: *Children hate sleeping.*

ENEMY: *To make phone calls.*

SONIA: *You're very stupid, enemy. Postage stamps are so cheap and cheerful.*

ENEMY: *To swear.*

SONIA: *Spitting's better.*

ENEMY: *To ask for help.*

SONIA: *From whom?*

ENEMY: *To pray.*

SONIA: *To whom?*

ENEMY: *To act in the theatre.*

SONIA: *Clowns that say nothing are the best of all.*

ENEMY: *. . .*

SONIA: *Do you give up, enemy?*

ENEMY: *To laugh and be told that you have an amazing laugh?*

SONIA: *. . .*

ENEMY: *So – you've got no answer to that. You got stuck on the laughter.*

SONIA: *You win, enemy. That's a good reason for having a voice.*

ENEMY: *I can think of another one.*

SONIA: *Another one?*

ENEMY: *Yes. To tell someone what your name is. To be able to say, "My name's Sonia. What's yours?"*

CHAPTER 8

Simeon Piertzovanis Remembers

1.ii–2.ii
Sunday 11.30 a.m.

"Happy new month!"

It was Rania, standing in the doorway, holding two plastic bags in one hand, with at least ten kilos' worth of newspapers draped over her other arm.

"Sunday papers," she chirped. "And croissants to suit all tastes. I pressed the bell with my nose!" she said, reaching up on tiptoe to give me a kiss.

I stood back to let her come in and put down her bags. She turned off the light in the sitting room and pulled up the shutters behind the French windows. "The sun's trying to shine outside, see?" she scolded and disappeared into the kitchen, ignoring Rina who, the minute she clapped eyes on Rania, started on her aria medley, frantically seeking a little attention. I took a quick look at the front pages, and was struck once again by the earnest conviction of our two prospective prime ministers, one the son and the other the nephew of previous national saviours. Each candidate discussed "work" in an enviably forthright way, despite the fact that the concept was completely alien to both of them. Rania came charging back into the room, bearing coffees, croissants and a big grin.

"Make yourself at home. The Hellenic Police have given us the day off," she said, tucking into the pastries.

She was wearing jeans, a white shirt and a black waistcoat. Her hair was pulled back from her face by the sunglasses perched on her head, and hanging from her left ear was a large red bauble, which sparkled like her eyes.

"Doesn't that make you lose your balance?"

"I gave the other one away last night," she answered through her pastry.

"Who was the lucky man?"

She gestured to me to give her time to swallow, licked the runny chocolate sticking to her lips and took a sip of coffee.

"It could have been you, you know."

"You flatter me."

"Do you want to know what I was doing last night?"

"No, but you can tell me anyway. Coffee is the perfect excuse for two people to have a chat."

She lit a filterless cigarette and started telling me all about her adventures. She was not trying to make me jealous; just trying to get closer to me. Her efforts were commendable. She was hurt by the fact that after the successful mission in Oropos, I did not invite her for a drink at 16. She did not complain; she understood that I did not want her to see me get drunk. But sitting at home on her own, it started to get to her. She phoned a friend and they went to the theatre in an old warehouse in Metaxourgeio. Three young guys she had never heard of were in a play she chose because the title intrigued her, Akis Dimou's "Flowers for the Lady". It was good – a bit amateurish, but very fast-paced. The heroes were three twenty-five-year-olds: one of them made wooden cages for songbirds, the second was a barman, the third a student. They were spying on the girl in the flat opposite and talked about her constantly. Talked, just talked, but in the end decided to invite her over. They sent her flowers, the eponymous flowers for the lady, but she never turned up. She probably jumped off the balcony because her lover had left her. That was probably it, because the girl never appeared on stage. Rania really enjoyed it and laughed a lot, but in the end, the question of whether or not the girl jumped off the balcony did not appeal to her. She and her friend grabbed a sandwich in Omonia afterwards, and then went back to his place. That's where the red earring ended up. This "friend" happened to be her boyfriend. Yes, she had a boyfriend. She had not mentioned it to me because it had never come up. He was a fellow student and worked part-time as a pizza delivery boy, and had played a leading role in setting up the first union representing this popular profession. They had been together for about six months and were getting on well. It was an easy-going relationship. He took care of her, and she enjoyed being taken out on his moped, liked him cooking for her in his bedsit, going to the cinema (never to the Village Multiplex, of course, as this young man was a member of the Anti-capitalist Front), and Rania even had the odd orgasm. She was not in love with him; she had been with two other guys while she had been seeing him (one of whom was me), but she had not told him because she didn't want to hurt him. He gave her a sense of security.

When I offered to be best man, she tried to stub out her cigarette on the palm of my hand.

"What title are you after: King Cynic?"

She was shouting, and Rina applauded this outburst, confirming the eternal female alliance against men. I was worried that my relationship with the canary had been irretrievably damaged, so I apologized to Rania; she picked up the mugs and went to the kitchen. The running water inspired Rina to experiment with other melodies and transported me to other times, when the sound reassured me, when someone would be breathing just a few metres away from me. Those days were gone.

"Can you answer something honestly?" she said, wiping her hands dry across her back pockets.

"I'm not in love with you," I told her.

"I know that, you idiot," she whispered and snuggled up next to me. "That wasn't what I wanted to ask you."

"What then?"

"Why don't you want us to make love?"

"We have."

"Just the once."

"At my age, sex needs careful forward planning."

"Fuck you, and your fucking awful jokes."

"Why is it so important to you?"

"Well, it's not because I'm insecure, if that's what you think."

I recalled some advice a good friend once gave me which I always follow to the letter: never try to fool an intelligent woman who is in love with you. She will read you like a book.

"Sonia."

She took my hand in hers.

"If she recovers, are you two going to be together?"

"She's not going to recover."

"She will."

"If she does, I'll ask her."

"And what then? Will you still want to see me? Will you want us to make love every once in a while?"

I looked at her sternly, as sternly as you can look at a good woman, that is.

"Is this Queen Cynic talking?"

"No, it's Rania, who turns twenty-five today, and isn't asking you for anything. Or rather, the only thing she's asking is for you not to disappear."

Somewhere I managed to find the strength to smile at her, stroke her hair, kiss her softly on the mouth.

"Happy birthday, Ourania."

"Ourania! That's what my mother calls me when she's feeling sentimental. Well? I'm still waiting for an answer. Is that a yes or a no? Are you going to disappear?"

"At my age, you don't make promises you can't —"

She suddenly smothered my mouth with her hand.

"Promise me you won't disappear."

I mumbled something.

"You promised! Rina's my witness."

I nodded. She laughed, let go of my mouth and leapt to her feet.

"As for the sex, we'll work something out," she said menacingly and started to unbutton her shirt.

She stopped at the third button, as soon as the lacy trim of her bra became visible.

"What are you getting me for my birthday?" she said sadistically.

"What do you want?"

She did up her buttons again, slowly, put on her coat and pulled her keys out of the pocket and played with them with her slender fingers.

"The sea," she said, slipping on her sunglasses.

*

The sea I gave my young friend for her birthday resembled another sea that I knew well, the one in the north, hundreds of kilometres away, just as murky, just as shallow and just as still. The old sea was scarred from the seagulls squawking in the rain; the new sea was disdained by tired herons wading around in the evening sun.

*

"Where are you sailing to, Captain?"

Rania had devoured two fried chicken thighs, almost all of the salad and chips and was cleaning her hands on a squeezed lemon. She whooped for joy when I told her that the only convenient place for us to go that she would like was two hours from Exarcheia. She liked driving, and as we went along she introduced me to the most melodic examples of hip-hop from Italy, Corsica and Senegal. When we got to the dirt track going down to the sea, she turned off the C.D. player and looked at her surroundings, totally lost.

"But this is the middle of nowhere!" she marvelled, scouring the landscape for some sign of human life among the scant, wizened olive trees.

I promised her that in a few seconds she would be looking at the pride of Argolida. When she saw the whitewashed building, which, like Fotini's place in Oropos, had clearly been erected overnight without planning permission, the yard with the bamboo roof and the three aluminium bistro tables, the garland of yellow light bulbs and the five chained-up dogs who welcomed us with angry barks, she turned off the engine and looked at me in terror. I got out of the car, held her door open with all due ceremony, walked her over to one of the tables and went into the small kitchen to attend to the rest.

"Where are we, Simeon?"

"This is the best and cheapest restaurant in town. You don't have issues with cholesterol, do you?"

"No, but Nafplion's across from here. Why don't we —"

"Doesn't Nafplion look amazing from a distance?"

"From a distance?"

"Only from a distance."

The dogs had calmed down. Rania lit a cigarette and looked at the sea, two hundred metres away beyond the mud.

"Are those herons or something?"

"Herons, yes."

"I've never seen one before."

"See how much you learn from being with me."

"Is this where you used to seduce your perverted girlfriends?"

"No. This is where I used to drink *retsina* when I was in the army – over there – a few years before you were born."

She gave me a quick kick under the table.

"So why, if you don't mind me asking, did you choose this place, Mr Piertzovanis?"

"I celebrated my twenty-fifth here." She believed me, and was moved.

I got up to fetch our third half-litre jug and some olives; the restaurant was self-service on account of the owner's irrational fear of people. A miserable fellow from Piraeus – God knows what past sins he was paying for that had made him end up here.

"Any waltzes on those C.D.s of yours?" I asked, returning with supplies.

"Waltzes? Don't think so. Why?"

"Nothing. It's not important."

"Wait. I'll have a look."

She bit on an olive and dived back in to the Polo. Opposite, the sun was approaching the sea. The herons had settled on the sand.

"I've got something, but it's not a classical waltz," Rania cried from the car.

"Doesn't matter. Shall we dance, young lady?"

"Certainly, Sir."

"Turn it up full blast and leave the door open."

She ran up to me, taking off her coat. I took her by the hand and led her around a circular concrete dance floor, decorated with dried-up weeds.

"How did this get to be here?" she said as I slipped my arms around her waist.

"What do we care?"

We danced to a popular old waltz, slowly, one from my youth, "Let's take a stroll one evening . . ."

She was a good dancer. She closed her eyes and I let her lead me to better times.

On the way back I asked her to hurry up so that I could be back in time for visiting hours. That did not stop her from chattering away like a small child after its first school trip. Just outside Corinth, she realized that I had not said a word. She asked if anything was wrong.

"I'm wondering where Sonia's going to live afterwards."

"Didn't you say you would ask her to come and live with you?"

"She won't want to. Even if she did agree, she would still need someone to look after her round the clock. The flat's small and . . . I don't know."

"Don't get me wrong, but if money's the problem, I can help," she said after a while. "My father can, that is. Even if you wanted to restore the old house."

"No. The house is history."

"Why don't you give it to a developer? You would get at least a couple of flats in the new block in return. Till then, Sonia could stay in my flat. I'm in Italy half the time anyway, and when I am here, I often stay with my parents. Think about it, Simeon. It's the way to go. My father can find you a reliable contractor and you won't have to do a thing."

"I'm not sure. Last year, someone . . ."

I stopped and lit a cigarette; my hands were shaking. She was looking at me out of the corner of her eye.

"What is it?"

A vague recollection was stirring in my drink-fogged mind. An image was slowly taking shape. But, no! That was insane.

"Are you alright, Simeon? What happened last year?"

"I'm trying to remember. Please don't say anything for a while and switch off the radio."

Rania turned all her attention to driving while I tried desperately to combat what my doctor friends at 16 early this morning were calling alcoholic impairment, wanting to prove that memory loss in a number of cases was not down to Alzheimer's but to excessive alcohol consumption at the moment a particular memory is formed. Inevitably, after their lecture, they had needed the barman to give them "one for the road".

I struggled to reconstruct the chain of events: it must have been a week or two before I left for Marseilles, March or early April at the latest. It was a time when my drinking was out of control. I thought that it would be good preparation for my meeting with the green-eyed brunette who had walked out on me eight years earlier, but more than that, to convince myself that I still loved her. One afternoon I had a visit from a lawyer who had been a fellow student up in Thessaloniki. I did not remember him, of course, and it was not as if I could see him very well either. He was telling me something about the house – it was all a bit confused – I didn't really get what it was all about. I forget how I managed to get rid of him; but I do vaguely remember him mentioning the possibility of taking the plot in consideration on behalf of some of his extremely wealthy clients who were very open-minded and took a thoroughly modern approach to investment. I can remember him now: he was short, swarthy, dark overcoat, dark tie, sunglasses. And I remember all of that because some poor, beleaguered brain cell of mine had retained the image of a highly unusual distinguishing feature: in the middle of that thick head of hair was a white tuft – and had not Agisilaos said that the well-dressed type who drove him to the monastery had a white tuft in his hair?

"Where are we?" I asked Rania.

"At the Attiki Highway toll. We should be at the hospital in twenty minutes – assuming we don't get shot at by a patrol car on the way."

"Change of plan. Let's go to Stadiou, to my office. Don't worry: you'll get to blow out your candles before midnight."

The lawyer with the white tuft's business card was nowhere to be found. I called Achilleas, my young partner. He had never seen it, he said, and did not recall my ever mentioning the man. I couldn't find a single unfamiliar name in our appointments diary. I sat down in my armchair and lit up. Rania tried to sort out the chaos I had created while searching for some trace of this mystery visitor.

"No need to despair; it's only a matter of time before we find him. A lawyer who graduated from the Aristotelian University the same year as you! Can't you talk to some of your contemporaries? Or to your bar association? There must be someone – think!"

I blew her a kiss and dialled Spiros' number. Spiros was my mentor – he had introduced me to the dark side of Thessaloniki and initiated me into a life of drunkenness and selflessness: he was the only creature alive who connected me to the city of my youth, now nothing more than a synonym for loss.

His wife answered, frosty as ever. She had always had the impression that I was responsible for corrupting her husband. I had never been tempted to disillusion her on that score; it had been quite a compliment to be assigned the role of scapegoat for one of the most degenerate men of the country's second city. She told me that Spiros was watching a P.A.O.K. match on television and could under no circumstances be disturbed.

"Tell him it's me and it's urgent."

I heard the receiver bang down onto the table, followed a few moments later by the savage voice of my friend.

"I've only got three things to say to you, you dog: first, you're bloody lucky that this is a Sunday and I'm at home. We're still playing in a closed stadium – that's why I'm not down at the match. Secondly, what a pleasure it was getting your postcard of the Marseilles docks. Thirdly, don't ever dare cross the Tembi pass again. I've been dry for three months now and have cut off all exposure to the virus. I'm listening – what do you want now? If you've phoned to snivel about some beautiful woman again, tell her Spiros will erect a public monument in her honour if she manages to finish you off once and for all."

Apart from being a brilliant lawyer, and a left-winger in the old sense of the word, he also had an encyclopaedic knowledge of the city – all the information contained in the phone directory, the records office and the secrets that lay hidden in them, Spiros had at his fingertips. I explained who I was looking for and he promised to get back to me within the hour.

"O.K.?" Rania said as soon as I hung up.

"We'll know in an hour."

She walked to the window and opened it.

"The 'A' is missing," she said after a while.

"What 'A'?"

"From the neon sign on the roof terrace across the road. Amstel. The 'A' bulb has blown."

"*When you were young, did you ever imagine you'd see your name up in lights? And on the main thoroughfare too?*"

"*So you mean I'm not young now?*"

"*When you were younger?*"

"When I was younger, I wanted to be tall. After that I wanted to be given a pair of patent leather shoes. After that I wanted to marry Vrasidas – he was the grandson of the best barber in Kypseli. Then much later I wanted to become a biologist. When I was eighteen —"

"That's not what I meant."

"I know what you meant. But we're just talking. We're talking while waiting for a taxi. What's wrong with that?"

"Nothing."

"What did you ask me? No, don't tell me. I know! How do I feel seeing my name up in great big lights?"

"For instance."

"I'll let you in on a secret. You can keep a secret, can't you? Of course you can. You're a failed lawyer and a successful card player, so you obviously can keep secrets."

"Thank you."

"Here goes: when I see my name up in lights, it frightens me."

"Frightens you?'

"Yes. You see: Sonia Varika. Just imagine if the bulbs on the second 'i' were to blow. Sonia Varka. Sonia 'Boat'. Can you imagine? Why are you laughing?"

"That would be hysterical. The great tragedienne Sonia Varka in a unique light show."

"You think so?"

"What?"

"You think I should change my name when I get older. Sonia Varka. It's got a ring to it. And if I become a boat, I might just find the ocean."

"Interesting retirement plans."

"Any 'interesting plans' for tonight?"

"I know a good fun fair."

"Any wooden boats?"

"Complete with oars."

"Let's go."

I phoned the hospital; a nurse told me that there had been no change, but that Sonia would be moved to her own room that afternoon.

Spiros was true to his word, as always. I put the telephone on speakerphone and said sweetly, "Simeon Piertzovanis, legal office, how can I help you?"

"Shut up, you little shit. Get a pen and piece of paper and make sure you don't interrupt. And then I'll tell you how you can pay for this confidential intelligence. Here goes: Phaidon Tsolakidis, member of the Thessaloniki Bar Association. Born 1958. Married; two children, two girlfriends. Member, in chronological order, of the National Communist Students' Union, P.A.S.P. – the P.A.S.O.K. student movement – before standing as right-wing adviser for our bar association in the elections before last: five years ago in other words. Loaded. When I say the man is loaded, I mean that he makes in one hour what it would take me two lifetimes to earn. Three years ago he started getting his hands dirty, taking on cases for construction companies while also acting as legal adviser to the municipality. You can imagine how big his cut was. My good friend who gave me this information mentioned something you would do well to remember: the only time he ever shook Tsolakidis' hand, he went home one cuff-link lighter. If you want more, it'll have to wait till Monday. That's all. Oh, and about my fee."

"What fee?"

"For getting you all this information, you prick. Listen: so that we can call it evens, when you decide to come up here to visit your friend who you haven't given a damn about for the last nine years, make a pilgrimage to the P.A.O.K. ground, get down on bended knee and publicly renounce Panionios to make up for your bare-faced cheek in taking us to a draw on our own turf. Bastards!"

"Fine. Have you got any numbers for Tsolakidis?"

"I renounce Panionios. Say it."

"I renounce Panionios."

"O.K. Have you still got that pen?"

I jotted down Tsolakidis' numbers and before I hung up, I suggested a spot of sightseeing in Athens to Spiros. He told me to go straight to hell, and drink to his health *en route.*

"I'd like to meet this charming friend of yours," Rania said, clearly impressed.

"You'd get on famously. Except that, unfortunately for you, he's been in love with his wife for the last thirty-five years."

"I like a challenge. So, when are you going to take me up north and show me the White Tower?"

"Get serious."

She got serious, walked to the coat stand and took her mobile out of her pocket.

"Find Chronis and bring him up to speed."

"Shouldn't I call my esteemed colleague?"

"Listen to what the professional has to say first."

Halkidis answered on the twentieth ring, blind drunk. By trying to drown his guilt over Dedes in *raki*, he had succeeded only in drowning himself.

"Funerals, baptisms, what the hell, Simeon? I'm going to resurrect Manolis, my lawyer friend, and you're going to help me. Listen,

I'm looking at his photographs now – don't hang up – I want you to look at them, one by one. This is his baptism at Aghia Marina, I met his godfather, he was the village schoolteacher here, you see. Here he is in the gymnastics display, and there he is with old Stavros in the fishing boat, these are all with the girl, I'll bring them back with me – it's easier if you can see them up close. I gave them my word. Simeon, are you listening?"

"I can't hear you. The line's gone funny," I said, having to restrain myself from hurling a second phone at the wall.

Rania looked at me as though she realized what was up. I was desperate for a drop to drink, but not half as desperate as I was to extricate myself from this nightmare.

"Say something nice about me, Rania," I begged.

"Just as I was about to start feeling sorry for you, you go and say or do something that makes me change my mind," she said without missing a beat.

It took two cigarettes for us to decide on some kind of a plan. I picked up the phone and dialled Tsolakidis. He answered at once. For people like him, mobile phones are what pacemakers are to heart patients.

"Hello."

Light voice. Thick northern "l"s.

"Good evening. This is Simeon Piertzovanis. I'm a lawyer. I hope I'm not calling at an inconvenient time."

"No, no. Go ahead."

"A while back we discussed the matter of a property which was of interest to you, I don't know if you remember?"

"Yes, of course. How are you? Of course I remember. How was your trip? Zanzibar was it? Or Mozambique?"

I could sense that he was trying to buy time by starting this affable little chit-chat. I decided to help him.

"Swaziland, actually. But there was a change of plan. Women, as I'm sure you're aware, are such unpredictable creatures."

He laughed, a little slow to respond to the cue. I improvised, and came up with a story in which I played the part of the astonished traveller who returns to find his childhood home burnt to ashes. The story was fleshed out with my feelings of guilt at not having provided for the safety of my tenants: how I should have visited more often and that my prolonged absence was a major mistake. I adopted my professional lawyer's voice, unnecessarily long-winded in its attempts to hide the truth from his clients. I rounded off my monologue with a hearty dose of desperation.

"I realize that this tragedy is still very recent, but I'm deep in debt at the moment, and if I don't do something about it quickly, I'm finished. That's why I thought I'd ask you if you still have an interest in the property – the plot, I should say."

He coughed.

"Yes, of course, Mr Piertzovanis, of course," he said after apologizing for the condition of his pharynx, brought on by the accursed addiction.

"Good!" I said, winking at Rania who was listening, biting her nails like a little girl waiting for Sakis Rouvas to come on stage and flash his abs.

"Would you like to meet tomorrow?"

"Tomorrow will do nicely."

"I'll be in my office after 2.00. 318 Kifissias. That's the offices of the construction company, Earth Development."

"I'll be there at 2.30."

"Excellent. You couldn't bring the deeds along with you, could you?"

"I certainly can."

"I look forward to seeing you again, Mr Piertzovanis."

"Likewise, Mr Tsolakidis," I said, wiping the sweat from my forehead.

"What a performance!" Rania squealed, stretching out her previously clenched fist.

"Now can I have a drink?"

"*A* drink, yes."

"We'll see about that," I said, slipping the piece of paper with Tsolakidis' address into my pocket.

"Two, and that's the limit. We've still got twenty-five candles to blow out and your breathing alcoholic fumes all over the place won't make that any easier."

"Let's do it."

"Stand up."

"Just a moment," I said. "Let's get this straight: this man represents a company that has been bankrolling neo-Nazis, paying them to hound four poor bastards out of a rundown old house – and the idiots go and burn them to death by mistake in the process? Who on earth would dare risk something like that?"

"Alcohol deprivation is making you very naïve. Stand up and I'll prove to you, if you can guarantee the right circumstances, somewhere quiet in other words, that innocence is lost the moment we exit the womb."

The originality of her approach did not temper my anger.

"You're right. But this world is getting more and more tiring by the day," I said and lit a cigarette. She promptly pulled it out of my mouth, emptied the ashtrays, threw on her coat and walked to the window.

"The 'e' has gone now. All the vowels in fact," she said sadly.

I got up and switched off the study light. She shut the window and gave me back my cigarette and followed me to the door.

"Let me buy you a drink. Name the place."

"There's a very up-market bar downstairs," I said, summoning the lift.

*

"What more do you expect from life?" she said, the vowels barely articulated. I remembered the vowels in the neon sign and smiled. Aristides made the best Margaritas in town, and Rania had already had three. I did try to warn her, but to no avail.

"Tell me. What more do you expect from life?" she repeated, squeezing my wrist and trying to look into my eyes.

"No more presents at any rate."

"What? Me, I, myself – do you think that's what I am? A present?"

Aristides looked over as if to enquire whether I needed any backup. I reassured him that everything was under control. We both knew that drunk women were a blessing and drunk men a curse. Women got drunk and celebrated their defeat, while men drank and gloated over imaginary conquests. The beautiful drunk made another assault, in hushed tones this time.

"Fuck! I'm not some kind of present, you know. Besides, they usually come gift-wrapped, but I came to you just like that, as I am, naked, from the very first day, well, night. And do you know why, you cowardly little man? Do you?"

246

"No."

"Don't suppose I do either. But if I did know, I wouldn't tell you."

She tried to laugh but did not quite manage it. Releasing my wrist, she started stroking my hair.

"It's so unfair, Simeon. Any woman you fall in love with can wrap you round her little finger. You're soft as putty. So why did you have to go and not fall in love with me? Bloody hell – why me?"

"Let's go and choose a cake."

"I don't want a cake. I hate cakes," she said, licking the rim of her glass.

"But I promised I'd get you a cake."

"No, you didn't. You promised to buy me candles."

"O.K. Let's go and find some candles."

She gave in. I paid Aristides, helped her into her coat to compensate for her appealing stagger and ignored the envious smirks of the customers of 16.

"I was thinking . . . but can my gorgeous date drive?" she stuttered, realizing she was unable to unlock the Polo.

"Where to?"

"I'll tell you. It's not hard. Somewhere we can find twenty-five candles."

She took me back to her place, set out an entire fleet of candles, and made me light them. She blew them out, jumping on the spot, and then curled up on the sofa, deserting the battlefield. I slipped off her shoes, went into the bedroom, pulled the duvet off the bed, covered her with it and kissed her hair. She opened her eyes.

"The other earring. The red one. It's yours. Take it," she whispered. "It's your birthday present."

She closed her eyes again and fell asleep. I kissed her again and left on tiptoe without taking the earring. Gifts given drunkenly have never done me any good.

Sunday, 11.50 p.m.

One love is not enough; it's never enough. That is why religions with only one god, monotheistic they're called, yes, that's right, that's why they're so terrible. We want many loves, as many as we can get, we hunger after them, one love cannot satisfy you. The colpo grosso *is how many you can assemble at your funeral. If your funeral was a ticket-only affair, how much would you make? If you make a lot then you have had a lot of loves. Empty? Not worth the trouble? What about my loves? I've got the timid card player, I've got him, he'd definitely turn up. Then I've got that . . . no, that's not the right way – it'll get confusing. Let's take it from the beginning, set the scene properly. An opening night requires careful planning, my love, what sort of bullshit P.R. is that? In the front rows are the V.I.P.s, officially certified loves. There's the mother, that's one. Two, the father. So that they don't fight. As for you, my dear Freud, you can bugger off. Then the grandfathers and grandmothers. Not them, they don't count, I never met them. No, actually they do count because I heard about them. So it's grandparents next. Never met them but front row seats even so. Now it starts getting difficult. Not now, because they have all always been difficult – all of them poor. Rich and greedy, poor aristocrats, accidental artists, athletes who really wanted to be hairdressers, musicians who were more jealous of Spanoudakis than Satie, directors-cum-hangmen, authors and actors . . . Bet none of them turn up. So how am I expected to fill the seats? Easy. It's all a game to you, my girl. We will fill the circle with innocent passers-by: the theatre barman, no, I mean all the barmen in all the theatres, with that Pakistani assistant to the carpenter who built the stage for Yerma, with the photographer from that magazine* Health and Happiness, *all the leading actors of lots of stupid plays . . .*

There is one serious person who will turn up. His name is Chronis. He left me because he couldn't take any more. That skinny one, Simeon. He'll come. I couldn't stand watching him collapse in front of me for no reason, because I wasn't the reason, I was always the means, the thread which held them together with what they desired and which would snap with the very first tear, from the very first perfunctory dutiful kiss, from the first empty gaze . . .

I'll invite them all. They must come, every one of them, and they must pay. I'll put on a fantastic last night, but it has to sell out and make a good profit because I'm being asked to cover a lot of the transport costs.

Monday, 2.30 p.m.

The reception area of the offices of Earth Development was an impressive greenhouse; the floors and ceilings and walls were all glass. It was filled with rare exotic species of the plant kingdom and was unbearably hot. Three young women in summery clothes, with long red fingernails and dazzling smiles, were there to receive us. All three seemed pretty accomplished. One of them put our coats on a coat stand shaped like a palm tree; a second recited a catalogue of coffees, teas and other refreshments for us to choose from, while a third went to announce our arrival to her bosses. Not one of them could have been a centimetre under 1.95m.

Rania had had the foresight to dress formally in a beige suit, her mother's low-heeled moccasins, her grandmother's gold cross round her neck, and an engagement ring. The perfect woman to sort out her failed lawyer of a fiancé and secure a comfortable future for him. It had not taken much for her to persuade me that she would be useful.

"A sly and greedy fiancée can ask any questions she wants without arousing suspicion. Don't forget my performance at the billiards club, and the rapid deterioration of your mind – I'm coming and that's that."

We drank our espressos in silence, admiring the local vegetation. After ten minutes, we followed three of the longest pairs of calves we had ever seen into Phaidon Tsolakidis' office. He stood up to greet us and told his secretary to hold all his calls. His face did not stir any memories at all in me. If it were not for the white tuft, his designer sunglasses, and his expensively cut suit, he could have been the reincarnation of Louis de Funès. We spent the first five minutes of the conversation exchanging information about our contemporaries from law school – not that I had seen any of them since – and on optimistic forecasts about the success of the forthcoming Olympics (which he pronounced with that thick northern "l" of his), and of course the tragedy of the fire.

"Darling, let's not waste Mr Tsolakidis' time, shall we?" said Rania the minute I pulled my cigarette packet out of my jacket pocket. "And don't even think about lighting it – you've already had three today."

"I gave up six-and-a-half years ago. I limit myself to the odd cigar," said Tsolakidis. "But of course, if you want to smoke, be my guest. Not a problem."

"I'm afraid there is a problem, a very serious problem. I'm not about to marry a man fifteen years my senior and spend my time rushing around to see the city's lung specialists."

My betrothed's stern tone saved the French gypsy woman between my fingers from the flames, and I deposited her back into the safety of the packet, winking at my fellow lawyer as I did so. He smiled uncomfortably and opened the file on the desk in front of him.

"Right. Here we have the offer made to you by my firm on March 16, 2003. €300,000 – in other words twenty-five per cent above its taxable value. I don't believe —"

Rania interrupted.

"Mr Tsolakidis, before we came here, I discussed this matter with my father, a retired civil servant from the Ministry of Agriculture. I trust him implicitly. He has seen the property, and in his opinion our share of a five-storey apartment building would be at least three flats of 100 square metres each. As for the plans, building materials and the rest of it, we would have to discuss that with the architect before we can sign any contracts."

"I see," he said, deep in thought. "It's simply that our firm has other plans. We see it as an investment opportunity, and would not be planning to build. In other words, at this moment, we have no interest in the property development sector."

"Meaning?" I said with genuine interest.

"We only want the land."

"Well, I can't agree to that," Rania said petulantly.

"Just a moment, sweetheart," I said crossly and turned to Tsolakidis. "Phaidon – let's be straight with each other. Whichever developer I go to, I'll have those three flats within a year. If I sell you the land, you'll just —"

"Just a minute, Simeon. I told you that we had other things in mind for the area, but I'm not at liberty to disclose the details. Let's cut to the chase. What would seem a reasonable price to you?"

I looked at Rania, so deep in thought she would have been a worthy subject for Rodin. Tsolakidis relieved the silence that followed, tapping his wedding ring with a gold Montblanc.

"I don't know, Phaidon. I wasn't prepared for this, but €300,000 does seem a bit meagre."

"Let's talk about it, then."

"Darling, we don't have to give him an answer right this minute," Rania waded in. "Why don't we go and talk to an estate agent first, advertise, and then take it from there?"

"Ourania, please," I scowled.

"Fine. You two are obviously the experts," she gave up in a sulk.

Tsolakidis slowly uncapped his pen, scribbled something down on a piece of paper, and said without looking up, "I'll be quite frank with you. My instructions are that I can improve the offer by fifty per cent of the taxable value of the plot. This gives us a ceiling of €480,000."

He snapped the top back onto his Montblanc and looked at me, biting his bottom lip. The ease with which he had raised the original offer gave me pause.

"What did you say you wanted to build on it?" I said casually, wanting to give him the impression that I was trying to buy time to consider this new offer.

"I did not say, but since you're so curious, what I can tell you, off the record, is that one option we're looking at is building a large cultural centre there."

"On so tiny a plot?" Rania said in surprise.

"We'll find a way, madam, don't you worry," he smiled.

"I don't know, Phaidon. Give us a day or two to think it over. But I have to say that your offer is still a little on the low side."

"Let's try something else then," he said, getting to his feet. "If you'd excuse me for a couple of minutes, please."

He left the office, closing the door behind him.

"A cultural centre? What a load of bollocks!" Rania snarled. "You said that plot was barely 500 square metres."

"There are lots of other old houses surrounding it," I whispered and lit up.

I would wager that one quick visit to the land registry would show that they had all been bought up by Earth Development. These people were no amateurs: they weren't desperate to get their hands on the house because they believed there was buried treasure in the garden, or because they wanted to put up a block of over-priced duplexes.

Tsolakidis was back, rubbing his small hands together. He sat down in his chair and gave us a big smile.

"How would you like to meet our president and managing director of our company? We'll have something to drink and talk this over in a more relaxed atmosphere. I've just come off the telephone with him, and he told me that there's nothing he relishes more than hard-nosed negotiations. Would 9.00 be convenient? He lives in Ekali; the girls outside will give you directions."

"Tonight? But shouldn't we think about this a bit first, darling?" said Rania, playing the part of the confused young woman to perfection.

"Ever heard the saying 'strike while the iron is hot', Ourania?" I said and got to my feet.

She reluctantly followed suit, ignoring Tsolakidis, who was hold-ing out his hand to her.

"Madam, it has been a pleasure meeting you," he said, overlook-ing my future wife's appalling manners. "You'll allow me a minute in private with my old college friend, I hope. It's a business matter."

Rania nodded and left the office. Tsolakidis closed the door after her and winked at me. His face was the starkest portrait of human corruption I had ever seen.

"I'm sure you won't take it amiss if I suggest that it might be better for all concerned if you were to come on your own tonight. I'm sure you understand. And you'll be allowed to smoke as much as you like!"

"Of course I understand. And I hope we can have a drink like civ-ilized adults too," I said giving him a friendly pat on the shoulder.

"I'm confident the president's wine cellar will make quite an impression on you."

"9.00 on the dot, then. I'll be there, as long as it doesn't snow and the roads aren't closed."

"If it does, I'll send out a helicopter for you," he said, laughing moronically. It was as much as I could do not to slap him across the face.

*

Halkidis was waiting for me in a café up at the end of Syngrou. He was a pitiful sight in his crumpled grey suit with a black tie spilling out of his jacket pocket.

"Let's ask the expert: how do you recover from drinking too much *raki*?" he said the minute I sat down.

"Drink more *raki*, chase it with a beer, and crash out for three hours."

"You think so? One thing's for sure – coffee's useless."

"Have you been up all night?"

"I really wouldn't know."

I ordered a toasted sandwich and a soda water. The police colonel was not brave enough to try my homeopathic remedy and opted for a glass of orange juice instead. I went into long and proud detail about the progress we had made over the last twenty-four hours. His expression hardened. He called his secretary and told her to find out everything she could about Earth Development and its president.

"The prosecutor is still getting Agisilaos' statement. She should be finished some time this afternoon," he said vaguely and lit up. It was obvious that his mind was elsewhere.

"So what do we do?" I said, chewing away at the plastic abomination that had set me back €5.

"You go along to the big boss tonight. That will buy us time. Play the greedy desperado and find out what you can. Even though I'm pretty sure everything's quite clear now."

"Clear?"

"Theoretically, yes. This company wants the land your house stands on so that it can erect some monstrosity on it. Its pisshead owner is too sentimental and doesn't get it. Our bad guys are unlucky because the owner goes and disappears for months on end. If he hadn't taken off to Marseilles, they would have been in with a chance of catching him sober and in the right frame of mind to go ahead with the deal. With half a million, he could have gone and bought himself a very nice house somewhere and everyone would have been happy – Sonia and everyone else. No fires, no nothing. Calm down, I never said it was your fault. It was just really bad luck."

"I wouldn't have sold it anyway."

"Why not?"

"They were so comfortable there. Sonia loved the peace, the quiet and that almond tree. Morenike had plenty of room, and Rosa would play outside in the garden for hours on end."

"Never mind. None of that matters now."

We sat there for a while, smoking in silence.

"Do you know what I think? Go along there tonight and accept their offer. Take the money and run. You've had more than your share of grief. It would be a great help to me if you did. It will take days for me to get together all the evidence I need relating to that company, the president and anyone else that might have their hand in this. And don't forget, they've got friends in high places, so I might never get to the bottom of this."

He was talking in a low voice, his head inclined and his fingers playing with the residue at the bottom of his glass. I had the sense that he was suddenly acting all exhausted and worn out because he was trying to hide something from me. What concerned me more was that I thought I knew what that something was.

"Suppose you do amass all the evidence you need and take it to your boss, what happens then?"

"You'll be the first to know."

His mobile rang. He listened carefully for a while, got out a pen, and scribbled something on a paper napkin.

"If you've got a secretary who knows her way around the inter-net and also has a stockbroker for a brother, things can happen quite quickly," he said, hanging up. "Earth Development was awarded three per cent of all Olympic contracts. Its stock is very healthy and its last annual report showed a twelve per cent increase in profits. It really took off in 2000. Does that date mean anything to you?"

"The millennium? That gigantic artificial tree in Syntagma?"

"It was the year after the big stock market crash. If you think back, you'll remember that not everyone was caught out. Some people made sure they got out in time."

I ordered a beer to wash away the lingering taste of that toasted sandwich and I let him resume his introduction to political economy.

"If someone has the right information at the right time, makes the right moves, they can put away a tidy few billion. After that, they can go and set up a nice company and everyone's happy. Can I have a sip?"

"Why don't you get some sleep?"

"Perhaps I should," he said, producing his wallet.

"Who's the man at the top?"

He glanced at the napkin.

"Apostolos Zacharopoulos – president and managing director. Low profile, former director of a shipping firm. Married, two kids. I'm afraid I've got to go. Can I drop you anywhere?"

"No. I'll finish my beer and move on to something more serious," I was about to say, but was pre-empted by my mobile. I listened to the news and gestured to the young man behind the bar who was mesmerized by a large, mute television screen.

"Whisky on the rocks," I shouted over the music.

"What's the matter?" asked Halkidis, holding out a banknote.

"That was the hospital. They haven't moved Sonia. There's been a deterioration."

"What kind of deterioration?"

"Heart failure."

"Let's go."

"No. The doctor said it wouldn't do any good. She'll be asleep for the next eight hours. Her condition is stable."

The policeman left the note on the table and walked out of the café with slow, deliberate steps, attempting to straighten out the creases in his crumpled, funereal jacket as he went. I stared after him for a long time. The young man brought my whisky. I stared at it for ages too, and then decided to drink it.

✶

A marble plaque next to the grey steel door, with the words VILLA NATASHA chiselled into it in dignified archaic lettering, announced the identity of the mansion. There was no bell. I caught sight of a small red light above me to the right. It flickered teasingly down at me. I could picture the owner of this pile adding my face to his collection of hand-picked visitors. The gate opened slowly and noiselessly. A heavily built thirty-something man appeared, holding a short chain with a miserable-looking Alsatian panting on the other end of it. He welcomed me politely, reassuring me that I need not be afraid of the animal – without specifying which one he meant – and asked me to come with him. We walked across a small, well-manicured spinney, which opened onto a vast Neo-Classical villa of almost palatial proportions, the kind you see in the northern suburbs. We walked up a dozen marble steps, the heavy, the dog and I, and they delivered me up to the slightly odd smile of a Filipina maid. She looked familiar. I didn't have time to work out where from, because she very quickly showed me into a drawing room, relieved me of my coat and motioned to me to sit down on a leather sofa. Next to me towered a standard lamp which could have been cashed in for enough money to secure early retirement for an accomplished burglar, his children, and their children. To my left was a small mosaic-topped table, with eight tarot cards on it.

"Do you believe in fortune telling?"

The voice belonged to the fourth woman I had seen in the last few hours who was taller than me. She was in her mid-thirties, and by far the most beautiful. Her long blonde hair reached almost to her waist; her eyes were the colour of honey and her body living proof of the physical superiority of the female sex.

I stood up and introduced myself.

"Nice to meet you, Mr Piertzovanis. My husband tells me you're a lawyer. Natasha Ermeidis, Mr Zacharopoulos' wife. You didn't answer my question: do you believe in tarot readings?"

"No."

"Wonderful."

She slid into the sofa and patted the empty cushion next to her. I sat down again making sure to leave a buffer zone between us.

"Apostolos is just finishing up with his lawyer and has asked me to keep you company."

"Do you mind if I smoke?" I said, scouting around for an ashtray.

"Of course we'll smoke," she said and pulled a minuscule silver ashtray from the pocket of her long woollen cardigan. "We don't have any ashtrays in here because our interior designer said that they would disturb the *feng shui* of the space."

"What's *feng shui*?"

"You're beginning to grow on me, Mr Piertzovanis," she laughed.

I took cigarettes out of my jacket pocket, and offered her one.

"Gitanes!" she squealed, as though she had just run into a long lost school friend.

"Are they your brand?"

"They were once. In Paris, at *Les Deux Magots* on St Germain. I'm sure you've been there."

"Can't say I have."

"Pity. All the big artists go there. I was first offered one there a few years ago by an important French director."

"Were you impressed?"

"No. He was boring."

"I meant with the cigarette."

"Yes, but I was young and I would have smoked anything."

I mirrored her laughter awkwardly and lit the two gypsy women. She drew on hers and blew out the smoke, without inhaling.

"How old do you think I am, Mr Piertzovanis?"

"Judging by the way you smoke, I'd say you couldn't be a day older than fifteen."

Clearly annoyed, she stubbed out the cigarette and looked at me intently.

"You've come here to sell my husband that house which burned down, haven't you?"

"Perhaps," I said equivocally.

A door was heard opening somewhere, then footsteps. She leapt up like a spring uncoiling.

"Barso in Kifissia. Please be there," she whispered just as the Filipina maid reappeared, with that peculiar smile that was something between sarcasm and menace still fixed across her round face. Even now I could not remember where I had seen her before.

"Sir is waiting for gentleman now, please," she announced in a sing-song voice, giving me a slight curtsey.

She waited for me to get up and then turned round. I exchanged glances with Natasha and followed the maid along the thick pile carpeting of the long corridor leading to the study. The president and managing director of Earth Development was standing behind a modern desk covered in documents and architectural drawings. Tsolakidis was sitting on a small sofa, holding a brandy glass.

"Do sit down, Mr Piertzovanis. I apologize for keeping you waiting. What can I offer you? I'm having a smoked malt and your fellow student over here Courvoisier. The bar can offer you anything you please. Just name your poison."

He must have been in his fifties, but he looked in very good shape. He had a fine head of thick grey hair; his impeccably fitting Lacoste polo shirt showed off his well-toned body; and his face looked at least twenty years younger than mine.

"I'm O.K., thank you. Perhaps a little later," I said brightly, and settled into the sofa facing his desk.

He topped up his whisky and sat down next to his legal adviser. A large black and white photograph of his wife on the wall behind his desk caught my attention. Beautiful, dressed in a black evening gown, and leaning against a wall plastered with graffiti.

"Have you met Natasha, Mr Piertzovanis?"

"Yes, we spoke briefly."

"What was your impression of her?"

"Adorable."

"She was twenty-five when I married her. I was still trying to establish myself. For the first three years of our married life we were living in rented accommodation. Imagine! She gave up a successful

261

modelling career so that she could look after the family. You don't get many pretty girls doing that these days, do you?"

I conceded the point and went on to extol her understated beauty. He was flattered and got carried away enumerating his spouse's qualities. Despite the little laughs, and his relaxed and friendly demeanour, it was very plain to me that the man was not at ease. His hands played nervously with his glass, he took very small and frequent sips as he cast his eyes around the room unsteadily. Tsolakidis took advantage of a short pause, coughed, opened up the file on his lap and suggested we get down to business. The developer agreed, put his whisky on the desk, picked up a document and quickly scanned its contents.

"Phaidon has explained to me that you have certain reservations regarding the sale of the site."

"Mr Zacharopoulos, it's not just the money, you know. I like the area. I grew up there and had it in mind to move back. But this morning Phaidon told me that you were planning a large cultural centre on the land – and I imagine on the neighbouring plots as well – and I started to wonder whether this would be such a good thing for the area. In fact, I thought it would go downhill. What can I say? I'm very confused."

"Mmm," he smiled, and launched into the classic and excruciatingly boring string of mini-lectures about progress, modernization, economic stimulus, essential investment for the national economy, the kind of development that would automatically factor in respect for the environment, the movement of money and job creation.

His company was indeed planning a large-scale entertainment venue that would cater to the needs of hundreds of thousands of people.

"The area needs it, Mr Piertzovanis. The golden days of the sleepy suburbs are over. Life is changing. People now want to find goods and services close together. You're an old romantic, and I sympathize with you, I really do. Just look at where my wife and I have chosen to live – isolated from every sort of noise, practically in the wilderness. But the vast majority of people want other things."

His speech was lacklustre, like that of a salesman, who one day, just before he retires, starts to sing the praises of a food mixer to an indifferent bachelor who has already decided to buy one. I did not interrupt. I was trying to work out whether his manner could be put down to the confidence his money gave him, or to something else, and I just couldn't get his wife's bizarre behaviour out of my mind. But then Tsolakidis broke in.

"Apostolos, perhaps we should let Simeon name his price?" he said obsequiously.

"Yes, of course," came the rather distracted reply.

I decided to risk it.

"Gentlemen, you know there is something else that is holding me back. You'll have heard that I was putting up some close friends in the house . . . this tragedy has consumed me, and sitting here, discussing money, seems almost —"

"Sacrilegious?" Zacharopoulos was barely audible. I nodded.

"Can I pour you a drink?" he said after a while.

"Scotch with plenty of water."

"Any preference?"

"None. As long as it's not malt."

He got slowly to his feet, prepared the drink without paying attention to Tsolakidis' empty glass, handed it to me and sat down at his desk.

"I was shocked by the event myself, Mr Piertzovanis. Let me say that building on a place where so many people died also seemed to me to be . . . wrong. As soon as I heard about the accident, I got cold feet, and seriously considered dropping the project. Call it *naïveté*, call it superstition, I don't know. But then I looked at it more calmly. We must do this. Life has to go on, don't you agree? Besides, what difference will it make?"

I took a hearty swig and looked at the photograph of his wife. The notion that this mild-mannered man knew what had caused the fire seemed quite plausible to me.

"You're absolutely right, Mr Zacharopoulos," I whispered. "Life does go on. A short memory is a blessing and a long memory a curse."

They nodded their heads, like little clockwork toys, in total agreement with this wise apothegm.

"€800,000 with the taxes covered by us – that's the best I can do, Mr Piertzovanis," said the boss before downing his smoked malt.

Tsolakidis appeared taken by surprise, but God only knows if the surprise was genuine. I lit up and thought for a while. The silence was broken by a knock on the door, and Natasha's beautiful face lit up the room.

"Darling, I'm just popping down to Kifissia to grab a bite to eat with Loukia. I won't be long. I hope we'll see you again, Mr Piertzovanis," she said and left, her delicate perfume lingering in the air by way of compensation.

Her husband was anxious to resume the discussion.

"So, my friend, is our offer acceptable?"

"Look. There is one last loose end here. I will have to discuss this with my mother. She retains the usufruct —"

264

"We have already discussed it with her," Tsolakidis interrupted. "While you were abroad. That aspect has already been taken care of."

"I see," I said, stubbing out my cigarette.

I could picture my precious mother putting her signature to those papers, which, together with a healthy dollop of cash, would buy her the certainty that she would never have to see me again. Even a guilty conscience has its price.

The developer rubbed his eyes while his legal adviser half closed his, trying to guess what I was thinking, like someone very short-sighted sitting on a bus trying in vain to read the newspaper over the shoulder of the person next to him.

"Then I think we have an agreement, gentlemen," I announced, by no means sure that this was the right thing to do.

Zacharopoulos remained impassive – unlike Tsolakidis who was shamelessly exposing his yellowing teeth through a broad grin.

"When can you have the contracts ready, Phaidon?"

"The day after tomorrow. Thursday afternoon at the latest."

We shook on it, and the developer showed me out of his study. The strange maid took over from there; she was carrying my coat and her eyes were sparkling. And then I remembered: not where I had seen her, but the words of a song, "Maria's Story no.2": "Asians have chaotic minds,/Especially when they're planning something."

A minor masterpiece of a song in which Vasilis Nikolaïdis pre-dicted the form the new class struggle was to take, telling the story of an Asian cook who had been raped by the male members of the family which had bought her, and how she quite literally brought various members of the *haute bourgeoisie* to their knees with her exotic dishes. Members of the ruling classes had come together at a big mansion like this one, confident that they were about to sample some genuine oriental delights, but the new working class decided to take revenge by assaulting their intestines with the most explosive gastric combinations possible. At the end of the corridor, the words of the finale came back to me too: "What can the guests say, and who can they turn to? / Now it's the turn of the shat upon to speak."

I took my coat from the maid and winked at her, as the young heavy took on the final leg of the process. I got into Rania's Polo two streets away, turned right and phoned Chronis. He answered at once. I told him about my meeting with Natasha. We agreed to meet up after that, at a bar near my house.

"Look in your mirror occasionally. If you get even the slightest sense that you're being followed, stop somewhere that's full of people and call me right away," he said and hung up.

*

The second I walked into the ancient patisserie I was overwhelmed by the smell of custard cream and various baked oriental sweets. It brought back memories of excruciating Sunday afternoons when my father used to drag me around the northern suburbs to treat me to the best rice puddings in the world, at the same time conveniently assuaging his guilt. I walked through the room with all the large baking tins and enormous refrigerators into the cafeteria section, occupied only by a single retired couple and the lovely Natasha. The pensioners looked livelier than she did. She was waiting for me at a table next to the murky windows, seemingly absorbed by the withering vegetation in the courtyard, which was bathed in a sickly yellow light. A cup of tea stood steaming before her. I bumped into the spectral-white waiter, who could not have been much shy of ninety. I ordered a whisky, proudly ignoring his puzzled reaction, and took a seat next to the former model.

"I'm cold," she said, pulling her dark raincoat in at the waist.

"Would you like to go somewhere else?"

"No. It's quiet here. Anyway, this won't take long."

I got out my cigarettes and offered her one, but she declined. The waiter arrived, and, with very slow movements, left a small metal dish with dry roasted chickpeas and a glass of brandy. I forgave him. Whisky in a place like this would have been as out of place as milk in a saloon bar in the Wild West.

"Maybe I should have ordered a brandy too," she said distractedly.

"Shall I put some in your tea?"

"Why not?"

She took a sip and smiled at me.

"So, Mr Piertzovanis, did you and my husband reach an agreement?"

"Yes. I mean, we've made a preliminary agreement," I said hesitantly. She sighed.

"Are you an honest man?"

"Yes, I am."

"If I hire you, will you be obliged to respect client confidentiality? What I mean is that you won't be able to repeat what I tell you to anyone, isn't that how it works?"

"Correct."

"Then I want to become your client."

I was taken completely by surprise. "You'll have to put me in the picture first."

"But how am I to know that you won't go off and talk to someone else about it if you don't take me on?"

"Firstly, you have my word. And then there's the sanction that if you reported me to the bar association, I would be finished."

"And how do I prove that I'm your client? I've seen a lot of your colleagues on T.V. talking about their clients' personal lives."

"I do not regard those characters as colleagues."

"Why not?"

"I wouldn't even hire them to water the plants on my balcony."

She tried to force a smile, but she failed. It was impossible for her to hide the fear in her eyes.

"I'm being silly, aren't I?" she whispered, sipping her tea. "O.K., fine, I'll tell you a little story, and then you can give me your advice. Alright?"

I agreed.

"But first, tell me, what is your connection to Sonia Varika? Why was she living in your house?"

"She had been having some financial problems over the last few years and —"

"Were you in love with her?" she broke in, raising her voice a little.

"What's that got to do with it?"

"The more honest you are with me, the more honest I can be with you."

"Then the answer is 'yes,'" I said, stubbing out my cigarette and lighting another one. "I loved her very much."

"Good. Now you can listen to my story."

She leant towards me and started talking in a low voice. After ten minutes, the brilliant investigator Simeon Piertzovanis had solved the mystery without having to lift a finger, thanks to the sense of security his harsh looks and determined chin inspired in other people.

Natasha was now thirty-four years old. She had started modelling at eighteen. The rest was predictable: money, trips abroad, eternal dieting, insecurity, and the slow but predictable descent into pills, cocaine, tedious threesomes, and therapy. At twenty-three she was on the brink of a breakdown. That was when she met Sonia, who at that time was at the peak of her career. The two of them became friends; Sonia assumed the role of big sister and taught her not to rely too much on her looks, to make the most of her time. Sonia also introduced her to some interesting people, including a few – exceedingly few of course – who did not just want to get her into bed to improve their image. Very soon Natasha had kicked all her bad habits and had understood what it meant to live a life appropriate to your age. At twenty-five she met the engineer Apostolos Zacharopoulos, who was fifteen years her senior and not particularly handsome. He gave her security, and when she got pregnant she decided to marry him. Sonia was not keen on the idea. She thought that the age difference was too great and tried to persuade her that beautiful women should not marry till they are in their prime – that is, once they turn fifty. Natasha did not listen. After the wedding, she shut herself away at home, and within a year she had given birth to their second child, and lost touch with her big sister. Natasha heard that Sonia had started drinking and playing cards, but did not dare challenge her about it. Meanwhile, her husband's business was thriving, and before she knew it, she had become totally isolated up in her Ekali mansion. The last time she saw Sonia was on New Year's Eve, 2002. They bumped into each other on the street and went for a coffee. Sonia had talked to her about me, about my suggestion that she move into the house, and how much she loved her weird lawyer Simeon. After that they lost touch again. When she heard about the fire she was devastated.

"I felt as if the earth had opened up under my feet. Sonia had rescued me from the jaws of hell," she said, her eyes moist.

"I understand," I stammered, stunned by the coincidence.

"I don't think you do," she said, rubbing her eyes. "My husband was involved in the fire at your house."

I asked the ancient waiter for a double and a single brandy, lit a cigarette and tried to come to terms with what I had heard. She helped me out.

"Earth Development is planning to build a huge shopping and entertainment complex in the centre, covering roughly twenty-five acres. It's a massive investment. I know all this first hand; my husband tells me everything. Besides, thirty-five per cent of the company is in my name. By March last year, he had managed to buy up all the land surrounding your house. I say 'your house', but back then I had no idea it belonged to you, or that Sonia was living there. When you didn't want to sell, and then disappeared, certain individuals got to my husband. They convinced him that if your friends moved out, you would hardly have any reason not to sell. When Tsolakidis came back from visiting you, he declared you a sentimental alcoholic, and therefore vulnerable."

"Why?"

"Why? Because you kept going on about how much you despise money, and under no circumstances would you tell your friends to move out. And you drank to their very good health."

Our drinks were delivered. Natasha took a sip and closed her eyes in reaction to the burning sensation. I, on the other hand, found it refreshing.

"Do you know exactly what your company did to encourage my friends to move out?" I asked her coldly.

"Mr Piertzovanis, I swear, on the lives of my children, that my husband did not tell me anything about that until two days after the fire."

"And what did you do about it when he did?"

She spun the stem of the glass around in her fingers.

"Nothing," she said, lowering her gaze. "I cried."

"Until it came to you that tears don't get results."

She ignored my sarcasm, and went on with her story. She was keeping the best for last.

"Please listen. I beg you. Believe me when I tell you that it's not my husband who's behind all this. Apostolos is just a pawn. He told me everything last Monday. He's in their clutches. You see, his business ventures over the years, well, they have not been as 'innocent' as I had assumed."

"Precisely how many 'innocent' people do you know who can afford to live in houses like yours?"

"I just thought he was a hard-headed businessman who —"

"Who now and then had to step on a few corpses. But when a figure of speech translates into three actual corpses, plus a friend of yours – who is now fighting for her life in Intensive Care, a friend who once dug you out of hell and saved your life – that's very moving, so you have a good cry."

Fortunately, the pensioners on the next table were hard of hearing and paid not the least attention to my outburst. I slowly swallowed half of my glass in an attempt to calm down. The lovely lady opposite me was sobbing silently.

"So who are these thugs who force your husband to go around setting fire to people?" I asked her after a while.

"The Church." She struggled to say it. "They are behind the

investment. Most of the money is theirs. Tsolakidis is in their legal department. My husband and our company are used as a front."

I digested my astonishment with the help of the remaining brandy and shut my eyes. Images were spinning inside my head, driving me insane: my father forbidding me to take communion on the pretext that I would catch germs from the other kids; Sonia buried in a forest of tubes; the footsteps of the Holy Mother leading up to the monastery; the abbot hiding the half-naked neo-Nazi in his toilet; little Rosa sobbing inside the trunk that once held all my toys; people hurling stones at women in the name of Allah; crusaders shouting and kneeling before banners dipped in the blood of innocents; latter-day devotees of the inquisition spewing forth advice and threats; young people crossing themselves outside churches while chatting on their mobiles; young brides stamping on their groom's patent leather shoes; murderers and exorcists of new born babies; images of a place inhabited by bipeds with worm-eaten brains . . .

"Will you help me, Mr Piertzovanis?"

I was brought back to life by her hoarse voice. I lifted my face and saw a faded, but in no sense pitiful figure. "Be honest – why are you telling me all this?" I said, returning my cigarettes to my pocket.

"I don't know. Perhaps because Sonia was the only person who never wanted anything from me. And she loved you very much. Perhaps because I felt guilty. Who else could I talk to about it?"

"I'm sure the prosecutor on duty the night your husband talked to you would have been willing to listen."

"I couldn't. There's nothing we can do. How can you possibly go to war with the most powerful firm in Greece? They'll crush us."

"I am not interested in helping you, Madam. I broke all ties with the Church the second I emerged from the font," I said with all the spite I could muster.

She looked at me as though in a daze.

"What am I supposed to do? This is not my fault."

"Pray and weep," I said. "Weep and pray. Take a nice holiday somewhere civilized," I added, leaving her to relive happier times, the days before dirty money, bloodshed and charred ruins.

*

Halkidis listened without interrupting, without touching his beer, and without lighting up, all of which I did. I worried that if I did not get hammered tonight, I might end up desecrating the cathedral. When I reached the end of my animated narrative, he stood up without saying a word and bolted himself in the toilet. It occurred to me that if he kept this up with the coke, he would soon be dead.

"Do you believe her?" he said when he got back, visibly rejuvenated.

"Yes."

"Me too."

"What are our chances of getting her to talk to the prosecutor – supposing we lean on her a bit?"

"Not a hope in hell."

"Not a hope in hell," he repeated and tried his beer.

I signalled to the waitress for a drink. The D.J. had discovered "Dance Me to the End of Love" and a drunken couple was trying desperately to sway in time. Experience and their hunched backs told me that the next morning, the more intelligent of the two would wake and flee in terror from the crumpled sheets of a pitiful

273

encounter, sparing the other from harbouring false hopes. The waitress elegantly placed the new glass of alcohol on the table.

"Any interesting plans for the future?" I asked Halkidis.

"Some," he said, smiling.

He stood up, put on his coat, nudged past the happy couple, who were blocking his path, and opened the door.

"Don't go doing anything stupid," I shouted after him, not minding the irritated looks I was getting from a group of young girls at the next table.

Monday, 11.55 p.m.

Colours. Lovely, relaxing colours. Ophelia's bright blue – I really like that. More than Yerma's grey or Emma's yellow, and I also like Iphigenia's dreamy red, even though I really prefer Blanche's deep blood red, Electra's brown, and Andromache's, well, it's so-so, like Lulu's black; Virginia's deep green suits me better than Antigone's orange, and that's why that young girl, what was her name, that young girl in "Speak To Me Like the Rain", I cannot remember anymore, she was a sort of diaphanous colour, and the ashen grey, whose was that? Anya's? No. Klara's? I'm talking nonsense – Klara was in the summer, and there are no ashen-grey summers. Oh, think . . . think . . . Maybe Sonia's . . . no, not Sonia's. Out of the question. It can't be Sonia, no ashes there, Sonia was always naked.

CHAPTER 9

Chronis Halkidis' List

3.ii–4.ii
Tuesday, 9.50 a.m.

"Morning, angel."

"Good morning, Mr Halkidis."

Fotini was looking proudly at the bunch of flowers on her desk.

"I got you some too," she said, pointing to a vase on top of the filing cabinet.

Her smile hid a certain bitterness.

"Where did you get them? It's the middle of winter."

"This morning I was walking through the market and saw them and thought about Manolis. He loved it when I brought flowers to the office. You know, it's not . . ."

She hid her eyes behind the palms of her hands. As though in a dream, I could see myself standing over Dedes' grave, telephoning her, rambling incoherently and sobbing.

"'What would I have amounted to on this earth without you?'" I sang, tunelessly. It didn't work. I picked up the vase and unlocked my office.

"Chief wants you over at Alexandras," she managed to slip in before I could close the door. I looked at her in bewilderment. One hand was rubbing her eyes, and the other was trying to work the mouse on her computer.

"What time?"

"Now. I've booked the driver. He's waiting for you."

"What's he playing at? If he'd called me on my mobile, I could have gone straight there."

"It's not only God who moves in mysterious ways," she said and pretended to be absorbed in her work.

It would take time for her to get over Dedes' death. As for me, maybe not so long.

*

I got in the back and told the young policeman to turn the siren on. He was thrilled, but despite his skilful manoeuvres, the short journey from Syngrou to Alexandras took almost half an hour. I ducked into the toilets on the first floor, gave my nervous system a little boost and went up to the Chief's office. One of his four secretaries told me he had visitors and asked me to wait. Two cigarettes later, the Chief's door opened, and the horizon darkened. Two clerics appeared in the doorway, the Chief barely visible behind them. One of them must have weighed in at at least 130 kilos; the other one I recognized. He was the abbot who had been hiding Agisilaos in his monastery. The Chief opened a path between them to get through to me.

"Chronis, you're early. Never mind. Even better. This gives you the chance to meet Archimandrite Eusignios and Abbot Nikolaos. I've just had a very interesting chat with them, and if there's any time left after we've discussed our own business, I'll bring you up to speed."

The corpulent one proffered a hand for me to kiss. I squeezed it instead and turned to the abbot, who was doing all he could to avoid making eye contact with me.

"Pleased to meet you," I said, in a suitably respectful tone. He gave me a look so threatening that he could have made a small fortune hiring out that face to the arms industry. I kept my thoughts to myself, reasoning that it would be wiser to allow him go on living on the pittance his noble calling secured him, for now. The Chief walked them out and came back to his office, leaving the door open. I followed him through, closed the door myself and sat in an armchair.

"There's a strange smell in here, don't you think, Yannis?"

"If you don't start taking things seriously, both our necks will be on the block," he said and threw a piece of paper up in the air.

I bent down to the thick carpet to retrieve it: it was a document with bicephalic eagles stamped across the top, but with no signature at the bottom. In almost incomprehensible yet vigorous pseudo-legalese it complained about my sacrilegious and unethical treatment of Abbot Nikolaos.

"They told me, or rather threatened me, that these charges would be sent to the Prime Minister, the Minister of Public Order, as well as the leader of the opposition three hours from now unless we apologize, and in an unofficial document give an undertaking never to interfere in Church affairs again. They are livid. The fat one is something like their head of finance – he is a really big gun."

"Is that all? That all seems very reasonable. Are you sure there was nothing else?"

"Such as?"

"I don't know. Perhaps they'd like us to book them a suite at the Grande Bretagne, and have some champagne sent up with a unit of our finest Anti-Terrorist chaps dressed in bikinis?"

"Are you out of your mind? You don't get it, do you? I was woken up last night by the prosecutor, who told me that you had arrested a man without a warrant, stashed him away somewhere in the countryside, tortured him and forced a confession out of him for crimes he hasn't committed. His lawyer's threatening to go to Strasbourg with this."

"He can go to the Hague for all I care."

"You've totally and utterly lost it, haven't you?"

"I quite possibly have," I said, lighting a cigarette. I decided to tell him my little story, leaving out certain minor details, such as Simeon's involvement, Rania's involvement and Fotini's involvement. I started with Piertzovanis' refusal to sell his house and explained the methods used by the construction company to intimidate those poor bastards living there. I outlined Berios' role in the arson and his connections with the legal adviser to Earth Development, with Agisilaos, and of course, with the Church. I left Dedes' murder for the end. Not so that I would force him to do the right thing; I had already worked out that he would not dare stick his neck out to accuse the powers that be without solid evidence. After all, he was himself one of the powers that be and understood the importance of maintaining balances within the family. I talked to him about Dedes because I wanted to remind him of all his fine words about his young colleagues' senseless deaths, so he would realize that from today his own hands would bear the stain of that blood.

Shrewd policeman that he was, the only thing he asked me was how I had worked out that Earth Development was a front for the Church. And, shrewd policeman that I am, I told him that I had tapped Piertzovanis' mobile, because I had initially suspected that he was behind the arson. Once I realized that he had nothing to do with it, I maintained my tail on him because I was expecting someone to contact him about the house. That was how I heard the conversation with the wife of the president of the company. I don't know if he bought it, but it really didn't matter that much anymore. He stood up and started pacing his large office. After a short while, he announced in a hoarse voice that he had come to a decision. Luckily he decided not to elaborate the theory behind it, and in the space of three minutes he had dealt with the police's delicate position in view of the forthcoming Olympics, the stranglehold of the Church on both political parties, and of course, the crucial run-up to the elections. He rounded all this up with a pregnant "this country cannot afford to be scarred any further by scandal" and came to the point.

"Listen. We haven't got any admissible evidence, correct? So this is what's going to happen after you walk out that door: Berios gets transferred to a nice little place just outside Didymoteichon. And Agisilaos, we'll have him up on some pretext or other some time soon – it shouldn't be hard to think of something that will get him eighteen months in Korydallos. We'll take it from there. We'll cover all the costs, whatever it takes, for your actress friend. Let that bloke sell his house and enjoy the money. The interested parties won't have any reason to concern themselves with what's happened: they wanted that house and they shall get that house. You will give me a list of the foreign police forces you have always wanted to visit, go off and come home with plenty of fresh ideas and examples of good practice. You'll be back in a month, in time to vote, but I know you always spoil your ballot, so you might as well stay away a bit longer. Before you leave, bring me the tape with Agisilaos' confession on it, and do not even think about making a copy. No T.V. channel will ever touch it."

He stopped pacing around, looked at me and slowly sat down in his chair.

"If you don't agree to this, and are thinking of going off and doing something stupid, then you'll have me to answer to."

A small laugh escaped me; Piertzovanis had also advised me not to "do anything stupid" last night. Just how stupid do people think I am?

"I don't like that laugh of yours," he said, drawing in his eyebrows.

"It can be lucky sometimes."

"Alright, Chronis. What do you want me to say? I'm upset too. I'm pissed off too. But this won't be the first time the bad guys win, or the last."

He stood up and offered me his hand.

"Do we have an agreement?"

I shook his hand.

"Yes, we do. But I want you to tell me something – as straight as you can be."

He looked worried all of a sudden.

"Go on," he said, without letting go of my hand.

"Why did you introduce me to that priest? The fat one, I mean, not the abbot?"

"I told you. He's a big gun, he's in charge of the team that's managing the investment."

"So what? Why do I need to know who he is?"

"What do you mean? This has been your case up till now, albeit unofficially. Besides, you're a very shrewd policeman."

"Meaning?"

"Meaning that I have absolute faith that you would never even contemplate breaking the law. Who knows? I might be wrong. We're only human after all."

He let go of my hand, went back to his desk, opened the file in front of him and started poring over it. I was certain that he was staring at a blank piece of paper.

*

Kourkouvelas was waiting for me in my office, chatting to Fotini. I had called him on my way back, telling him to drop everything and round up all the officers in the meeting room.

"Everybody's inside. Everybody's here," he said as he got to his feet.

I asked Fotini to come with us and we went down to the third floor. The four heads of department at Internal Affairs welcomed me with forced smiles. The late Dedes might not have been their style, but he was a colleague nonetheless, and they all needed a bit of good news from me. I disappointed them. Within five minutes I had told them, without going into detail, that the case was soon going to court, and that it would be business as usual round here. I tasked Kourkouvelas and the best educated of the four heads with drawing up our annual report, which would probably occupy Parliament for at least half an hour. I explained that I was to be sent abroad for an indefinite period on police business, wished them luck and bade them farewell. Not a tear was shed; nobody realized what was really going on and nobody asked any questions. Then Kourkouvelas and I had a brief chat: his rank entitled him to fill in for me until my deputy recovered from his skiing accident. I asked him to destroy what little evidence we had on this case. He was honourable enough to ask me what was going to happen to Berios. I assured him that the Chief would be taking appropriate action. He shook his head, hesitated, then tried to force a smile, failed and headed back to his office. I realized that I had fallen a long way in his estimation. I ducked into the toilet, and emerged a couple of lines later having successfully avoided looking in the mirror after giving myself a small extension – one month, maximum, and I would be clean again. I had walked that wire before and made it to the other side. Back in my office I called Fotini and told her to come in and sit down opposite me. She straightened her skirt and looked at me, her eyes spilling over with questions. She was a fantastic woman, someone who knew how to hide her wounds, her mistakes and her contact with filth.

"Sweetheart, I'd like you to listen without interrupting. Whether you believe me or not is up to you, but I swear on Dedes' grave that what I did today, I did it for your protection and for Piertzovanis' protection, and for that young girl who helped us out at the pool club the other day. I don't think I could survive another funeral."

She nodded and smiled sweetly at the sight of the cigarette clamped between my lips. I lit it and went on.

"It's a difficult situation. I've spoken to the Chief; told him everything. We had a very friendly chat and saw eye to eye on everything.

Without being aware of it, we have been up against huge business and political interests. Circumstances are such that we have no choice but to shut up shop temporarily, with the emphasis on temporarily. This case is not closed. Far from it. The Chief has got all the evidence, and as soon as the Olympics are over, it will go to court. We thought it wise for me to make myself scarce for a while, both for reasons of safety and to make that lot think we've thrown in the towel."

She actually put her hand up, like a timid schoolgirl asking for leave to speak. I nodded.

"You don't have to explain. I'll do whatever you ask of me to make sure that nothing happens to you."

"Don't worry, I'll be fine. These are just precautions. Now listen carefully. I want you to forget everything you know about this case. Wipe the computers, get rid of that new mobile, and remember, you've never met Piertzovanis, or Rania, or that blond fascist at the billiard club, nobody. And you did not give me the keys to your house in Oropos. Is that understood?"

"Understood."

She looked frightened, but there was nothing I could do about that.

"And one last thing. Get me an open return to Rome, book me into a cheap hotel and pay enough money into my account to keep me going for six weeks. Use the travel code 'fact-finding.'"

"Right away," she said and stood up. "But promise me one thing?"

"Fine! I promise. I'll go easy on these damn things."

"No, you won't. We both know you won't. I want you to promise me to be careful."

"That's why I'm going, sweetheart."

She closed the door gently behind her and left me admiring the flowers in the vase.

"*I found three camellias waiting for me at reception this afternoon.*"

"*Did you like them?*"

"*No.*"

"*Sorry. I didn't know.*"

"*Aren't there any wild flowers in this hellhole of a town?*"

"*I didn't ask. I saw the camellias and I really liked them. Besides, Hania is not a hellhole. It looks fine to me.*"

"*Well, it would, wouldn't it? All these half-naked tourists everywhere.*"

"*What have you got on this evening?*"

"*Have you seen the theatre? Did you realize that it has absolutely no acoustics whatsoever? Nobody will be able to hear me past the fourth row.*"

"*That's what you said about Rethymnon a couple of days ago.*"

"*Yes, and I nearly shattered my vocal cords there. Shit. And those bloody camellias were shit too.*"

"*Did you bin them?*"

"*What do you think?*"

"*I think you probably did.*"

"*Why? I might be fucking a younger man, but I'm no whore.*"

"*And I suppose the chamber maid is?*"

"*No, but she's Russian, and Russians read a lot.*"

"*So?*"

"*She's read Alexandre Dumas. And she likes the bloody 'Traviata'.*"

"*What of it?*"

"*Bring some wild flowers to my room, 309, at midnight. I'm not in the mood for staying out late. And in the theatre I want you right at the back, next to the lighting box, where I can see you. And I want you to forgive me at once."*

I unlocked the bottom drawer and hid my treasures away inside my desk. I picked out the silver Zippo with my initials engraved on it, her nineteen messages, and the only photograph I had of her. It all fitted very easily into the left-hand pocket of my coat, but my 9MM posed a problem. It was in good nick, and unregistered, an unexpected find from an "unofficial visit" to some bent junior minister. I put it in my right-hand inside pocket. Everything else, I just chucked it into an old leather bag that I never used. Fotini gave me the address of the travel agent and my hotel in Rome, wished me luck and gave me a peck on the cheek, avoiding every opening for melodrama with immense dignity. I got into my Golf, hid the pistol under the seat and started the engine. I was not feeling so much sad as empty. I no longer had anywhere to go.

Simeon Piertzovanis saved me from this dead end.

"Chronis? Simeon. Where are you?"

He sounded out of breath.

"I'm just leaving the office."

"Come to the hospital."

"Why? What's happened?"

"It's Sonia."

I then realized that he was not out of breath; he was sobbing.

*

Piertzovanis was on a bench tucked away behind the hospital's open-air café. He looked suddenly old, his bony shoulders hanging down, his eyes two red slits, and his lips trembling as though he were trying to pray. Rania was rubbing his hands, trying in vain to revive a frozen shadow. I sat next to her so that I would not have to look at him.

"She's inside. Do you want me to take you in to see her?" she said.

"In a bit. Tell me what's happened first."

Her voice was low but steady. She did not want Simeon to hear.

"The hospital called about an hour and a half ago. Sonia wasn't doing well. Simeon asked me to go with him. The consultant said that there had been kidney failure after the heart attack. They did everything they could. He took us to see her. She looked as though she was sleeping. Simeon asked them to give him a sedative, an injection. Then he called you. He hasn't said a word since."

"Take him home. I'll take care of everything else. I'll call you later."

She let go of the lawyer's dead hands to take hold of the policeman's frozen hands.

"She's still really beautiful," she said.

I stroked her hair and left her, confident that she would be able to manage the empty shell of a man she had taken on. I finished everything in less than an hour, thanks to a very accommodating official, who was readily persuaded to overlook certain bureaucratic details. I jumped into the old wreck and set off for home, without daring to go and see my lady.

*

"Why don't you want us to go to your village? I want to see where my little Chronis grew up."

"It's a dump. Just a dozen houses and a dive of a kafeneion."

"Good. We'll drink some tsipouro *there. You do make* tsipouro *in your village, don't you?"*

"Perhaps. I can't remember."

"Liar. You know what I think? I think you're ashamed. You're too ashamed to show your humble origins to the big star who's in love with you."

"I have a horror of small villages. They're ugly."

"That means you have a horror of your childhood."

"I have absolutely no memory of it."

"Liar."

"I wouldn't have made much of an actor, would I?"

"How many times have I told you that actors aren't liars?"

"Many."

"I love you. Do you believe me?"

"Yes."

"Do you love me?"

"Yes, I do."

"Liar. If you loved me, you'd take me to your village."

"I will take you."

"When?"

"Next summer."

*

I do not know how long I stared at her photograph. She was dressed in Electra's brown rags, laughing. The gap between her two front teeth, the lock of hair that fell in front of her eyes and her hand on my shoulder obliterated the stone seats rising behind us. I was in a pair of loose white trousers, a white shirt and a red cap. "After murdering her mother, Electra went to the fun fair and had her picture taken with the ice-cream seller", she had wanted to write on the back. I would not let her. I turned the picture over and copied my list on to its matt surface:

Agisilaos, Berios, Abbot Nikolaos,
Phaidon Tsolakidis, Apostolos Zacharopoulos,
Archimandrite Eusignios

I filled my silver Zippo, replaced the flint, put my coat on, stuffed the photograph in my pocket and went out.

*

Piertzovanis was doing a bit better. His eyes were still red but were open a little wider. His hands did not shake when he tried to light his cigarette and his speech was very clear from a distance of about a metre. Rania was in the kitchen making a spaghetti sauce.

"Did you see her?"

"Yes, I did."

"And?"

"And what?"

"Nothing," he mumbled and went to the fridge to get some ice. He was fine.

"So, partner, there's no reason to hide it anymore. You were in love with her, weren't you?"

"I can't imagine anyone between the ages of fifteen and eighty who would not have been."

"So when?"

"You'll have to wait for my memoirs to come out if you want to know more."

"Alright." I backed off.

I tried the wine Rania brought. The lawyer's gaze was trapped deep inside his glass.

"Where's the canary?" I said after a pause.

"She's asleep on my bed."

The cook made a brief appearance to ask us if we needed anything and disappeared back into the kitchen. Our silence worried her, I expect. Simeon lit another cigarette.

"What arrangements have you made for her funeral?"

"I spoke to the consultant. The hospital will make an official announcement on Thursday. I managed to convince him that this was necessary in view of the ongoing police investigation. The funeral will be civil, three o'clock in a village in Evia. I gave something extra to the vultures, but it's all been paid for."

"Why Evia?"

"There's a village there she'd always wanted to visit."

"Your village?"

"Yes. Did she say . . . did she express any other wishes to you?"

"Alcoholics think they're immortal," he said clinking glasses with me. Whisky and wine splashed on to the table. "Anyway, you did the right thing."

"I'm not so sure. I'm just thinking that there were a lot of people who admired her and loved her and —"

"That's not what I meant," he said. "She would not have wanted a religious ceremony. I never once saw her crossing herself."

I went to the coat stand, took the photograph from my pocket and showed it to him.

"Nice picture. When was it taken?"

"July '97. Kavala – at the ancient theatre of Filippi."

"So you were young once too, eh, Officer?"

"Look at the back."

He turned it over and froze.

"Well?"

"Is this a complete list?" He took a sip of whisky and looked at me sadly.

I nodded.

"O.K., Chronis. I'm listening."

I told him about my encounter with Abbot Nikolaos and Archimandrite Eusignios and my chat with the Chief. I assured him the case was being wound up, leaving the road right open for the two of us. He didn't say a word, just kept on looking at me sadly.

"What do you say, partner? Should I finish the job?"

He took a look at the photograph, handed it back to me and turned towards the kitchen.

"Is this spaghetti made of bone?"

"Ready in two!" Rania chirped with forced jollity from the kitchen.

Piertzovanis drained his glass and smiled at me.

"She studies in Italy; ought to know a thing or two about pasta."

He was right. The spaghetti was wonderful, but nobody had much of an appetite, either for food or for conversation. Rania did her best to lighten the mood by putting on some Neapolitan love songs, as well as a bit of Caruso, and telling us funny stories about Italian lovers who won't have sex without their mothers' permission, about the time she almost got to dance the tango with Paolo Maldini. She even woke up the canary and tried to sing a duet with her – Gabriella Ferri or someone. By the end of the meal she was drowning her failure in wine. Shortly after midnight, Piertzovanis came out to the lift with me and pressed the button."

"I'm waiting for an answer."

"Are you mad?"

"I'll make all the arrangements. Yours will be an auxiliary role. You won't appear anywhere. I've thought it all through. I'm flying to Rome on Saturday, and I'll drive back on Monday on a counterfeit passport. Everyone will think I'm lazing around in Italy, but all the time I'll be here. It's a good game."

The lift arrived. Simeon opened the door and we both got in. I closed it. He laughed and leant against the wall.

"I'm a bit drunk, but I do know what I'm saying. There are two names missing from your list, and if you move them to the top, you'll save yourself a lot of trouble."

I opened the door, grabbed him by the collar and thrust him up against the mirror.

"She's dead, you prick – get it? Don't you see that time's running out?"

As soon as his first tear landed on my wrist, I let him go.

*

"*Chronis?*"

"*Yes . . .*"

"*Are you awake?*"

"*I was dreaming.*"

"*What about?*"

"*I forget. I was walking. No, you were walking.*"

"And?"

"I'm tired."

"Never mind. Let me tell you. Are you listening?"

"No."

"I was walking to meet you. You were waiting for me outside the Aigli Hotel. The town was by the sea. You were holding a big, old key – you know, one of those ornate ones our grandmothers used to have hanging from their aprons. These days, grandmothers limp along with plastic supermarket bags. Anyway, you are listening, aren't you?"

"I'm tired."

"Don't be angry, young man. It's your dream – what harm can it do?"

"I'm not angry."

"You can't even lie properly, but I don't care anymore. So, you're waiting for me with this key, and behind you is a flickering neon sign, saying, 'Volos Hotel Aigli presents . . .' Do you want me to tell you the title of the play? You're pretending to be asleep. I'm going to carry on undeterred. And the title of the play is . . ."

"Stop. You can't turn the whole of life into theatre."

"Whoa! The young protagonist throws the sheets off and gets up, in a rage. Yes, that's it, perfect, I've seen it done in lots of American plays – this poor young thing who is admiring a wonderful back for the last time, the back of a man who's pretending to be tired, looking out of the window, looking down onto a deserted avenue, which —"

"That's enough."

"I know it is, young man. In my dream you hand the key back to me, the key I'd given you."

"Are you out of your mind?"

"No, I'm making it easier for you. But I'd like one last favour. When

*you leave in the morning, throw my house key into water – the sea,
down the toilet, I don't mind. But hang on to the key ring. I bought it
from an adorable Pakistani. I can still remember his smile."*

"Sonia, go to sleep."

"I will. Goodbye, and take care."

4.ii
Wednesday, 9.00 p.m.

Just before the Volos intersection, I pulled into a dark car park for
a couple of snorts and a smoke. I got out of the car and sat on the
bonnet. The radio was crackling, but I liked the sound; it suited the
moment and the scenery. It had been a busy day, but I had managed
to get everything done. I had a car now fitted with a new exhaust,
tyres and oil, a suitcase with everything I needed for my trip, tickets
and travel guides for Rome, twenty grammes of coke and enough
weed to record a double album of *rebetika*. I had a travel bag with
my toiletries and two top-of-the-range wigs. I had a shotgun with
a telephoto lens, a good-quality commando knife, two lengths of
strong rope and two brand new unregistered Berettas in the boot. I'd
given my son his pocket money, told him to study hard, always use
a condom, and stay away from drugs. I had also given myself plenty
of time to plan my new life.

I tossed my cigarette to the ground and stamped on it, started my
super new Golf, turned up the interference on the radio, and twenty
minutes later was taking the key to my room from the smiley receptionist at the Aigli Hotel, a swipe card for Room 223. My other hand
was clutching the old key to the old room with the same number.

I opened the door, threw my travel bag down on the bed and

walked out onto the narrow balcony. The sea had not changed at all since that first night.

"*What a tiny room my young bodyguard's got!*"

"*It's fine. I like it.*"

"*Like a nest, eh?*"

"*Refuge.*"

"*Yes, it looks safe. What are you going to treat me to?*"

"*The fridge is full.*"

"*Of what?*"

"*Tiny, multicoloured bottles.*"

"*What foresight, Mr Halkidis.*"

"*My job is to look ahead.*"

"*Quite right.*"

"*Isn't that why the lady hired me?*"

"*Yes, that is why. No ice?*"

"*I'll have some sent up.*"

"*Don't worry; I'll put some cold water in it.*"

"*To your very good health.*"

"*To our health. Bottoms up.*"

"*Bottoms up?*"

"*Of course. Can I test your bed now, please?*"

So had I remembered correctly? Is that what happened?

"*What a tiny room my young bodyguard's got.*"

It wasn't exactly a question, it was more like flirtation, or provocation, something along the lines of "show me how flexible you can be in this five-star-hole"; "what kinds of tricks can you perform on my body and imprint on my memory?"; "how can you combine asphyxia and pleasure?" She lay down, her full skirt covering the bed. I undressed her, kissed her, and caressed her hair. When she drifted

294

off to sleep, I pulled the covers over her, and just sat there watching her for ages. It might have been then that it dawned on me that she always went to sleep sad.

I closed the balcony doors and turned off the light. A street lamp bathed the walls in yellow. I knew I would not get to sleep, but then I had not come all this way to sleep. I lit a cigarette and lay down on our marital bed.

CHAPTER 10

Simeon Piertzovanis
Confesses His Love

The cemetery was small and well maintained. Apart from Rania, Noni, myself and the four grave diggers, Sonia's coffin was followed by the village idiot, who every now and then would doff his thread-bare summer hat, cross himself and replace his hat, and beam beatifically up at the leaden sky. Halkidis was not there. His mobile had been switched off since morning. His secretary told me that he was away on leave, and I did not have the strength to worry. Rania was being very discreet; she did not take my hand at any point. She stood ten paces away from the grave and it was only when the coffin was lowered into the ground that she approached, dropping a single white rose onto it. I could not remember whether Sonia liked white roses. Noni pulled a cloth charm from home out of his pocket, brought it up to his eyes, wiped away his remaining tears on it, kissed it and then passed it on to his good friend. The village idiot offered his condolences, accompanied by a deep bow, and ran to catch up with the gravediggers who were in a hurry to get back to Athens. Rania and Noni moved away slowly, leaving me to try to walk across the damp soil alone.

*

"Happy birthday."

"Thank you, beautiful."

"Does it bother you, Simeon, getting old?"

"Of course it does."

"Not me. So what if I'm getting older? Sometimes I swim very gracefully, sometimes very clumsily. That's all."

"I'm still working on my style."

"Oh, I like your style – on your back."

"Are you calling me lazy?"

"'Don't call me lazy and demoralize me.' Remember the song?"

"I thought you didn't like popular music."

"That's where you're wrong. Deep down, I'm a working-class girl. At drama school, I always had to play the maid because I was short."

"Sing me a song."

"I don't care to be laughed at."

"Just a chorus. It's my birthday and I want a present."

"But I bought you a sweater."

"Clothes don't count. Clothes are essentials, not gifts."

"And I gave you all Luis Sepúlveda's books."

"Yes, but you didn't write a dedication in them."

"I don't want you to think about me if I die."

"Your penalty for that particular piece of bullshit is that you have to sing one song."

"Tease. Which one do you want?"

"'Your Black Eyes'."

"That's a man's song. Think of a woman's song."

"'Why did you give me that tobacco tin?'"

"Too soppy. And I've never cared for tobacco tins."

"'Love – A knife that cuts both ways'?"

"Can't be doing with knives either."

"'You can't do that because of an old mistake of mine'?"

"Too whiney."

"'Have I Driven you to Drink?'"

"That's a good one, but not really suitable for tonight. I've had more to drink than you. Think of another one."

"The one about the crazy woman in the moon?"

"What!"

"'Crazy Woman in the Moon'."

"It's not called that!"

"What is it called?"

"'The Castles of Digenis'."

"Whatever."

"That's too hard."

*

Rina and I were watching a riveting documentary about the consequences of climate change on the lives of lemurs when my mobile rang.

"Were you sleeping?"

"Trying to."

"I'm outside. Come down."

"Forget it."

"Let's drink to Sonia. This is the last time I'll ask anything of you. Please."

"I've had as much as I need to get to sleep."

"Please."

"As long as you promise to carry me to bed later."

"Promise."

I stuck my head under the tap, threw on the first thing I found, left the television on so Rina would have some company, and went downstairs. Halkidis was sitting waiting for me on the doorstep outside. He had parked on the pavement opposite, the radio full-blast, with the most god-awful interference.

"Don't worry, I won't bite," he said, turning off the radio and starting the engine.

"Why should I worry?"

"I've been doing a lot of thinking, yesterday and today."

"Where to?"

"We're going to a place I'd always wanted to take her to but never got round to it."

"Why didn't you come to the funeral?"

He chose not to answer. I chose not to press him.

*

The place he had never got round to taking Sonia was an *ouzerie* in a working-class area, with some extraordinary sea creatures painted on the walls, and two polite young waiters with pierced ears and T-shirts with Jim Morrison and Metallica emblazoned across them. A charming grey-haired man was frying whitebait in the background while Michelle Pfeiffer as a waitress who falls in love with grill cook Al Pacino in a New York diner played on a mute television set. Chronis ordered something vague and I asked for a small carafe of *tsipouro*. His face betrayed the fact that he was playing a risky game, and was on the brink of spectacular defeat. While we were waiting for our order, I took solace in Michelle's tired smile. I tried to remember how many tired smiles I had counted on the faces of supposedly carefree young women, their feet swollen from all those hours on their feet, but Halkidis interrupted my train of thought.

"The funeral director told me everything went smoothly."

"Yes, it all went off without incident."

He chuckled.

"Who told you it was all over?"

"Pull yourself together. Sonia's dead."

"Some jobs only start after the funeral."

The combination of cocaine and guilt had driven him off his head. He started talking like someone delirious with fever. I struggled to identify any logical thread in his monologue. He mixed up all sorts of enchanted moments from some distant summer with improbable lines from Sophocles' "Electra". He was bringing up names and room numbers of dozens of hotels all over the country, rain next to the sea, strolling under the stars. When this romantic squall finally abated, he moved on to the chapter entitled "Justice and the Various Methods of Dispensing It," and as if by magic, he suddenly metamorphosed into a sober orator. I was sure he had passed the jurisprudence exam at law school with flying colours. He brought up examples from the past in order to prove the relativity of the value of human life over the centuries, and the still unsolved problems which so-and-so had posited, and the fearsome colossus that is the law.

I was smoking, drinking, and now and then would nod to give the impression that I was paying attention. I knew that after the theoretical underpinning, we would soon move into the minefield. And that is exactly what happened.

"Simeon, I've never so much as trodden on an ant in my entire life. But things are different now. I have thought about this carefully. It is me against them. I cannot back down now."

He took two sips of water and licked his lips. He looked at me, but he found it impossible to fix his gaze on any particular point. I decided to make an effort. I owed him that; after all, we had almost become friends.

"My dear Halkidis, you're in danger of going over the edge. You need help, psychological support. I have got a really good friend who is a brilliant doctor. He really helped me out once."

The explosion was instant, as though someone had sent a few thousand volts through him.

"What did you say?"

"Sonia has died. There's no comfort to be had, I know that. You'll live through your memories – that's healthy. It's what we all do. Tough but healthy. You're young. You've got a child."

"Sonia did not die. She was killed by that gang," he said, pulling out the photograph with his list on the back.

"There are loads of gangs who kill thousands of innocent people every day."

"One fewer won't hurt," he said, looking at the photograph. "You have to help me."

"Forget it, Chronis."

"You're full of shit," he said in a low voice.

"How long did it take you to work that one out?"

"I bet you take that money, and spend the rest of your life drinking it away, supposedly to forget."

I leant towards him, resting my hand gently on his shoulder. He took his eyes off the photograph and looked across at me.

"This afternoon, as soon as I got back from the funeral, I called that lawyer Tsolakidis and told him I'm not selling."

He shook his head, pushed the untouched plates of food to one side, and laid the photograph face up in the table between us.

"Don't you carry a picture of her with you?" he said casually.

"No."

We got through a second carafe in silence. Michelle was in bed with Al by now. We split the bill, staggered out into the night and said goodbye to each other with the certainty that we would never meet again. He did not offer to drive me home. Thank God.

As I got into the cab, I realized with horror that it was snowing. Back home, Rina welcomed me with a cheerful chirrup. I drew the curtains and moved her cage close to the window so that she could see the snow. I poured a whisky in the vague hope that it would get rid of the taste of *tsipouro* in my mouth, changed her water and confessed my love to her. As soon as she told me she felt the same, I stuffed my finger through the bars and let her chew my fingertip until she drew blood.

CHAPTER 11

Chronis Halkidis at Confession

10.iv

Saturday, 3.00 p.m.

"Father Eusignios, I have come here today because I know you listen to the faithful and give them comfort."

"All of the fathers our Church give comfort to the faithful, my child."

"I am weighed down by sin, Father."

"Unburden your heart, my child. Only then can you save your soul."

"I am weighed down by many sins, Father Archimandrite."

"I am here to listen to you and to entreat the Lord to forgive you."

"May I kneel?"

"As you wish."

Hearing confession was Archimandrite Eusignios' favourite

pastime. Although his job of overseeing the financial activities of the Church occupied most of his time, every Saturday evening he would sit in a small church somewhere in the Mesogeia area waiting for the faithful to come to confession. A young priest would drop him off in a modest Ford, presumably so that he would not outrage the local congregation with the spectacle of the black limousine he used for all his other business. Three weeks of surveillance had been enough. I pulled up outside the church on an old Kawasaki 250cc that I had stolen a few days earlier. The archimandrite's young driver did not give me any problems: chloroform did the trick. I installed him on a bench at the back of the church and waited impatiently for the two elderly ladies to detail their transgressions to one of God's finest representatives on earth.

It was easier than I had anticipated. Agisilaos had been harder work; he had put up quite a fight in the toilets at the pool bar. Berios had opted to jump from the roof of his building rather than take a bullet in the mouth and Abbot Nikolaos proved too weak to put up any resistance, while Tsolakidis swallowed practically his entire swimming pool. As for the managing director of Earth Development, he needed five bullets – the distance was out of proportion to my skill as a marksman, but in the end he collapsed on the bottom step of his company's headquarters, so I was not such a bad cop after all.

"Father, I can speak to you in confidence, can't I?"

"Of course."

"Father, I have killed five men. I murdered them in cold blood. I administered a shot of pure heroin to the first in the toilets of a club of ill repute; sent the second hurtling to his death from a great height; strangled the third; drowned the fourth; shot the fifth with a precision rifle. What must I do get absolution for my sins, Father Eusignios?"

I lifted my head and flashed him my warmest smile. He went ashen.

"Father, whatever is the matter? It's a simple question. What do I have to do to get your chief executive to absolve me?"

"Who are you?" he whispered.

With my left hand, I removed my blond wig and false moustache while my right hand pointed a .45 straight at his fat stomach. He did not recognize me, probably because I had shaved my head. I gave him some clues.

"Chronis Halkidis, Head of Internal Affairs, Hellenic Police. I am here to confess. My sources inform me that you too are desperate to save your soul, which is troubled by the deaths of five innocent people, four of whom were burnt alive."

"I don't . . ."

"Oh! Father, are you shaking? What a pity. I was hoping we had have time for a serious theological discussion."

"I was not responsible for that fire."

"My detective's instinct tells me otherwise."

"Wait! We can make a deal. I could make you a very rich man."

He stopped dead when he saw the pistol pointing at his forehead.

"Oh! Fuck me!" he whimpered.

"Make your own arrangements," I said, and shot him.

CHAPTER 12

Simeon Piertzovanis at the Crime Scene

Saturday, 10.30 p.m.

Halkidis was sitting in a blue Niva, smoking. As soon as my taxi pulled away, he got out of the car, flicked on his torch and stepped into the garden. He had shaved his head and looked ten years older. I followed him. We sat on the charred steps. We must have looked like a nervous couple on their first date. He spoke first.

"Well, my lawyer friend, I have finished. I killed the last one this evening."

His eyes were shining in the darkness. He rested the torch on the step next to him and the cold, bluish glare licked the charred almond tree.

"Congratulations."

"You have to hand it to me: all done and dusted in sixty-three hours exactly. Preparation is the key. Make everyone think you're off having fun in Rome while all the time you are here. Invisible. You become this enormous eye, monitoring all targets. But you have to strike fast, before the enemy gets wind of what's going on and gets a chance to regroup."

"Why did you want to see me?"

"What's the hurry? Don't you want to know all the gory details?"

"No."

"It's your loss."

"Why have you really dragged me here?"

"Work it out," he said, putting his hand in his pocket.

"Come on, Chronis!"

"You were her last, weren't you? The last man who could have saved her."

"Do you want us to talk about who really left Sonia?"

"You were fucking her, weren't you? Why won't you admit it? I've looked at the dates. It all works out. She met you while I was still with her. She was seeing you on the sly, and then she came back to me, drunk. Dead. What did you have that I didn't, you bastard?"

"Nothing," I whispered and stood up. "I didn't love her enough, I didn't love her enough either."

He pulled a small pistol out of his pocket.

"I could kill you. Easily," he said, thumbing back the catch.

"Let me ask you something, Chronis."

"What?"

"If I were pointing that gun at you, would you ask me to kill you?"

"I'll do that myself, later."

"I'm going home."

I walked slowly across the garden, stepped out onto the street and started walking in the direction of the main road. For one fleeting moment which seemed like an eternity to me, I thought I could smell something resembling spring in the air.

12.vi

Saturday, 7.45 p.m.

I never saw or heard anything of him again. Nor did I seek him out. Meanwhile, the municipality had requisitioned the plot in record time, and in a few months the courts will determine the level of compensation I am paid, and then I will become a well-to-do alcoholic lawyer rather than a struggling alcoholic lawyer, and the Church's construction company will finally get to build its breathtaking multiplex entertainment centre, no doubt satisfying the wishes of both the Lord and the market economy in the process. From what I can glean from the papers, the state is being re-invented and the Olympics will herald a new era for Greece. I drop by the office now and then and pretend to work. More often, I go and play cards, and most of all I take refuge at 16. Rina is still chirruping away and enjoying the views out over Eressou. Young Rania sent me a letter decorated with wonderful Italian postage stamps. She has moved in with her pizza boy – apparently supporting him financially to write a comparative thesis on Julio Cortázar and Italo Calvino. Noni has got a transfer to Panionios, but I expect that he will spend the season on the bench. I promised to go and see him after the matches on Sundays and take him for *souvlaki* at the place next to the stadium. I have written a will. I am leaving everything to him. To be honest, I did have second thoughts, just before I signed, and considered all the many worthy, revolutionary causes in the world, but in the end decided on Noni. I have finally come to realize that it is not money that is the obstacle to revolution after all.

I still see Sonia occasionally. She is looking good for her age. She has finally given in to my pleas and wears only dresses. After her visits, I walk up to the ruins of the burnt house, a plastic water bottle full of vodka for company. It's nice, especially the moment when the sun goes down, and then resurfaces again briefly with that special shade of red, a cheap, melodramatic red, something like a spell that would go with her smile. Now that I look at it, not caring that the ash from my Gitane is making a mess of my linen trousers, I am absolutely certain that that is the red of Sonia's smile. What else could it be, since I can see her before me, her right hand on her heart, trying to locate a pair of kind eyes somewhere in the audience, and refusing stubbornly, even tonight, to acknowledge the rapturous rounds of applause with a bow?